# CHARM CITY

A novel by

C. Flores

Life Changing Books in conjunction with Power Play Media
Published by Life Changing Books
P.O. Box 423 Brandywine, MD 20613

This novel is a work of fiction. Any references to real people, events, establishments, or locales are intended only to give the fiction a sense of reality and authenticity. Other names, characters, and incidents occurring in the work are either a product of the author's imagination or are used fictitiously, as are those fictionalized events and incidents that involve real persons. Any character that happens to share the name of a person who is an acquaintance of the author, past or present, is purely coincidental and is in no way intended to be an actual account involving that person.

Library of Congress Cataloging-in-Publication Data;

www.lifechangingbooks.net
13 Digit: 978-1934230459
10 Digit: 1934230456

# Dedication

*To my cousin, Rell, who lost his life to gun violence. I love you and I hope you're watching over the family!*

# Acknowledgements

I want to acknowledge my team first off, my Publisher Azarcl and LCB. Thanks for the opportunity to show my talent and make my passion bleed through the pen. I was, and still am, dream chasing. They saw the hunger in me and gave me a shot at success.

I have to give thanks and acknowledge my city Philadelphia, and Black and Nobel bookstore; Hakim, Tyson, Dr. Leslie, and all the good people over there that have been holding me down since day one.

Free Smoke, Free Black, Free A.J. R.I.P to all mine.

To my cousin Rell up above, I miss you, and I named my newborn after you and big cuz: Jarell Ernest Flores.

Keep rocking with me I'ma put on for the city!

# Prologue

**1999**

While the music in the Cherry Red S Class Benz pumped the tunes of Mobb Deep, Science smoked a freshly rolled Dutch dipped in honey. He stopped at a red light just before a police car pulled quickly from the gas station and rolled behind him.

"Shit!"

He blew the smoke and slowly reached for his seatbelt, locking it, while glancing in the rearview mirror. Science placed both hands on the steering wheel and turned down his radio. He thought about the drugs in his stash box. He thought about the possibility of getting locked up again. He thought about going in and not being able to see his one-year-old son again.

The horn honking brought him back to reality. The once red light was now yellow and about to turn red again. Science looked in his rear view mirror and locked eyes with the white, scraggily haired police officer who signaled unpleasantly for him to pull over.

"This some bullshit, yo!" Science shouted.

Once the light turned green, Science pulled into the gas station. He placed the Dutch in the ashtray, knowing if the police found it things would turn out bad for him. The thing that worried him the most was the sixteen ounces of crack cocaine in the stash box under his glove compartment. He looked up at the shabby looking white officer chewing tobacco with regret.

"What's the problem, son? You don't know your colors?" the heavy-set cop asked.

"I just found out I lost my father, sir. I'm sorry for holding up traffic."

Science hadn't seen his father in almost ten years and wouldn't even know what he looked like if he walked right up to his car at that moment. He just hoped that answer would let him get on with his business.

"I smell weed. You getting high, boy?"

"Like I said, I just lost my dad who was a firefighter for the city for almost fifteen years. He had cancer and I thought the weed would help. It's in the ashtray. I'll throw it away though, sir. I'm sorry."

"Shut the engine off and get out the fuckin' car, slowly. And I don't want no slick moves either," he told Science with his hand on his service revolver.

Science let out a sigh in frustration and cut the Benz off. He stepped out of the car and watched, as the cop looked him up and down.

"You some kind of rapper, boy? What's with all the gold?"

Science had two chains on with iced out pieces, an icy Rolex watch, and a sixty thousand dollar diamond bracelet that occupied his wrist. He attempted to remain unruffled as the cop probed every inch of his body asking more questions about the rap industry. "You had any dealings with that boy, Tupac?"

"Actually, I'm a producer. I've been in the music business for a few years and it's been good to me."

"Producer, huh?"

He spat a wad of tobacco at Science's feet then began examining the car, which sent chills through Science's body.

"Ain't this the new Mercedes that just came out?"

"Yes, sir. Do you like it?" Science teased. He knew he'd gone too far.

"I'm asking the got damn questions," his voice roared. "Put your hands on the hood while I call for back up."

Science began to sweat. "Whoa, do we need all that, sir? I have a meeting to get to and I really don't have time for this. Please, can you just write me a ticket?"

"Boy, I call the shots. You see this badge? Put your hands behind your back!"

The cop forcefully gripped Science up and placed the cuffs tightly on his wrists. He called in back up faster than his spit could hit the cement, and asked for the K-9 unit. Science knew what that meant and prayed that the dogs wouldn't sniff out the drugs.

"Alright, spread your legs, boy. Do you have any drugs on you, or weapons?" the officer asked as he slammed Science up against the hood of the car.

"No, sir. But can you loosen up these cuffs, please?"

"What about that damn car?" the officer asked, ignoring his question. "Any drugs in the car?"

"No sir."

The police officer patted him down with force, pulling two huge wads of cash from his pocket and a couple of condoms.

"What's all this money?"

"I was just on my way to the bank to deposit that."

"Yeah, yeah it looks like drug money to me. All you muthafuckas yap the same ole lies."

Before Science knew it he was in the back of the squad car. He watched as two more police cars rolled up, one with an oversized K-9 dog. Science held his head downward as the search began. Minutes seemed like hours. He just kept shaking his head. All Science could do was hope for the best. He hoped that his stash box was worth the money he'd paid to keep the dog from sniffing the product.

Soon the inevitable happened. Science slowly saw his life flash before his eyes when he heard one of the cops say, "We found something." The dog started barking ferociously and jumping around wildly. The police officer that pulled him over wore a huge smile as he pulled the brown paper bag out and looked inside. He walked over to Science and knocked on the window.

"Producer huh, I see what you producing alright. I knew I'd get your ass. See you in twenty years."

Science gave him a fake smile and turned the other way.

The trip downtown was quick, and with his only phone call Science called his baby's mother and girlfriend to give her the scoop.

"Ay shorty, call the bondsman up," he instructed, "I'm booked under the name Sean Dixon. Hurry up before my prints get back because I got a warrant. Go to the stash spot and get what you need," he told her with hopelessness in his voice. He figured shit was about to get crazy.

$$$$

"Big baller, let's go!" the burly correctional officer yelled.

"Go where?" Science responded.

"Does it matter?" the C.O. shot back. "Just be glad somebody came to see your punk ass."

Science stood up, giving the officer the once over. He should've been glad that he'd finally gotten a visitor. He'd been down three weeks with no word on bail and no one coming to see him other than his lawyer. Sadly, his baby's mother, Damya never called the bondsman. Since then, his case had gone from state to federal. Science was sick in his gut. He hoped the visitor was his baby's mom so he could curse her out. In the three weeks he'd been down, the streets talked and news spread about the way Damya balled out of control on shopping sprees and spending money without rhyme or reason. As Science walked toward the visiting room all he could think about was the two hundred grand that Damya had access to.

When the officer directed him in a different direction from the visiting room he felt uneasy. Science stopped in his tracks and looked at the C.O.

"Where the fuck you taking me, yo?"

"You have a special visit," the C.O. said with a smirk.

Science knew what that meant. He put his game face on. The C.O. opened the door and Science saw the two federal agents with wide smiles on their faces.

"Cecil, how are you doing?" one of the agents asked sarcastically.

"Science yo, you don't fuckin' know me! Don't call me by my government."

The C.O. left them alone while Science reluctantly took a seat.

"Alright then, Science. Let me get to the point. You looking at a lot of time. Sixteen ounces of crack with prior convictions will get you double-digit numbers. You like football? Because you'll get Reggie White's number. Work with us and you'll do eighteen months. That's all. Take a look at some pictures and let me know if you know these faces."

The other agent passed him a black book and opened it slowly. The first pictures were of Sheek, some ruthless hustler from Philly who was on the come up in the drug game. Science knew him well considering they'd battled for some of the same territory.

"You know him?" the agent pointed.

"Naw, never seen him before, yo."

The agent continued to flip through the book, passing by several images of hustlers and dope dealers that Science knew. However, they'd eventually gotten to the end without Science identifying even one person. Flipping on anybody to get himself out of a bind wasn't in his blood. He couldn't snitch; it just wasn't him. He lived by the G-code and he decided to die by it.

"Take me to my cell yo, I ain't got shit for you."

"You're digging your own grave, son," one of the agents remarked.

"I'd rather die than talk like a bitch," he responded as he left the room headed back to his cell.

It didn't take long for him to doze off. After tossing and turning in his bunk half the night, Science got up around four o'clock in the morning with thoughts of Damya running wildly through his head. She still hadn't gotten his lawyer, or bond money together. He hoped she wouldn't leave him for dead like most chicks did when their nigga had to pull a bid. He thought of his son growing up without him and being raised by another man. He even thought about the possibility of having to leave both her and his son behind for a very long time.

Science knew that he'd not only disappoint Damya, but his mother, too. Another incarceration would damn near kill her. A tear fell from his eye, as his heart was full of frustration and anger. He'd left his mom once again after promising her he would never do more time. He closed his eyes and wished the hurt would go away. He had time ahead of him and whatever the sentence he received, he would stand up like a true soldier. Paying his lawyer every few months wasn't just for fun. He prayed that he could get him a number that would still get him home young enough to still live a wealthy life.

As if his cellmate knew exactly how Science was feeling, he leaned over and asked, "Bruh, you good?"

"Not really," Science responded in despair. "Nigga, this shit real. Let me see that phone you was telling me about earlier. I gotta call this bitch."

His cellmate quickly went under his pillow and retrieved the phone he'd paid a sexy correctional officer $300.00 to smuggle in. As he passed the pre-paid phone, his comment threw Science for a loop.

"Bitches ain't never what they seem, Bruh," he told him. "Just do your time all by your damn self if you wanna make it with no heartache. Bitches snatch whatever pride you have left when you locked down."

Science shot him a crazed look and dialed Damya's number with all types of anger pumping through his veins until a familiar male voice answered throwing his mind off track.

"Yo, Yo," the voice answered.

"Hello…hello," Science fired back. "Who the fuck is this?"

Science assumed he'd dialed the wrong number. He took the phone from his ear to double check the number he'd dialed. The line had gone completely silent. "Hello," Science roared again. "I know this nigga ain't fuckin' my bitch," he said, then hung up to redial.

# CHAPTER 1

**2007**

Science stepped onto the concrete as the gates of prison closed behind him. He felt energized and refreshed. Even though he wasn't a stranger to being incarcerated, this was the first time he had done a really long stretch.

Eight years and nine months on a crack charge almost broke his back, but he stuck it out like trooper and a real G. Prior to this bid, he had done four years; then there was the eighteen month bid, the 365 day bid, and ninety day bid, but he always came home like he never left. He was doing major numbers in the coke game before he got booked, but everything he possessed was snatched away and sucked dry by the government. The Feds seized his house, vehicles, and every dollar in his bank account. His baby's mom, Damya acted like his stash over her house never existed. Word on the street was that she'd run through that two hundred grand within the first year of Science's incarceration.

He didn't tell his mom, brothers, or Damya when he was coming home. He wanted it to be a surprise. He hopped on the bus with two other convicts and the C.O. took them to the bus station. While putting his plan together to get back on top, Science looked out the window at his grim surroundings.

"Alright, get ya asses off the bus and don't come back!" the C.O. yelled, stopping at the bus station, with the doors flying open. Science moved slowly allowing the other guys to get off first. He fell back when the C.O. called his name. "Science, look-a-here. You a good dude. Don't come back. Leave that game alone out there, man. It ain't worth it."

Science looked at the C.O. with sincerity and nodded his head. "I hear you."

"I'm serious. Change your life, or you'll be back."

Science stepped off the bus with his ticket in his hand, a bag of mail, and photos he received during his bid. He had about $2,500 dollars from hustling cigarettes and weed. He walked into the bus station with his du-rag tied tightly over the deep waves he'd spent precious time brushing in prison. After looking around for a few minutes, he went to a newsstand to get a few things for the ride. He noticed the looks he got from the townspeople, mostly whites. A few blacks were mixed in, but not that many. The other convicts had clothes sent in; they looked normal. Science, however, was wearing tan khakis, black boots, and a wife beater that showed his inked up body. The women gawked at the large scripted letters B-MORE written on the side of his neck. To Science, those words meant everything, along with the images of the tombstones covering his arms, honoring his dead homies.

"Damn, you fine," a woman announced as Science entered the store.

He attempted to ignore the unattractive clerk who had her boobs hanging from her shirt.

"Let me get a box of blacks and that XXL magazine," Science stated, as he pulled a twenty from his fat wad of cash.

The young clerk, who was about eighteen, passed him his items and received the cash. The young woman drooled as she passed Science his money back. Science put his change in his pocket and pulled his baggy pants up on his waist. He paid the clerk no mind as he saw his bus boarding to Baltimore, Maryland. Science hurried to get to his bus hoping he could get the backseat to stretch out. Luckily, he got on the bus just in time. He went to the empty backseat, sat by the window, and put his bag on the other seat. He couldn't believe how many people were going to B-More. Every seat was filled in a matter of minutes, except the two next to him. The driver closed the doors and slowly pulled off.

"Yo, bus driver! You got a female running you down!" Somebody yelled out causing the bus driver to stop and pick up the late straggler.

Science's attention was out the window and back home. He was thinking about how he was going to shit on Damya for spending his stash money, and not bringing his son to see him at all; not even once during the entire 8 years. He had some vicious payback ready for her.

"Excuse me, can I sit here? There aren't any more seats," a light voice sounded.

Science's thoughts were interrupted. He looked up and spotted a female with exotic looking skin standing over him. He let out a sigh, picked up his bag, and placed it on his lap.

"Thank you," the female said politely and took her seat.

The scent of her lovely perfume tickled Science's nose. He looked her over from head to toe. Her hair was wrapped in a Louis Vuitton scarf; she wore gold hoop earrings and a diamond nose ring. Her face was naturally pretty, especially with the mole on her thick lips. He could tell she was thick by the look of her thighs in the jeans she wore. Her blouse was giving him a good look at her breasts, which had to be D's. Science felt his dick jerk in his pants. He kept an eye on her through his peripheral.

"So, you just got outta jail, huh?"

Science looked at her like, *Damn is it that obvious*? "Yeah."

"How much time did you do?"

"I did eight and some change."

"You were at the Fed joint up the road?"

"Damn yo, you ask a lot of questions. Look, I'm just tryna take this time to relax and enjoy the sights."

"Well shit, a bitch was just making conversation. I would think after doing eight years you would want to talk to a sexy girl like myself. It's a nice little ride until we get to B-More. I guess you was on them boys in there, huh?"

"What? Look yo, don't come at me like that. I was never on no fucking punks. I'm just chilling. Why don't you call your boyfriend and talk to him?"

She started laughing while Science sat there confused. "What's so funny?"

"You! That was so corny. If you want to ask if I have a man, just ask. Don't throw no indirect comment like that. It was cute though." She chuckled.

"I wasn't trying to… you know what, you got that, yo. You right, it is a long ride, and I do miss talking to a pretty face. So, what's good? My name is Science, what's yours?"

"I'm Jasmine," she said, extending her hand.

"Okay Jasmine, I see you on the bus to my city. What's your story?"

"Nothing dramatic, I'm just tired of this little ass town. I'm about to go to B-More to meet up with my cousin to dance. I'ma do that and stack my money up to go to school."

"Same ol' stripper story I see. You'll definitely make some money though," he said, looking her up and down like a salivating dog.

"Thank you. Is it because I have a nice body and a cute face?"

"Nah yo, you a new face and that mean new pussy. Them hoes in those clubs been ran through a thousand times over. New pussy in any club make stacks. That's the advantage, and plus you do have a nice body and a cute face. Just don't get turned out."

"I'll try not to; maybe I can hire you as my bodyguard? You all diesel and shit, I know you'll knock a nigga out," she commented, admiring Science's chiseled upper body.

They both laughed. As the ride progressed, they got to know each other a little more. Science was already feeling her boldness. Jasmine didn't hold back. She kept it real and spoke her mind, talking about niggas who'd given her the best tongue job and who'd dicked her down the nastiest. Her talk game had Science almost nutting in his pants.

Eventually Science dozed off, until the bus stopped waking him from a vicious dream. He was coming through the hood in a Maybach with the music blasting and a bad chick with her lips on his shit. Damya and other haters were outside with their eyes wide open and their jaws to the ground. He wished like hell that dream was real, and that he could speed off blowing dust in Damya's face. Science looked down at Jasmine realizing his reality, and that she was sleeping with her head in his lap. She was drooling way too close to his dick, making it rock hard. She looked so beautiful sleeping; he didn't want to wake her.

Science just glared at her.

"You got ten minutes at this rest stop," the bus driver called out. "Make those snacks quick and the smoke break even quicker."

Everyone exited the bus with the exception of Science and Jasmine.

"Ay, yo Jasmine, this is a rest stop. Wake up," he said nudging her slightly.

She slowly moved her head causing Science to get even harder. She opened her eyes, noticed his bulge, and the drool coming from her mouth. Her face brushed past his stiffness as she wiped the drool from her face. "My bad," was all she managed to say.

"Don't trip yo, I'm good."

Jasmine didn't look up; she surprised him by grabbing his massive wood, then reaching in his pants and removing his manhood. Science reared back allowing Jasmine to tease his manhood with the circling of her tongue. His throbbing penis stood at nine inches as she slowly took him in her warm mouth.

"Aww shit!" Science moaned.

Within seconds, Jasmine had deep throated everything Science had to offer. She bobbed up and down on his dick, assaulting it, sucking it like a pro. He couldn't believe the backseat action he was receiving, or the way Jasmine's lips made him feel. She deep throated him over and over again until Science began losing control.

"Ooooooooohhhh shit, girl."

Science pressed his feet into the floor as his eyes rolled to the back of his head. "Suck this dick, damnnnnn," he uttered grabbing a patch of her hair.

Jasmine never let up. It wasn't long before he exploded in her mouth. She took in every last drop as he held the back of her head, holding on for life. When she came up for air she spit his nut on the floor letting him know she was no rookie.

"How long we got? I'm horny as hell. C'mon let's go," she instructed.

"What? Right here? You don't want to go in the bathroom?"

Jasmine looked at him like he was crazy. "I ain't going in that pissy, cramped-ass bathroom. C'mon, right here is good. I need to get mine, too." Jasmine quickly removed her tight jeans and laid back on the seat with her legs in the air. She moved her thong to the side giving Science easy access. When he saw how fat her shaved pussy was he wanted to get a taste.

"Noooo, I want the dick. C'mon, let's fuck!"

That was all Science needed to hear. He was ready to go. He couldn't believe how flexible she was as he entered her, stroking her insides ferociously. He had her legs behind her neck as he pounded away at her tight, wet pussy.

"Mmmm…fuck this pussy, fuck me, Science!"

She clawed his back as he continued his rampage.

"Aaaaah, shit," she hollered. "That's it. That's it!

Science lifted his head slightly to make sure no one was coming, but Jasmine yanked him back toward her. Immediately, Science plunged back in, making her tremble. He felt her body shake and saw thick white cream on his dick as he thrust deeper. It was far from over as he went harder and faster to get his second nut.

Out of the blue, Science felt someone's presence. He turned to see the bus driver looking on as he punished Jasmine missionary style. Jasmine was in such ecstasy, she didn't look up, or even care that they were being watched. Science looked at him still keeping his pace, wondering how to handle things. The bus driver looked back at him like, 'nigga, don't look at me, do you.' Science pounded some more, feeling his climax near as the driver walked back to the front, mumbling a few crazy words about sharing pussy on the bus. The moans from Jasmine only made him come faster. He was about to pull out, but quickly threw the thought away, and erupted inside of her. He rolled over after hearing chatter from the front of the bus, knowing he had to quickly pull up his pants.

"Yo shorty, that thang official! Damn!" Science said, wiping the beads of sweat from his forehead and trying to catch his breath. Jasmine slowly sat up feeling weak and fully satisfied. She tried to put her leg through her jeans, but her legs felt like noodles. Science saw her struggling and reached down to help.

"Thank you," Jasmine said genuinely.

"Nah, yo. Thank you."

"I had to test you out to see if you lost your touch. All those years could have fucked you up."

"My pipe game official, yo. Some things you don't lose."

"I see."

Jasmine and Science spent the next two hours getting to know each other better. He enjoyed being able to talk to a female face-to-face again; especially one who understood the streets. By the time the bus pulled up to the Baltimore bus station Science knew he'd want to get up with Jasmine again. Everyone gathered their belongings and made it to the exit.

"Yo, Jasmine I just…"

"Science, you ain't about to get all emotional on me, is you?" she stated with her hands on her hips. "That was just a good friendly fuck. It wasn't nothing more, right?"

"Nah, you right. Just take my mom's number down in case you want to do that again."

"If it's meant to be, we'll meet again. It was just fun, Science." Jasmine grabbed her bag, then traced his tattoo on his neck with her hand. "It's been real," she said as she walked off the bus leaving him standing there.

What she'd pulled made him want her even more. But like she said, if it was meant to be they'd see each other again. Besides, Science wasn't in a rush to wife some chick he fucked on a bus the first day he met her anyway. When he finally stepped off the bus, he inhaled the air of his city. He was back. Immediately, he began thinking of ways to get money again.

For Science everything seemed simple. The notion of being free had him spellbound. It took several minutes for him to start moving his feet. By the time he focused again, he was stopped dead in his tracks by a vision that had him wondering how to play things. From afar, he could see two guys slouched down inside a black Impala, glaring directly at him. One wore a baseball cap, pulled deeply over his eyes; while the other had long, thick dreads. Their cunning eyes locked with Science's. It was a look that warned trouble, maybe even death. For minutes they stared each other down until Science stuck his hand in his pocket and moved in their direction.

Quickly, the youngest of the two picked up his cell and put it to his ear, continuing to watch Science's every move. As he mouthed a few words, Science wondered if he'd had dealings with them in the past. Who were they? And why were they watching him? Science's first thought was to head directly to their car, proving he was no sucka, until the driver lifted his hand, transformed it into the shape of a gun, and mouthed the word, pow!

Science paused, dreading the fact that he'd have to get his hand on a weapon on the first day of his release. He took a deep breath vowing to keep himself out of harm's way. Before Science could make his next move, the car's engine ignited, whipped a U-turn in the middle of the street and sped away, with the passenger hanging from the window, shouting.

"Welcome to my town, Science! You're on a visitor's pass, nigga!"

# CHAPTER 2

"I'm back, baby! I'm back!" Science shouted, despite the shocking encounter with the young boys in the Impala.

He hailed a cab and headed home to see his mother and brothers. He couldn't believe how much the city had gone downhill since he'd left. Even though it was full of poverty before, it now looked like a war zone. As the cab passed through the streets Science use to roam, dope fiends, crack heads, bums, and dealers flooded the neighborhoods as he sat in the backseat observing, surprised by it all. Soon, the cab came to an abrupt stop.

"This is as far as I go, youngblood," the cab driver stated, stopping at Hollins Street.

"Whoa, yo! I gotta walk like fifteen blocks if you let me out here."

"I ain't going no further, youngblood. This area is a battlefield. I might get snatched out my cab and have to walk my damn self. This is as far as I go!"

"Oh fa real, yo? That's how you doing it?" Science opened the cab's door and stepped out.

"That's $41.50," the cabbie said, extending his hand.

Science looked at him with a smile, and then slapped his hand away. "You making me walk the rest of the way so fuck you and your $41.50!" Science stated with authority.

The cabbie slightly opened the door, but seeing Science's grimace, he closed it back.

"Whatever, youngblood. I ain't got time for games."

"Nah, you ain't got time for an ass whoopin', yo. Get this raggedy ass cab outta here before I get these young niggas to strip this shit."

The cabbie hit a quick U-turn and sped away yelling out the window as he drove like a madman "You lil' thievin' ass nigga! I want my damn money, asshole!"

Science shook his head and started walking, seeing familiar faces sitting on the stoops of row homes, and hanging out on the corners. Older females were smoking cigarettes and playing cards outside. Children were in their diapers with no socks on, running around near broken glass, baggies and needles lying on the ground.

"Science, is that you?" a voice called out to him.

Science turned around and couldn't believe his eyes. Roneesha was walking up on him with her hair all over her head; a dingy white T-shirt, some old shorts, and a cheap pair of flip fops. When she got within arm's reach, he noticed the track marks on her arms and her brown teeth. She still had those green eyes that attracted him to her back in the day. He used to snort raw with her on the low and they would fuck like animals afterwards. Never did he think she would end up a junkie.

"What up, yo? Damn Roneesha! What the fuck happened to you?"

"Don't look at me like that, Science. I'ma get back on my feet. I'm about to go to rehab. I just was stressed out when my baby father got killed. But, it's cool. I'll be back, watch. All these niggas gonna be back on my heels again."

"Yeah, I bet they are," Science said under his breath.

"You looking good as shit. Damn, boy. You been pumping that iron?"

"Something like that."

"Science, you got a couple dollars so I can get this monkey off my back?"

"C'mon Roneesha, I just came home and you asking me for money? I thought you was going to rehab?"

"I am, but I'm sick right now. And the doctor said I shouldn't drive. Plus, I got diagnosed with claustrophobia, so being in Rehab might not be a good thing right now."

Science just shook his head at all of her excuses.

"Please, all I need is like twenty."

Science reached in his pocket and passed her off a twenty-dollar bill. He knew how dope fiends got when they were sick.

They would steal from their momma on her deathbed to get a fix. He gave her the money and kept going about his business. As he walked he could hear a car coming up on him. Old habits never die; he turned quickly so no surprises came his way. Sneaking up on him wasn't an option.

"You need a ride, yo? I see ya feet look like they hurt. It's hot as a bitch out here right now."

Science studied the black on black G-wagon with the black rims shining in the hot sun. The fact that his man now rocked a fade haircut and had a swoop part embedded in the middle made him question if it was really who he thought it was. After minutes, he realized, it was really Gwop, one of his old workers from the neighborhood. Gwop was all about a dollar, and by the looks of his Benz, he was doing real good. He'd upgraded his entire game; swag and all.

Damn yo, this you?"

"You know it," Gwop boasted from the passenger seat. He pulled closer to the curb. "When you come home, nigga?"

I just got out," Science said, leaning to talk through the window.

"Nigga, why you ain't let nobody know? Hop in. I'll take you home," Gwop said, urging Science to get inside.

Science quickly hopped in and felt the plush leather seats rub against his back. It was clear how far Gwop had come by the diamond fronts in his mouth. Eight years ago he barely made enough to buy himself and a few bitches the latest gear. Now he rocked a pair of five hundred dollar jeans, the latest kicks, and diamonds covering from his wrist. Science immediately saw the touch screen TV in the dash and the jewels around Gwop's neck.

"I see you shinin' like a mafucka. Damn, my nigga, you movin' fa real."

"You already know, yo. The game been good to me. I see you home now, so what's the move? You gettin' back down, or you about to be a workin' man? You know that's what all niggas say when they first get home."

They both laughed crazily.

"Nigga, I'm about get down," Science uttered while checking out the interior of the car. "Damn Gwop, you stuntin' in this shit. Yeah, put a nigga down immediately, yo," he said, feeling some type of way about the way the roles had been reversed.

"Yeah, we gonna see. I know you trying to get ya mom out this fucked up neighborhood, but you need to holla at ya brother, Donte. That nigga twenty years old and don't do shit but play video games and fuck bitches. And he wild out too much. Calm that lil' nigga down. Ya other lil' brother at least pumpin' the weed."

All Science could do was nod his head as he listened to Gwop's version of all that had gone on while he was locked down. Finally, Gwop stopped in front of Science's mother's house and double-parked. They both stopped to glare at the desolate situation that Science's mother lived in. Science knew at that moment he needed to make some major paper and get his mother out of there.

"Look, come down to the club tonight. I'll holla at Sheek and see what's good. He runnin' shit."

"Oh, so that's who you dealin' with now?" Science asked, not really feeling the fact that Gwop switched teams. Sheek and Link used to be their competition; now Gwop acted as if Sheek was his savior.

"Hell yeah! That's my man. That nigga makin' shit happen in B-More. But I'ma make sure he put you down," Gwop said with confidence. "He trusts my moves," he added, while eyeing a big booty passing by his door. As Gwop continued to talk he never allowed his eyes to leave the girl's ass.

Immediately, Gwop's door swung open. "My dick stay hard," he told Science excitedly. Open that box and peel off a few thousand as your welcome home gift."

While Gwop hopped out to run down the woman who switched so hard past his ride, and would need a hip replacement soon, Science popped the glove box to peel the bills off the stack just as Gwop instructed. Science saw wads of cash and a P89 Ruger gun, fueling his anticipation for getting back in the game. But to his surprise, he also saw a piece of paper with his government name on it, Cecil Walters. Before Science could process the info, Gwop was back in the car grabbing a pen to get the chick's phone number.

Science sat for a few minutes trying to understand why his name was on a document in Gwop's car. He remained silent while he contemplated his next move. The next thing he knew, Gwop was passing him a gun. "You need this?"

"Nah yo, I'm good for now," he said, snapping from his daze. He held his hands in the air, making sure not to touch the gun.

"Look, come down to Club Shopz tonight. It's Sheek's spot. All the hot jawns be in there. You can get your shit sucked off, ass-hole licked, or whatever you like. Plus, you can handle business all at the same time." Gwop laughed loudly, holding his crotch just like he used to do before Science went in.

"Ayo Gwop, I appreciate that, yo. Good looking out," Science stated, knowing he had to get another look at that paper in the glove box.

"Shit, nigga we go back. Besides, you passed off when I came home from doing that little three years. You coulda snitched. It ain't a lot of real niggas out here no more, Science. I ain't forget that shit. The game changed and it's all about self now. But come through tonight. I know you tryna get some pussy."

Out of the blue, the girl who'd been talking to Gwop earlier strutted back over, and seductively signaled for Gwop to get out of the car. Gwop got out and arrogantly walked over to her, instantly placing his lips on her right, oversized tit.

"I'm hungry, baby. Whatcha got fo' me?" he asked while laughing.

The woman was thoroughly enjoying the attention she received in the middle of the street. Science took the opportunity to quickly pop the glove box, and pull out the paper with his name on it. Shockingly, his release date was on the document. His mind began spinning. Why would Gwop lie, pretending he didn't know about him coming home? What was the purpose? Science wasted no time in hopping out of the car. He grabbed his things and made his way around the hood of the car when Gwop stopped him.

"Yo, I was just getting full," he joked.

"Man, let me get in here and holla at my mother."

"I understand that, yo. I sent my mother away from here. Too dangerous. Niggas always wanna rob a nigga and shit. I love my moms too much for that."

"I feel ya, yo. I'll see you later on tonight."

He shook Gwop's hand and walked towards his house wondering how much Gwop had changed. He quickly reminisced about the times when Gwop worked under him. He trusted him. He used to be his right hand. Now, things had changed.

As Science had visions of the past, he thought back to the many nights he'd spent with his homies, spending stacks of money, surrounded by chicks and hard liquor. The partying never seemed to end. At times he and his crew even headed up to D.C. to the Go-Go spots where he'd floss, showing off his line up of cars, jewelry and endless cash supply. Those days were long gone. But he was going to get everything back and more. He promised himself.

Before long, Science was at his front door, trying to open it, realizing it was locked. He rang the doorbell and heard his mom yelling, "Who is it?" loudly. As she opened the door in amazement, she couldn't even speak seeing her oldest son standing in front of her.

"Can ya son get a hug?"

She displayed a huge smile. "Boy, get in here and give me a hug. Why you ain't tell nobody you was coming home?" They hugged tightly; with his heavy-set mother rubbing all over his back.

"I missed you, Cecil. I hope you learned your lesson this time."

"I did, Ma. I did."

She sniffed him closely and shook her head.

"What Ma?"

"I see you ain't waste no time with the sex. Go get in the shower, coming in my house smelling like pussy. I swear, if you ain't like ya damn daddy. Both of you won't turn down nothing but ya collar."

He tried to kiss her on the cheek, but she moved her face.

"No, you won't kiss me with that nasty mouth! Go on and wash up. I'll make you something to eat."

Science walked upstairs and passed his old room. He cracked the door and peeked inside. He saw someone lying in the bed. It had to be Donte because Mooch had school. Walking over to the bed, he snatched the covers back and saw Donte with a pretty little light skinned girl with nothing on. Tits and ass was all he saw.

"Okay, lil' bro, I see you doing it big."

Donte opened his eyes and saw his big brother. He jumped up in his boxers to give him a hug. "Oh shit! What up, Science? When you get out?"

"Hold up, calm down Donte, chill. I got out today. Let me put the cover back on ya girl."

"That bitch ain't my girl. She just a freak from Mooch's school. You tryna fuck?"

Science studied the girl who was knocked out cold. Even with them talking over her, she never woke up. She even let out a light snore every few seconds.

"Damn, you must've put her ass in a serious dick coma," Science said.

"You know it, nigga," Donte bragged. "Now, are you tryna fuck or what cuz I can wake that bitch up."

"Nah, I'm good." Science placed the covers back over the girl's body and began to walk out of the room.

"Yo, where you going?" Donte asked, running toward the door.

"Just chill and get me some boxers and socks to wear. We about to go shoppin'. You got a car?"

"Nope!"

"C'mon, yo," Science replied noticing the low cut waves in his brother's head. "You twenty years old and ain't got a car? What the fuck you been doing while I been gone?"

"Smoking and fucking, fucking and smoking. I was waiting on you to come home."

"Six foot three niggas shouldn't be waiting for no handouts. You gotta get off ya ass and get it. And what the fuck is that on you face," Science questioned. He actually knew the answer. Donte's two teardrop tattoos on the corner of his left eye conveyed the life his brother now lived. *Damn, he'd taken another man's life.* Science knew he had work to do with fixing his brother.

"So, you a gangsta now? You bangin'?"

"I'm just doin' me, nigga. I'm not the same lil' brother who used to follow you around. I'm a soldier just out here tryna get what's mine. And take that Daddy shit back behind them prison walls."

Science could tell the conversation wasn't headed in the right direction. Donte's expression had turned sour. His intent wasn't to start problems with his brother the first day out, but everything his mother had been telling him about Donte being out of control proved to be true.

"I just don't want you to end up like me. I can't see mommy makin' it through your funeral, yo. C'mere nigga."

He pulled his brother in for a brotherly hug. "Look, I'ma throw some clothes on and we can drop shorty off and go to the mall."

"A'ight."

"So, let me handle something real quick and jump in the shower."

Science went into his other brother's room and closed the door behind him. From the looks of Mooch's room, he kept it up. He had almost twenty pairs of shoes lined up under his bed, a few posters of some thick model chicks, his fitted hats hung on the wall in a straight line and he owned a nice flat screen TV with a Play Station and DVD collection.

He sat on the bed, pulled out his money and began counting it out by thousand stacks.

"I see you back at it and on the grind. Here are some fresh boxers, socks, a T-shirt and a wife beater. Fresh out of the pack. Look, while you get dressed, I'ma drop shorty off. Mooch got the green in the top drawer in the Polo socks. That's his official stash, not that bullshit he be selling. Roll up."

Science grabbed the clothes and headed for the shower. "Just drop shorty off 'cause we got to talk."

As Donte walked out, Science's mother yelled upstairs and told him to pick up the house phone. He hadn't heard it ring, and wondered who would be calling him.

"Yeah, what up?"

"Oh, so you are home," the voice blasted. "I know you got some money for me?"

"I ain't got a muthafuckin penny for you, yo. I just came home."

Obviously you wanna go back for murder. Don't play with me, nigga. Get at me, fast."

Science hung up and plunged his head into the palm of his hands.

*Damn, after all these years, this shit is still haunting me*, Science thought to himself.

# CHAPTER 3

Donte beeped the horn from outside of the house. Science rushed downstairs worried about Gwop's motive, knowing he would confront him when the time came. It had been on his mind for hours along with going to see his son. He hoped Damya had at least showed him pictures or talked about him while he was away. As soon as Science hit the bottom step, his mother met him at the front door.

"I made you some food, Cecil. Ain't you gonna eat before you leave?"

"Thanks, Ma. Just put it in the microwave and I'll eat it when I get back."

"Alright now, don't get in no trouble. Oh, and please talk to that brother of yours. His ass is as lazy as it gets."

He kissed his mom on the cheek and gave her a tight hug before stepping out. "I gotchu, Ma."

Science stepped outside into the beaming sun and was glad he decided to wear the wife beater, some of Donte's shorts and the boots the prison issued him. His feet were too big for either of his brother's shoes.

"Who the hell you beeping at, yo?" Science asked Donte. "Ain't nobody ya bitch."

"Yeah, yeah. Let's go Science, this the time all the hoes be at the mall."

"Fuck them hoes, they ain't ride that eight out with a nigga, yo. Scoot ya ass over, I'm driving."

Donte climbed over to the passenger side of his shorty's Charger. Science got in, moved the seat back, and adjusted all the mirrors.

"C'mon, man. This ain't no driving test. Did you get the trees from Mooch's drawer?"

"Nah, I can't smoke. I got to see my P.O. within 72 hours. Plus I'm on five years paper. Fuck that weed."

"Scary ass nigga, everybody come home from a bid and blow."

"That's the thing. I ain't everybody. I'm Science." He pulled off speedily and turned the corner. The cell phone that was hooked up to the car charger started ringing immediately. Donte looked at the number and cleared it.

"Ain't you gonna answer that?"

"That ain't my phone. That's my little shorty shit. If it ain't her number to the crib I ain't answerin' it."

"Why you got her phone and not your own?"

"Nigga, I'm a pimp. You see I got her car and phone. This what I do," he said, beating on his chest. "And she's not my girl. She just like the way the pipe touches her stomach." Donte paused to laugh crazily at his own joke. "She do her and I do me. We got that understanding. She don't trip on my hoes, and I don't trip on her niggas. This car she got is new though… so I gotta keep the pussy satisfied since I drive this bitch more than her."

"You know the sad part about that, yo?"

"What?"

"You actually think that's thorough. You a scrub ass nigga," Science nagged. "You twenty years old with no job. You didn't get a diploma, and you ain't got your own car or phone. You think you pimpin' but you really just leechin'. Your sixteen-year-old brother making moves and you playing games, smoking ya life away. You a scrub, yo!"

Donte reared up in his seat with anger pumping through his veins. He was known to be a hot head but had never gotten out of line with Science.

"Nigga, fuck you! You don't know me," Donte roared with his deep brown eyes narrowing even more. "You been in and out of prison my whole life. I'm a scrub and you a fucking jailbird. That makes us both fucked up!"

Science could tell from his brother's body language that he'd lost his temper. "You, you better unclench yo fist, nigga. I'm not the enemy. I'm just keeping it one hundred."

"What I'm supposed to do, sell drugs like you? Huh? You want me to go to prison like you?" You don't know shit!"

"Yeah, I may not. But I tried to get my moms out the hood every chance I got. She loves that crappy house and she won't leave. That's where her and ya scrub ass daddy raised their kids. So she feels like it's some connection she got with him since he died. I looked out for everybody when I was home, everybody! Yeah and you too, yo! But when I did that eight ain't nobody send me shit. Not a letter, a picture or a damn cent. But it's cool 'cause I'm a man, and I chose to do wrong. I'm back now, yo. And prison won't see me no more. A nigga shootin' his way out this time. If the Feds see me again it's football numbers."

The rest of the drive was silent as Science let Donte's venting sink in about him not being around to be a role model, or look out for him like a real brother. They both made mistakes and only the future would show how they would overcome it. Science was always jealous that Donte and Mooch had their father at home because his wasn't around. Even though Mr. Ed wasn't his dad, Science still listened to him occasionally. Deep down inside, Science was really hurt that he'd never met his father, or even seen a picture of him. When he would ask his mother she would say, "Your daddy chose them streets instead of being a father to you."

At an early age Science started rebelling against his mom and getting in trouble at school. He would stay out late with the dope boys and ended up selling drugs full time at the young age of thirteen. He dropped out of school and chose the life of a drug dealer. He saw the dope boys with the cars and females, and it amazed him how they didn't have a care in the world. His old-head, Beef, taught him everything from shooting a gun, to fucking, to cooking up crack. That's how he received the name Science. His skills over the stove were impeccable. None of that had changed.

Science stopped reminiscing the moment his eyes spotted the familiar Impala following him three cars back. It was clearly the same car, and same guys he'd seen when he got off the bus. He kept his eyes glued on the vehicle from his rear view mirror as he made the sharp turn into the Mondawmin Mall parking lot. Like clockwork, the car turned, too.

"That's them nigga's right there," he said pointing.

"What niggas?" Donte inquired, turning around to the back of the car. "Where?"

"Two niggas watched me way too close when I got off the bus. Then they crossed the line when that nigga right there with the dreads acted like he was shooting at me with his finger. You see 'em?"

By the time Donte spotted the vehicle, it turned off and sped in a different direction. Luckily, Science had gotten a better view this time. He wasn't afraid though. He was used to the streets and the danger it brought. He just had to get his hands on some fire. Immediately, he picked up the phone and called Gwop as they parked and walked into the mall. The moment they entered, Donte was already trying to get a number from some chicken head.

"Yo, Gwop, I need some fire. Can you handle that?" Science asked anxiously into the phone.

He kept turning around, watching his back. The fact that he had no idea who was following him sent bad vibes through his mental. Science walked off as Gwop ran down a list of guns his boy had access to.

"Price don't matter," Science told him as he walked into the sneaker store to get the prison boots off his feet.

There were only two choices; Jordan's or Timberlands. Everything else just didn't fit him. "Let me get five pairs of the newest J's and three pairs of them wheat colored Timbs in a size ten," he told the young lady in the referee shirt. He could tell the sales girl was checking him out, but Donte walked in talking loudly.

"Ayo Science, I told you I was a pimp. We been here ten minutes and I got four numbers already," Donte boasted as he waved the small pieces of paper in the air with the proof.

"Good for you, but step ya game up and stay away from the birds. All them hoes are chicken heads. You my lil' bro, everybody know I deal with dimes."

"Yeah, let you tell it. Damya ain't no dime and that's ya B.M. Shorty might be under inspection on being a seven."

"She don't count. The bitch trapped me off," he responded while picking up another pair of shoes off the shelf. "Shorty put a hole in the condom. Check my jacket lil' nigga, all my hoes bad. I was the first to bring Spanish bitches in the hood."

The young girl chimed in to tell him his stuff was ready. "Is there anything else?"

"Damn, you ain't get me shit?" Donte questioned with his hands opened widely.

"Did you pass me off some change?"

"You foul yo, you know I'm in a financial bind right now."

"Oh, so you broke? Don't front nigga. Ya pockets light. Hold my bags and I might get you an outfit."

Donte laughed it off and grabbed his brother's bags, following behind him. "You got dat, Science. But I won't be broke for long. My plan 'gon make yo head spin."

They continued their shopping. The trends had changed so Science switched it up with the old and the new. He copped a few throwbacks, jeans, button ups, and lots of tank tops to show off his hard work. His body was more than impressive since he'd worked out like an animal while on the inside. He had muscles like a trained body-builder, and was ripped like a bag of dope. He planned on flossing for the haters to hate, but most importantly so the ladies could bite. By the looks he'd been getting throughout the mall from the females, he thanked himself for staying in shape.

"I'm hungry, yo. You got me carrying all this shit. Let's go to the food court and get some pizza or something."

Science was hungry; he was ready for some real food in his stomach. All those years of bullshit mixed together with a side of Jell-O were the worst. They got pizza and sat down to watch all the ladies pass; of course Science was still semi-paranoid without a weapon. But he sat down anyway, at a table with his back toward the wall. While Donte munched on his extra cheese pizza, his cell phone rang in his pocket. He knew the number and picked it up.

"Where you at, nigga?"

"Word, me and ya Incredible Hulk looking ass brother in the food court. Aight, come through." Donte hung up and continued his massacre on his pizza.

"That was Mooch?"

"Yeah, he with his girl. They comin' right now. He loves that little bitch. That nigga stay buying her whatever she wants. She got that nigga's nose wide, yo. That nigga even bought her a dog, yo."

"A dog?"

Donte couldn't stop laughing. "Yeah, my nigga. Some lil' dog that she wanted. That bitch carries that muthafucka everywhere, too. Just like white people and shit."

Donte laughed so hard he almost choked on his food.

"Yo, you a'ight?" Science asked with a smirk.

"Yeah, I'm straight. Anyway, she like twenty-two so you know she throwin' that pussy on his ass," Donte continued.

A few moments later, Mooch turned the corner with a sexy, Black and Spanish mixed breed vixen. Shorty had the low-rise jeans that were super tight; a low cut T-shirt that said 'I'm Spoiled', and some stilettos that showed her pretty toes. She had silky hair down her back with the sexiest lips Science had ever seen.

"Damn yo, I see why he open. That's the type of bitch you need to get. Leave them around the way ass birds alone," he jokingly told Donte.

As Mooch approached them, Science checked out his swagger. Mooch was definitely fresh from head to toe. He was wearing a 76ers Wilt Chamberlin throwback with the matching fitted hat to the back. His cornrows were past his shoulders and his Air Force Ones were brand new. He even had a little necklace with a nice shine to it. Science stood to greet his little brother who without a doubt was way more attractive than Donte, just significantly shorter.

"What up big bro? You got big as a mafucka."

Science bear hugged him and lifted his 5'8 frame off the ground. The moment he let him down, Mooch fixed his hat back toward the back.

"Damn yo, I see you fresh like you supposed to be."

"You already know! It's good to see you, yo. I hope you stay out this time, son. Niggas tryna get a dollar, and I'm glad you home."

"Best believe I am, yo. So, who is this sexy ass little lady you got?"

"Oh, this my wifey. Vita, dis Science, my brother I was tellin' you about."

Vita extended her hand with a cute smile showing the sexy gap between her front teeth. "Nice to meet you, Science," she said eyeing him, sexily.

Science couldn't help but smile when he suddenly saw a small dog poke it's head out of her purse.

"Same here shorty." Science's first thought was that Vita was way too friendly with him.

"Yo, you ain't supposed to bring no dogs to the damn mall," Donte said with a huge smile. "You ain't in no fuckin' Beverly Hills."

Vita gave him an evil glare. "Shut the fuck up, Donte. Pepper ain't bothering nobody."

All Science could do was shake his head. Even the dog's name was white. He glanced at Mooch who had a 'don't ask me shit about that' look on his face.

"So, what kind of dog is it?" Science asked, trying to calm Vita down.

She looked at Science with a seductive pair of eyes. "It's a Yorkie."

"*It's a Yorkie*," Donte mocked.

"Shouldn't yo broke ass be at work? Oh…that's right you ain't got a job," Vita countered.

Science decided to change the subject before things got heated. "So, what's good, Mooch? We about to bounce. Y'all staying or what?"

"Let me drop Vita off and I'll catch up a little later on."

"Aight then, I'll see you back at the crib, Mooch. It was good to meet you, Vita." Science hugged his brother again and watched them walk off, wondering how he'd keep himself off his brother's girl.

It didn't take too much longer to finish up shopping and get back home. The rest of the day Science sat with his mother enjoying the collards, macaroni and cheese, fried chicken, and yams she'd made. They talked and caught up on a few things as Donte called one of his jump offs over and locked himself in his room. Science didn't care. He wanted that quality time with his mother.

"So, what you going to do about Lil' Cecil?" she asked. "You know Damya just hopping around to every dope boy that she can manipulate. You need to get your shit together and get your boy."

"I know Ma, but he don't even know me. He was only a year old when I went in. I tried to call and write, but she ain't accept calls or write me back. I don't even think he knows what I look like."

"Cecil, that fast ass girl is no good. I told you about stickin' ya dick in every hole that opens up. These girls just out for a dollar nowadays. They don't know what love is. But I made sure your son knows about you. I walked around to that girl's house and picked my grandbaby up. I showed him pictures and videos of you at the beach with them nasty girls you left here. He knows you, and now you need to get to know him."

He held his moms hand tightly as he felt himself about to get emotional. Science loved his mom. She was a strong, independent black woman, and he respected her for being a great mother. She didn't fall victim to the crack epidemic like most blacks in the 80's. She raised her kids to go to school and do the right thing. Science just chose the other path because it was so enticing. At a young, impressionable age, he'd seen too much of the glam life. It seemed like the fly thing to do. Boy was he wrong.

"I love you mom, you're the best mother a man could ask for."

They hugged each other and sat on the sofa in silence for what seemed to be a lifetime. Mooch came through the door and looked at the special moment his mother and brother were having.

"Can I get some love, too?" He went over and joined in, but his mom playfully pushed him off of her.

"You need to talk to Mooch, too, Cecil. He's skipping school, messing with females twice his age, and smoking that reefer. I ain't crazy, he smells like it every day. He tryna be like you, Cecil. Please guide that boy before them streets swallow him up like it did your daddy and you." When she mentioned his daddy, it made him feel uncomfortable.

"C'mon yo, let's go to your room and talk." They walked upstairs only to hear Donte fucking loudly in his room.

"Quiet that shit down, nigga! Ma is in the house!" Science shouted after banging on the wall.

"Yo, Science, that nigga Donte burnt out," Mooch complained. "He's gotten so out of control lately. He ain't been himself. And…" Mooch stopped talking when he walked in his room and saw Science's clothes laid out on his bed.

"Where you going tonight?"

"I gotta handle some business at some club called Shopz."

"Oh, that's Sheek's club. That nigga got the whole game on lock over East."

"Oh yeah?"

"He getting money," Mooch boasted like a fuckin' cheerleader.

Science didn't expose his feelings to Mooch about Sheek. It seemed as if the entire city now thought he was famous; including his brother. Eight years ago, he and Sheek played on even ground. They both bodied plenty of niggas, and was rising in the coke game at the same time. When Science was home Sheek only had a couple blocks over East, and to hear he had the whole thing on lock now was crazy. They used to compete back in the day with the cars and bitches. But they never really crossed paths with the drugs because Science did his dirt over West.

"So, I hear Gwop be with Sheek now. What's the word on Gwop? Anything shady?"

"Gwop's straight. He's Sheek's right hand. All I know is them niggas gettin' that paper."

"So, what you doing?" Science questioned.

"I got a connect out of New York who sells me pounds of haze for four grand and pounds of dro for $3,200. It keeps my pockets good. I pass it off to mommy, but she don't take it all the time because she says she knows where it came from. I still toss her a few dollars in her dresser on the low."

"Look yo, once I make this move we gonna be straight. I'm a holla at the nigga Sheek and see what's good. You got a car?"

"Nah, but I ride Vita's Lexus Coupe. It's out front if you need it. I ain't makin no moves tonight. I'm tired as shit. What's good with Lil' Cecil?"

"I'm gonna try to see him tomorrow. Drop him a couple dollars and chill."

"Don't get trapped off by Damya. Ever since she had the last baby, she got extra thick. I mean that ass lookin' like that video bitch, Buffy. But we all know she ain't shit."

"Last baby? Damn how many kids she got?"

"You don't know? That bitch got six kids and all of 'em by different dope boys. Three of them dead, one doing life, and the other one on the run from the feds right now."

Science couldn't believe his ears. Damya was an official hood rat for real. No wonder she never wrote him, visited, or picked up the phone. She had too many dicks to juggle. He shook his head while getting dressed, wishing he'd never gotten her pregnant. It would make it easier to get rid of her since she was the one person who knew the one murder Science committed that would send him back to the Pen if anyone ever found out. He wanted her dead, but somehow still had feelings for her; feelings he needed to die, fast.

# Chapter 4

It didn't take Science long to get in the shower and jump in his clothes; black Sean John jeans, a blue button up with the black and blue retro Jordan's. He took a fitted hat off Mooch's wall that matched. He scooped the keys from Mooch's nightstand and checked the time. It was 11:45pm. When he passed Donte's door, he heard loud moaning, more than before. He knew what it was; his lil' brothers were running a train on the girl that was there. He smiled and laughed to himself as he left the house.

The black Lexus Coupe out front was sitting on 20-inch Lorenzos. He hit the alarm and hopped in. The inside smelled like a female, some sort of strawberry vanilla fragrance. He looked through the CDs, which consisted of Beyoncé, Ashanti, Keyshia Cole and other female divas. When he came across Lil' Wayne's The Carter II, he grinned, popped it in, and rode smoothly bobbing his head to the music.

When he pulled up to the club, he noticed a lot of young dudes on big rims doing real good. The last time he was home they were either on the porch, or looking out for the police. He couldn't believe how much things had changed. The females were still chasing the next baller. He parked and did something he had never done in his entire life. He waited in line with the rest of the club hoppers. Usually he would tip the doorman and he and his .45 Smith and Wesson would be in.

He noticed some loud music coming up the block and saw a cherry red S600 speed through the lot. The Benz pulled up on 22-inch rims blaring Young Jeezy's, 'My Hood'. Science recognized Sheek's tar looking ass instantly when he hopped out with an exclusive white female resembling ICE Tea's wife, CoCo on his arm. The chick's Double D's and ass looked like they belonged in a magazine. Instantly, bystanders showed

Sheek major love by either calling out his name, or giving him dap. Waiting in line wasn't going to cut it. Science stepped out of line and went straight to the front after Sheek went in.

"Whoa, playboy. You gotta wait in line," the heavyset doorman said. He stood around 6'6 and was easily three hundred pounds.

"Look yo, I gotchu." Science passed him a hundred dollar bill, causing the doorman to step aside, letting let him pass.

The music was blasting and the ladies were fly. Science saw Gwop and Sheek in the VIP area, but decided to grab a drink from the bar first.

"Henny straight, no ice."

The sexy bartender wearing a tight tank top with Shopz on the front got his drink with a smile. "You just came home?" she asked with her huge tits spilling from the shirt.

"How you know?"

"You know when y'all niggas come home. You got that glow and you buffed as shit." She grinned. "I'm Angela. I would love to be your first. Why don't you give me a call when all this shit clears out?"

*Damn, chicks bold as hell*, he thought to himself.

Angela wrote her number on a napkin and slid it to Science.

"I might do that, yo. I'm Science."

"Science? Oh shit. You mean Damya's baby daddy, Science?"

"Yeah, why?"

"Oh my bad, I can't do that. That's my girl, she ain't tell me you were home."

Science downed his drink and slid her a twenty across the bar.

"That's because she don't know. I'll holla." Science walked through the thick crowd of pretty dancers shaking and popping their booties. He got to the VIP and tried to go straight through but the bouncer stopped him.

"Nah, yo. We full up here," the big black bouncer said, placing his hand on Science's chest.

"Hold up yo, don't fuckin' touch me! I'm here to see Sheek. Tell him Science is here."

"Oh shit! Science, what's good?" Gwop shouted the second he laid eyes on Science. "C'mon baby, we got bottles and bitches, however many you want. Yo Bolo, let my nigga through with ya congo looking ass."

Laughter erupted in the VIP area. Science was let through and greeted with pounds and a manly hug by Gwop who was iced out. "Hope you got my piece out in the car?" he asked immediately.

"I gotchu, nigga."

Gwop walked Science over to Sheek who was wedged between his white chick and a chinky-eyed dime piece. Seeing Sheek up close made Science realize just how much Sheek had changed. He was more muscular now, and obviously rocked more expensive gear than he did before. It seemed like he'd gotten even darker, damn near the same shade as a dusty chalkboard.

Science extended his fist. "What up, boy?"

"Okay, I see Science home. What's really good, Scrap?"

"You tell me," Science asked, while pouring himself a drink from the array of bottles and alcohol that lined the table. "Y'all niggas doing big things, I hear."

"Depends on who you hearing that shit from," Sheek responded with arrogance.

"Let's quit with the games. I want in."

Gwop grabbed a bottle of Cristal and sipped on it as he sat down, throwing his feet on the table. "We definitely makin' major moves, playboy. You think you ready to get back in so soon?" he asked, showcasing every detail of the diamonds in his grill.

"What's up, Science," a female abruptly announced.

"Aye, bitch! Don't you see us having a personal conversation? All y'all hoes get the fuck outta here and let us talk."

Science had just about forgotten how cocky Gwop was. Without warning, he kicked every lil' bitch out of VIP, sending them scurrying off, even Sheek's broads.

"So, like I was saying, you think you ready?" Gwop questioned.

"I'm saying, you know how I get down. I make shit happen 'cause I'm a hustler by nature. Everybody in this city know that. I need to get on my feet and I know I can get the West Side on lock again like before. I know my peoples still makin' moves. So hit a nigga with like ten joints and I'll be straight. I'll hit you with ya paper in like a week or two. Then we back in motion, yo."

Sheek looked at him and burst into a loud, hysterical laugh. Science wanted to smack his chipped tooth out his mouth for laughing at him like he was a nobody. *How the fuck is a nigga with major paper walking around with one gold tooth, and a chipped tooth,* Science thought to himself.

For minutes there was silence between the fellas. Just music.

Loud music and glaring.

Finally, Sheek broke from his evil trance. "First off, my man Link runs that over on the West. Almost everything that comes through there, he gets a piece of. So I really don't need you," he spat. "Then you just got home from the Feds, so you hot right now. You can't just jump right back in the driver seat."

Science thought back to the night of his arrest when the Feds asked him to identify Sheek. He knew he'd never become a snitch, but wanted Sheek to know he did have options that night.

"Nigga, I'm always gon' be a stand up guy. Your photos been flashed before me a long time ago. I manned up, did my time, and acted like I never seen you before."

"You want a prize?" Sheek asked sharply.

Science just shook his head in amazement at his conceit.

"And another thing, what makes you think I'm hittin' you with ten birds? Is you crazy? You gotta grind like any other nigga did, from the bottom. I can probably hit you with nine ounces or a half a joint to get on ya feet."

Science looked at Gwop and back at Sheek. He couldn't believe the man he thought of as a clown was trying to play him like a peon. He had bricks before he went in. They came in twenty or better at a time. Now, Sheek wanted to play him with nine ounces. He kept his composure like a G and shot back the same slick grin. He'd calculated his profit at being a joke. That definitely wasn't what he was looking for.

"Yeah yo, you right," Science said standing. "Nine ounces it is. Well, since all that's cleared up, let's party with these bitches." He paused, checking out the area. "What's good with that white bitch?" Science asked with a smirk.

"No sir Scrappy, that's my bottom bitch. You can have all these hoes, but not that one," Sheek stated as he sipped from the bottle of Grey Goose.

"Damn yo, you making these hoes wifey now, Sheek? You slippin', baby."

Sheek ignored him purposely.

"Shit, I'm tryna get me a snow bunny tonight like you. It seem like them white bitches takin' over. They gettin' thick as hell, thighs, and ass. I gots to get me one. But fuck it. Let's party. I just came home. I'm tryna get drunk and put a bitch in the hospital after I pipe the shit outta her."

Science grabbed his crotch while everyone laughed except Sheek.

"Bring the bitches back. My nigga home!" Gwop yelled over the music.

Just like that the bouncer let all the ladies through. Unfortunately for Science, he didn't have a chance to focus on the ladies. His eyes zoomed in on the guy with the dreads at the bar, standing about three yards from him. It was one of the guys from the Impala. Science got Gwop's attention quickly. His heart rate increased as anger sped through his veins.

"Aye, you know that nigga right there?"

"Where?"

"The light skinned nigga with the dreads," Science said while pointing.

"Hell no. Yo, lets get back to the pussy."

Science wasted no time asking Gwop for the gun he'd seen on his waist. "I need it! Now give it to me."

# Chapter 5

With fire in his eyes, Science stormed through the crowd with fire in his eyes and Gwop's gun stuck inside his jeans. "Nigga, you got something you wanna say to me, yo?" he shouted, headed in his stalker's direction.

The crowd parted frantically knowing things could get ugly. Seeing Science moving on him instantly made him nervous. With wide eyes, he attempted to put his drink down, but Science swarmed him within seconds. Up close and personal, Science made his presence known.

"Here I am, nigga! Now what?" Science roared. "Point yo muthafuckin' gun now." He roared like a beast that had finally gotten loose.

"I'on want no problems, homie," the dread head announced. "It ain't me that got the problem with you."

Science wasted no time gripping him by his shirt and pressing his body against the bar. "Who sent ya punk ass? You doin' somebody else's dirty work?"

The music abruptly stopped and all eyes watched as they tussled slightly. The dread-head talked major shit but apparently lacked heart. Science could see security coming but didn't let that keep him from putting ol' boy in a choke hold.

"So, who tryna get at me?" Huh?" he asked, gripping his neck even tighter.

"Nigga, you'll see. I swear you'll see, homie."

Sheek's security and Gwop reached Science at the same time. Immediately Gwop stepped in trying to settle the situation. Sheek's club had been in the news too many times for violent fights, sex in the club, and so much more.

"Let 'em go Science," he shouted. "Whatever it is, it ain't worth it. We got these bitches over here, yo. They ready to fuck."

Science paused to stare at Gwop, letting his words marinate. He then loosened his grip slightly. Rage filled his voice as he spoke. "The nigga been following me, yo. He been playing games, pointing with fake guns and shit. Now he saying he not the one tryna get at me. The nigga got some answering to do."

Out of the blue, Sheek walked up, overhearing the conversation. Immediately, he agreed with Science. Although he wasn't a fan of Science, he was big on loyalty and respect. "Take him out back," he ordered.

Just like that the music re-started as Science, Gwop and two of Sheek's goons walked to the back of the club , exiting into a dark, murky alley. The entire time, Gwop was against wasting any time on violence and fooling with a peon. "Yo, let's get back to the bitches," he kept repeating. "Whip his ass, take the nigga's money, and let this muthufucka go."

"Hell naw! This my life, nigga. I can't be havin' muthufuckas followin' me around and I don't know why."

Within seconds, Science had flipped into a rage that no one could stop. He'd kicked the guy to the ground, stomping his head into the concrete forcefully. Blood poured from both his head and face as Science continued his brutal attack. No one did a thing, not Sheek's boys or Gwop. There was only more begging from Gwop to end it all. From the ground, the guy soon lifted his eyes, and pleaded silently for Gwop to convince Science to let him go.

"Yo, we gotta talk about this shit," he begged. "You gotta help me," the dread head called out to Gwop.

"Yo Science, leave this nigga alone," Gwop sounded.

Science felt like something was fishy with Gwop. He was too antsy. Too forgiving. He wasn't acting like the Gwop that Science rolled with when they were gettin' money together.

"Gwop, you sure you never seen this nigga before?"

"Hell no, yo! I told you that!"

Science asked the guy on the ground with the dreads just to confirm his suspicions.

"Naw, man. Just let me go, yo. I'll take you to the people who hired me."

All kinds of thoughts ran rampant through Science's mind. Abruptly, he turned around and passed Gwop the gun.

"Do him."

Gwop refused to take the gun. "If you wanna kill a nigga, do it yourself."

"Yo, I'm on paper. You know how it goes. Three strikes—you out. Handle that, for old times sake."

"Hell naw," Gwop shouted and began pacing the alley. Immediately, Sheek's boys rushed back inside the club. They knew no witnesses made more sense. "Just let 'em go," Gwop said once again.

Science cocks the gun and kneels down to the ground. "Tell me something. Why the fuck you been following me?"

With a face full of tears, the young dread head turned to plead for his life when Science emptied his clip into his chest and head with no remorse. Gwop backed away and watched as his body jerked back and forth. He was clearly dead from the first shot but Science wanted to prove a point to Gwop. He'd given him the eye earlier letting him know he could get it too. He was either with him or against him.

"Nigga, why'd you do that? I got enough bodies on that gun!"

"My life on the line, nigga. I'm blastin' anything that ain't official.

He glanced at Gwop to give him the evil eye. It didn't take long for Sheek to have his boy's dispose of the body. He didn't want heat brought to his club, so everything was done quickly and on the low. Eventually, emotions had calmed down, and Science had gone back inside to gulp down a bottle of Ciroc all by himself. The club closed down a little after 2 a.m., but the party was far from over. Science, Gwop, Sheek and a few of Sheek's soldiers stayed back with some ladies to get a lil' extra partying in.

Science was tipsy, but he managed to grab one of the pretty ladies and got his two-step on. Meanwhile, Gwop was getting a lap dance, and Sheek was smoking a big blunt watching the females dance with each other on the dance floor. *Candy Shop* by 50 Cent blazed through the speakers with force. The girl Science was dancing with, in her intoxicated state, got real close and spilled her drink on his shirt as she tried to pop her pussy on him.

"My bad Science," she said with an innocent voice.

"Don't trip yo, it's cool."

Science peeled off his button up shirt and tossed it toward the barstool, revealing his inked up body. The tattoo on his chest showing the City of Baltimore always impressed anyone who saw it. When the rest of the ladies saw how cut his muscles were in his wife beater; titties and ass suddenly surrounded him. Science was in the middle as butts swarmed him like killer bees and began grinding on him. He squeezed whatever he could. He didn't realize that Candy, the white bombshell Sheek was with was one of the butts he fondled. Her presence commanded attention, moving the other women away as she bent over in front of Science, claiming him for herself. When she grinded her round ass against his dick, Science hardened even more. He was tipsy and the liquor had him smacking that ass as she popped it.

"Go Candy, Go Candy!" the other females chanted as she went to work on Science.

"Yo Candy! Get the fuck over here!" Sheek yelled over the music, stopping the freak fest on the dance floor.

Candy walked over to Sheek with her head downward as the rest of the girls went back to putting Science in a sandwich.

"What's wrong, Daddy? I was just dancing a little," Candy said with fear. He snatched her closer to him, yanking her dark brown and blonde, streaked hair. Sheek pushed her down on the plush leather seat next to where he was sitting.

"Sit ya ass down, you had enough drinkin' and dancin'."

"I was just dancing, Sheek, damn. You be on that jealous shit too much," Candy said with an attitude.

"What? Bitch who you talkin' back to? Remember who you speakin' to like that. Remember what happened the last time. And don't make me snap in this mafucka, ya'mean?" Sheek gripped her face and looked deep in her eyes. "Bitch, act right, or else!"

Gwop was still getting a lap dance out of this world. From the outside it looked like a normal lap dance but Gwop had her skirt lifted, while she rode him viciously. He was sipping on a bottle of Cristal just watching his dick go in and out of her nest.

"I gotta piss ladies, I'll be right back," Science said, trying to make his way to the men's room.

"Nooooooo. C'mon Science let's finish, I love this song," one of the females with the bright red juicy lips and light bronze eyes stated. She kept rubbing her hands up and down Science's muscular arm as she whined.

"We got all night," he told her before strutting off the dance floor.

Science looked over at Candy who watched his every move. He winked at her then noticed the sweet glare in her eyes. She was feeling him and he knew it. There seemed to be a connection, outside of the fact that he always wanted a white chick. In time, Science knew he'd fuck Sheek's woman. He simply strolled to the back where the bathrooms were, knowing it wasn't the time or place to get at her.

Sheek was rolling up another blunt when Candy stood up fixing her mini-skirt. "I gotta use the bathroom, Sheek."

He looked up at her and rolled his eyes as he licked the blunt paper. "Hurry the fuck up!"

Candy sashayed to the bathroom area and stopped in front of the men's room. She thought about it and decided to go in the ladies room instead. She walked inside thinking about going into the other bathroom, until a strong arm grabbed her. Science gripped her waist, squeezing her soft fat ass, and deep throated her with his tongue. He didn't care who else was in the ladies bathroom. Their tongues caressed each other wildly until Candy broke their passionate kiss and wiped her mouth.

"Are you crazy? Sheek is right out there! You gonna get yourself killed. We can't do this," she exclaimed nervously.

"You can't! I can. Fuck that nigga. I see the way he treatin' you, yo. That ain't how a queen supposed to be handled. You too fine to be mistreated, shorty. Look, I want you to meet me at the Ramada downtown tomorrow night around 10:30. I'll be under the name Devon Tower."

"Candy, Candy, Candy!" a loud, angry voice shouted from outside the door. "It don't take that long to piss, bitch!"

"Oh shit that's him! I can't meet you. He won't let me leave."

"You can and you will. I know you tired of being less than what you are. Be there! 10:30," he added just after feeling underneath her skirt, and sliding his fingers between her pussy lips to feel her wetness.

"Be there," he said firmly. He hurried into a stall and stood on the toilet seat as the door burst wide open. Sheek came in with the blunt hanging from his lip and raging. "What the fuck takin' you so long? C'mon, bitch! Let's go."

"Ohhh. Okay," she stuttered.

Sheek obviously thought something was fishy. Candy's face was flushed, and hardly had any color left in her face. "You in here by yourself?" he asked.

"Stop it, Sheek. Of course I am," she said turning on the water faucet. "Let me wash my hands and I'll be out."

Candy went over to the sink calmly and proceeded to wash her hands. She kept looking into the mirror hoping like hell Science didn't do anything stupid. Candy knew Sheek's track record. She didn't want a repeat from the time when he drug her through Macy's all because a few guys were flirting with her at the cash register. She thought about the many hospital visits all because of his powerful fists.

She turned away from the mirror hoping like hell Science hadn't got her caught up. Out of the blue, Sheek began pacing the floor, looking around the bathroom causing Candy's heart rate to increase even more. He bent down to see if any feet were in the stalls.

"C'mon Sheek," Candy said. She grabbed his hand seductively, allowing her tongue to trace the outline of his neck, following by kissing him in the mouth. She hated his gold tooth but licked it like she loved it. She pushed him into the first stall and closed the door behind them. Sheek didn't resist. He sat on the toilet seat and pulled out the dick that Candy viewed as too little. Candy almost laughed with all the alcohol she'd consumed, but she played it cool while she thought about Science. She lifted up her skirt around her hips and sat on his dick. Hearing the moaning from Sheek, Science crept out of the stall and then out of the bathroom knowing Sheek's girl would soon be his.

"What took you so long, Science?" one of the ladies asked, grabbing his hand the moment he came back to the dance floor.

"Big dicks take longer to release," he said sincerely.

The girl's face lit up, but Science wasn't really interested in her. He looked over at Gwop who was putting his dick back in his jeans and the freak he had was fixing her tight dress.

"Yo Gwop, I'm about to break out, yo!" Science yelled over the music.

"Call me tomorrow so we can talk, nigga."

"No doubt, yo. So what's good shorty, you coming with me?" Science asked the short brown skinned stallion with light eyes.

"Yeah, but can Djuana come, too?" she asked, pointing to her friend.

Science looked over at the light skinned shorty with bright pink lipstick spread thickly on her lips. She had freak written all over her face, causing his dick to instantly get hard. After the night he'd had, he needed something to make things better. Pussy was the key.

"Let's ride."

# Chapter 6

"Guuuuurrrrl, was y'all at Shopz last night? Hmm, I heard it was some ballers in there," Kim boasted as she braided her customer, Amira's hair.

Kim's was a local salon that always kept gossip and drama flowing. Some people came in just to get the scoop on the who's who around the city of Baltimore. Some females came with hopes of seeing if their man or baby's father was in the mix. One way or another, names always came out. Kim's had four regular stylists and five when her sister Damya needed to make a couple dollars. The shop was packed on this particular Saturday afternoon and all ears were wide open.

"Bitch, did you see Gwop with his wild ass last night? He sent us like five bottles and didn't even come over to holla. I swear that nigga is too cocky for his own good," one of the girls said.

"Naw bitch, that nigga is a dog! He thinks he the shit," Kim shot back. "Everybody knows he's Sheek's flunky." Kim instantly threw shade.

"Flunky? That nigga got just as much gear and paper as Sheek," Damya chimed in.

"Damya please, you just saying that because you fucked the nigga a couple months back. He copped all ya kids new scooters and sneakers," Kim stated with her hands on her hips. "So, now you on his cheer team?"

Everyone started laughing as Kim put her sister on blast. Damya didn't care though because it wasn't any shame in her game. If a nigga pockets were fat enough he could get the pussy if he gave up the right amount of dollars.

"Where was you at anyway, Damya? A nigga you would have wanted to see came through lookin' like a Mandingo Warrior," Amira said with a grin.

Just as Damya was about to ask, Diamond pranced through the door with a Louis Vuitton scarf on, and some Gucci sunglasses. She was wearing some Victoria Secret sweats, flip-flops and a blinged out tank top that read 'Baller Bitch'.

"Kim, gurlllllll. Can I please squeeze in somewhere? I gotta get this weave fixed."

Diamond always thought she could get special treatment because she gave the best deals to Kim when she boosted. Since Diamond wasn't your average booster, Kim most times fit her in the schedule, knowing she'd get a deal on some Prada or Gucci in return.

"Now Diamond, I just did ya shit yesterday for the club. What happened? You got in a fight or something?" Kim asked, trying to be nosy.

Diamond took a seat and removed her shades, then sighed. She had huge, puffy bags underneath her eyes like she had been up all night. Every time Diamond came to the shop she had a crazy sex story. Damya envied her for that. Diamond would say who she was about to trap with her pussy and Damya would say she had him already. It was always war.

"Whose dick you suck this time?" Damya interjected sarcastically as she sent one of her clients under the dryer and started on another.

"Well, before I was interrupted by a hater, I was about to tell everybody. If y'all was at Shopz last night you'd know Science just came home."

All eyes were on Damya to see her reaction to hearing his name. Everybody knew she took his money and blew it on a bunch of bullshit; trips with other niggas, jewelry, clothes, and that old E-Class Benz she bought. The entire city knew how she'd pretended to be faithful, but had never been. As Diamond began her story, Damya didn't give off any signs of nervousness as she continued doing hair, but listened intently.

"Well, after the club closed, Sheek kept it open on some private party shit. Gurlllllll, bottles, weed, pills and whatever was jumpin' off. So it was me, Djuana, Candy and like five other bitches I didn't know. We were all dancing and having a good time. Some bitch spilled a drink on Science's shirt so he took it off. Ladiesssssssss," she said dragging out her words. "When I say 50 Cent and LL don't got shit on this nigga's body, I ain't lying. So we all start throwing our asses on him 'cause he fine as hell, and was the only nigga on the dance floor."

"What other niggas were there?" Damaya cut her off, giving major attitude, and swinging her long, signature ponytail.

"Oh, it was Gwop, Science, Sheek and a couple of his soldiers standing around acting real stiff. Candy was throwing that ass all over Science until Sheek checked that bitch. But anyway me and Djuana won the prize. We took the nigga to the hotel room and we fucked like wild animals all night. We just got done like thirty minutes ago. I popped an E, and girl my pussy was on fire. He was just as horny from the Henny and all those years of no pussy. That nigga pulled my tracks out and tossed us all around that room from four o'clock in the morning until just a few minutes ago. The nigga dick game is official."

"Damnnnnn, Amira said, lifting herself almost out of the chair and drooling at the same time. "Where that nigga at now!"

Everyone burst into laughter.

"Oh and get this. He was fuckin' that bitch, Djuana's pussy so good, she tapped out. She had to go to the emergency room so me and him went at it by ourselves the rest of the morning."

Diamond made sure she gave Damya a shiesty look while she whipped out her make-up bag and applied some gloss to her lips. She wanted Damya to know she fucked her baby's daddy real good. The rest of the ladies in the salon were on the edge of their seat waiting to see what Damya would do.

"These dirty bitches love my left overs. It's only one Damya and they want to be my ass so bad. It's sad," Damya finally stated before storming off to the back office, but not before hearing Diamond's last comment.

"Science ain't think I was dirty the way he ate my pussy!"

Damya slammed the door behind her and closed the office blinds.

"Diamond, you know you wrong, girl. Why you do that?" Kim asked.

"That bitch shiesty as shit. She took the nigga money and left him for dead while he did all those years in prison. Besides, she fucked both my baby's daddies and got a baby by one. Fuck that bitch!" Diamond snapped.

"Chill Diamond, that's still my sister. Don't dog her out like that in front of everybody. You ain't no fuckin' saint. You love fuckin' a bitch's man, too," Kim stated, as she grabbed some hair, ready to sew tracks into Amira's head. Her scowl warned Diamond that the conversation needed to end.

Diamond didn't even respond because she knew Kim was vicious with the hands. Plus she needed her hair done since Science had snatched her shit right out, promising a round two later in the week.

$$$$

Science pulled up to his mother's house shortly before noon. He was dead tired from the ménage-a-trios from the night before. He hopped out of the car and went inside, flopping onto the couch. Mooch was watching some videos on B.E.T. when Science tossed him the keys to the Lex.

"I see you had a crazy night," Mooch said, turning the TV down.

"If you only knew, yo. These hoes lovin' a nigga," Science commented, rubbing his goatee. "And where mom's at?"

"She at work. The hospital called her in this mornin'. You know she the head nurse."

"I know that, nigga. I been gone, but I still know what the fuck's been going on," Science said, leaning forward to untie his shoes. "If you still here later, wake me up at five. I got a few things to do," Science said, kicking his shoes off.

"I'll tell Donte. I'm about to go out with my girl in a minute. Ya baby's mom called like fifteen minutes ago asking about you."

"How the fuck she know I'm home?" Science asked.

"You know you was at the club last night, yo. Them bitches talk."

"Did she say she was at home?"

Science wanted to see his son badly. He refused to let the day slip away from him without taking that trip to Damya's house. Seeing Lil' Cecil without smashing Damya's brain in would be difficult. He had so many bottled up feelings and need for revenge swirling through his brain.

"Nah, she at the shop," Mooch confirmed. "She said come by her crib at two," Mooch informed.

"She still at the same spot?"

"Yup, three bedrooms and six kids. I heard that house stay junky. Nothing but clothes and toys everywhere," Mooch said, shaking his head in disgust.

"I'ma get me some rest. I'll holla at her later."

Science closed his eyes. It didn't take too long before he was off to La La Land. He was beat. He had forgotten how sex really drained his energy. His brother Mooch watched him closely wondering how his brother had dealt with doing over eight years in prison. He respected him totally and admired the way he came back home and hopped right back into the life of chicks and money.

Donte came downstairs in his boxers and walked over to Mooch. "Lil' bro, let me get $250 until I make this move," he asked, hoping Mooch would pass off.

"Nigga what move you gonna make? Every time I pass you off a few dollars you don't ever pay me back. Fuck that shit, get it how you live." Mooch laughed and put his attention back on the television.

"So, it's like that? $250 dollars, you on that type of time, yo? I'm making a major move tomorrow."

"You ain't got shit coming, Donte. You burnt all ya bridges with me," Mooch said with his back to his brother.

"You got dat! When I come up don't ask me for shit!"

Donte stormed off with Mooch giving him the peace sign. Before long, the house was quiet allowing Science to sleep for several hours. When Science awoke the house was empty. No sign of Mooch or Donte. He quickly hopped in the shower and got dressed. It was almost three o'clock and he still had other things to do besides chasing Damya down. She only lived a few blocks from his mother's house so he walked, even though the July sun beamed down on him like crazy.

The moment he spotted Damya's house, he shook his head. Her front lawn had big wheels, scooters, and candy wrappers scattered about the lawn. It looked as if a tornado had hit, spreading debris across the withered grass and nobody bothered to clean the shit up. He knocked on the screen door a few times until a little boy with a small, nappy afro came to the door in his pamper.

"Wassup lil' man? Go get ya mommy for me, yo."

The little boy didn't respond. He turned around and screamed for his mother. "Mommy! Somebody to the door!"

Damya came to the door shortly after with another little boy in her arms and a nasty attitude. She'd changed a lot. Her once short hair was now long, and bronze colored with bangs. Her skin was still smooth and resembled an islander. Seeing her brought back a lot of memories; mostly the good times they had when money was flowing.

"It's about damn time you came to see your son, nigga! He upstairs, come on in," she said, rolling her eyes hard and repeatedly. She looked Science up and down the entire time.

Damya unlocked the screen door. Except for her hips spreading, and more weight to her round ass, she hadn't changed a bit. Science walked up the steps and stepped inside. The front room had toys and clothes everywhere as the first little boy and three little girls ran around playing tag, shouting and yelling. Kool-Aid and spaghetti stains adorned the walls and trash filled the floors.

"I told y'all to stop runnin' around in my damn house. "Lil' Cecil, come down here and clean up after your brothers and sisters!" Damya yelled.

Lil' Cecil came down quickly with the same attitude and a hard frown. "Why I gotta clean up they mess, mommy?" He walked downstairs not even acknowledging his father. "Why do I gotta do it all the time?"

"Because you the oldest, nigga and I said so. Now don't talk back to me, boy. I'm a smack ya ass back up them steps." She put the baby down, glared back at Science, and pulled the booty shorts from the crack of her ass.

Science looked at his son who was the spitting image of him. He had his slim nose, light eyes, good hair, and even his muscles popped out like his father. Science couldn't help but tear up. Missing all the precious years of his life cause water to fill both eyes. His only child was now nine years old.

"Damn, yo. You been drinkin' ya milk I see. Lil' man don't miss no meals, do he?"

Lil' Cecil turned around and dropped the toys he had picked up from the floor. His eyes widened after intently listening to the voice. "Daddy, is that you?" he asked in amazement.

"Yeah C, it's me. C'mere and give ya daddy a hug."

Lil' Cecil ran into Science's arms and embraced the father he had dreamed about for all these years. Science squeezed him tightly and kissed his forehead. He couldn't help but to think about all of the birthdays and special events he'd missed. His son was handsome, strong and reminded him so much of himself when he was younger.

"I missed you, son. I'm sorry I was out ya life so long."

"It's okay Daddy, you here now."

The special occasion ended when Science released his son from his grip. He noticed the cap gun in his waistband. "Yo, why yo got a gun?"

"I'm strapped up in case niggas get outta line," he said with confidence.

Science's heart dropped to his stomach after hearing his only seed talk that way. At that moment he made himself a promise that he'd get his money right and take his son away from Baltimore. "Look son, gimme that gun."

Lil' Cecil handed it over with no problem. Excitedly, he asked, "I'm coming with you, right, Daddy? You not leaving again, right?"

Science sniffed and looked at his boy. "Yeah, you coming with me. Go pack a bag so you can come spend the weekend with me." Science let him go and just looked at him shocked that he wanted to be with his daddy.

"Excuse me Science, but you can't show up and make shit happen. You didn't even ask me if he could go. I run shit around here. He got stuff to do, like clean this house up and do the dishes." Damya put her hand on her hip. "Don't you move, Lil' Cecil," she told her son.

"Hold up, Damya. He coming with me today. I ain't tryna to hear that mess you talkin'. He ain't no slave, he ya son. You need to clean this junky ass crib up ya damn self. All these kids in here, it don't make no damn sense." Science checked her with authority.

"Lil' Cecil, change your brother while me and your daddy talk. If the phone rings for me tell them I'm busy. C'mon to my room Science, 'cause you don't run shit, nigga." Damya started toward the steps after passing her one year old son off to Lil' Cecil. She turned around half way up the steps and noticed that Science wasn't following her.

"C'mon Science!" she screamed.

At first, he glared at her, remaining frozen. Then he started up the stairs, noticing how much her ass shook. The rumor was true about her shit being like Buffy The Body. Her ass had him hypnotized for a minute, but he snapped out of it, and looked down at the bottom steps. She stood by her bedroom door with her arms folded, covering parts of her exposed breast. Science went in, and she slammed the door behind them.

"Why the fuck you have sex with Diamond and Djuana, huh?" she badgered. "I know you know they know me. You tryna get back at me or something, nigga? That's fucked up, Science. Real disrespectful." She pushed him in the chest, but realized he didn't budge. Science was cut up like that. It would take more than a push to move his body weight.

"That's what you called me up here for? Bitch, get out my way before I slap ya ass to the playground."

Damya stood in front of the door and pushed him again. She loved the firmness of his chest and instantly got moist. "No Science, you wrong!"

"I'm wrong? Bitch, you had five more kids after I went in. You blew all my fuckin' money and never came to see me. You ain't send me one picture of my son, or respond to one letter I wrote. You better be glad I ain't knockin' ya teeth on the floor.

"You wrong!" Science pushed her on the bed and went to open the door.

"So, I can't get none before you go?" Damya said in a sensual tone.

Science looked back at her, realizing she was coming out of her T-shirt. Her breast sagged a little bit but they still looked good.

*I can't fuck dis bitch. C'mon Science, think with your big head*, Science thought and closed the door. He walked over to the bed and pulled out his semi-hard dick. "Is this what you want?" He stroked it a few times, making her mouth water.

Damya smiled and crawled to the edge of the bed.

"Don't nut in my mouth, Science. Hold it in so I can get you inside me. I know you miss this pussy."

Science wasn't trying to hear it. He grabbed her head and gave her a mouth full of dick. Damya took every inch of him in her mouth, sucking the head of it really hard. She twisted her tongue in the hole of his penis remembering that made him go wild years before. She held his balls with one hand, and his dick with the other as she devoured his stiff member. She slurped and spit not letting anything free as she went up and down and jerking him all at once.

"Mmmmm… Shit! I'm about to nut yo, AHHHHH!" Science pulled out and squirted his cum in her eye and the rest in her freshly cut bangs. He wiped the remaining cum on her titty and tucked his dick back in his boxers.

"Ewww, Science, why you do that? I just got my hair done." Damya said, wiping the nut from her eye. "Where you going, Science? I thought we was gonna fuck."

"You thought wrong. Get my kids out ya hair."

"Fuck you, Science!"

"Fuck you, too! You lucky I ain't kill you for spending up my money."

"Nah, nigga. You lucky you didn't go down yet for that cop killing. They say the gas chamber is usually the judge's first choice. And I still got the proof."

Damya's words cut hard. That murder was a secret that only Damya and a few of Science's soldiers from years ago knew about. Science had been pulled over by a racist police officer one early morning after coming from the club with Damya and one of his boys. It was the same officer who'd been taking money from Science, and blackmailing him for years. The officer intentionally began taunting Science, and pulled his gun on him as he reached for his driver's license.

Science had been drinking and wasn't in the mood for his torture. He grabbed the officer's gun telling him, that night his bullshit wouldn't work. As the officer leaned in the window, the two of them tussled for the gun until it went off, shooting the officer in the chest. Science knew he had to finish him off so that he didn't live to tell a different story. He left the scene unnoticed and passed the gun off to Damya, making it clear that it would be a secret they'd both take to their graves.

# CHAPTER 7

Science spent some time at his mother's house with Lil' Cecil, but it was cut short when Gwop stopped by and picked him up. He asked his mom to watch his son while he headed out with Gwop. He knew Gwop wanted to know if he'd really gotten rid of the gun that was used to kill the dread-head the night before.

"Yo, before you ask, I told you I took care of that," he told Gwop firmly.

"Bet, I'm just making sure, yo. I don't want no heat coming my way." He paused as they both opened the doors to Gwop's ride. "Look yo, Sheek ain't tryna come up off no birds for you. He told me hit you with nine ounces and see how that work. He say you been down for a minute, and half the dudes you use to serve is locked up or dead."

"Are you fuckin' serious?" he asked with a frown. "That nigga, Sheek's a clown. How you work for him?"

"Yo, dude the boss, so I can't really challenge that."

"Mannnnnn, I held it down when them feds put his face before me. I could've ratted him out. Don't that shit count for anything?"

Gwop shrugged his shoulders.

"Dude actin' like he can't be touched," Science ranted while throwing one fist into his hand over and over again. He fumed inside. "For real the way he carryin' it, a nigga like me can take that whole shit over." Science clenched his fist and nodded his head. He wanted to hear what Gwop thought but couldn't get him to say anything bad against Sheek.

"Look at dis ma'fucka on my pinky." Gwop poked out his pinky that showed the canary yellow diamond. "Two hundred grand! Most niggas won't see a that in a lifetime, let alone be able to put 200k on his pinky. You can't beat dat with a bat, yo. We gettin' money over here!" Gwop said pulling into traffic.

"Yeah, it sounds good," Science fired back. "But niggas know if you ain't number one then you really just in the way out here. Sheek gettin' all the real money."

Gwop hated hearing those words. He wanted to be top dog but was clearly the underboss to the entire organization. Sheek's empire was well over twenty million. He basically ran the city of Baltimore's drug trade. Dope and coke distribution was all Sheek, and if you didn't get it from one of his associates, workers, or suppliers, you didn't get it period.

"Look, enough about Sheek. Let's just go make money at Ms. Tammy's crib. You know she stay having the liquor house poppin'," Gwop suggested.

"She still got the dice games and dollar shots going hard?"

"You know it; you got some cash on you?" Gwop asked.

"Yeah, I got a couple dollars. You know my dice game still official. In the bing that's how I ate besides sellin' cigs and shit."

$$$$

Ms. Tammy had all the fellas in the back room shooting dice and kept the drinks coming. One room was for the dice, another was for poker and the front room was just a lounge area. Ms. Tammy made a lot of money with her twenty-four hour liquor house. She had been going on fifteen years without being raided by the police once. She had people in the hood wondering how she pulled that off.

"Nigga, bet whatever, yo! Everything on the wood good. I'm about to roll, yo, so place ya bets. I do dis shit!" Science shook the dice and rolled them against the wall and watched them roll a five and two.

"Yeah nigga, get me!" Science scooped up all his winnings and began stuffing his pockets. That was the lick he needed because he was down five stacks and before that roll. He started shaking the dice again, talking more trash to the local corner boys and other mid-level dealers. Gwop stood by his side betting with him. "I'm tellin' y'all yo, I do this for bread and meat. If I don't win, I don't eat!" Science said, and shook the dice again.

Just as he released the dice from his hand the door came crashing down and two masked men with big guns came in aiming. One had an SK and the other had a .40 caliber handgun. They were in black Dickie suits with black ski masks.

"Get the fuck on the ground. Get down and this shit gonna go smoothly," the taller of the two men barked.

Science couldn't believe what was happening. He had every dollar to his name in this dice game, but he wasn't about to jump out there with these guys. Everyone did as they were told and got to the floor. The one with the SK watched the other dude's back as he scooped up all the visible money, and ran in everyone's pockets.

Science could hear that there were more people in the other room as he listened to a raspy voice say, "Don't fuckin' move!"

The masked man stuffed a small duffel bag with money and guns and came over to Science. "Run ya pockets, nigga!"

Science couldn't help but notice that the voice sounded familiar, but he couldn't put his finger on who it was. He emptied every dollar from his pockets not trying to chance getting killed or pistol-whipped. He knew how thirsty goons in the hood got down and he wasn't about to test their gangsta. The man still checked his pockets and pulled his wallet from his back pocket.

"Oh shit, dis nigga got a wallet. What you a 9 to 5 nigga, yo? You a hard worker? Gimmie dis shit!" Science attempted to make out the voice, but his adrenaline rushed as the guy walked over and pointed the gun at Gwop's head. Science could see the fear in his homie's eyes as the cold steel pressed against his dome.

"I see you iced out yo, gimme dat fuckin' chain!" The robber snatched Gwop's platinum chain from around his neck as they headed out.

"All y'all mafuckas count to one hundred and then get up. If I see somebody look out the window before then I'ma blast this shit up, yo. Everybody gonna catch a bullet." The masked men made their exit with a small fortune in their sacs.

After hearing tires screech, Science got up without thinking about counting to a hundred.

"Yo, nigga they said a hundred not ten!" Gwop yelled to Science who was standing up brushing himself off.

"Them niggas gone, c'mon we out."

Gwop looked around still counting in his head and slowly got up. Following his moves everyone else in the house simultaneously stood up also.

"Fuck yo! I paid fifty stacks for that chain. I knew I shoulda left that shit at the crib, yo." Gwop snapped.

"Tammy!" Science walked in the front and saw Ms. Tammy at the small bar area nervously taking a shot of some brown liquor.

"Yo, Tammy what the fuck! You let them niggas in without checkin' to see if you knew them cats?" Science asked really ready to smack the shit out of her for slipping and causing him to lose his money.

"Science they took my money, too! They emptied my safe out. I was getting a lot of traffic and when Sleepy came in someone yelled hold the door. I looked out and this nigga I ain't never seen before pulled out that big machine gun. He said hush and then him and all these other dudes hopped out, masked up."

Ms. Tammy shook her head and downed another shot as her hands trembled holding the glass.

"We out yo," Science said, ready to roll.

"Nah, fuck that shit! Where Sleepy at? He came in right before them niggas. He probably set it up," Gwop added over Science's shoulder and grabbed Sleepy off the couch.

He grabbed him by his dirty shirt collar and shook him back and forth. "Who did this shit, Sleepy? Did you set us up to get hit? Don't fuckin' lie to me." Gwop was ready to put Sleepy to sleep.

"Nah mannnn, I don't get down like that Gwop," Sleepy said with his lingo sounding like a player in the '70's. Gwop punched him twice in the mouth drawing blood. Sleepy fell to the floor and received a few kicks to the ribs from Gwop who was irate and needed to let loose his frustration.

"Chill yo, c'mon we out."

Science stopped the beating and pulled Gwop out of the house just as mad if not angrier. He just knew beating up a dope fiend wouldn't solve his problems. As they exited the house,

Science had Gwop stop him by "Willie's", a neighborhood shop that sold pre-paid cell phones. He knew with the plan he had in mind he couldn't move without a phone. Little did Gwop know that Science's plan wouldn't be good for him.

$$$$

Gwop had given Science nine ounces of cocaine and $2,500 dollars a couple hours after the robbery. He eventually dropped him off at the Ramada hotel where Science said he would set up shop. They parted ways and Science checked in his hotel, waiting for his special guest. Suddenly, Science remembered that he needed to call his moms and Lil' Cecil. The moment his mother answered, she wanted to know where Science had been.

"Mom, I need you to look out for my boy for a couple days. Don't send him back to Damya just yet."

His mother fussed for at least five minutes describing in detail all of the threatening messages Damya had left before putting his son on the phone.

"What's up, son?"

"Daddy, where are you?" Lil' Cecil uttered. "Why you ain't take me with you?"

"Cause I'm working, son."

"That's fine 'cause I know how to put in that work. I coulda helped you. What you got, coke or weed?"

Science hated hearing the sound of that. He gave Lil' Cecil his cell number and told him to call him if he needed him. He hung up, then separated the cocaine into small baggies. He thought of all the times he'd bagged up. Starting from the bottom wouldn't be hard for him. He was gonna sell grams for $100 to the white folks that loved that nose candy. Then he planned on finding his old crew, re-establishing himself. After an hour of thoughts and work, he began to think his date wouldn't show up until the knock at his door proved him wrong.

"Yo, I see why Sheek got you on a short leash. Damn, Ma. You gotta be mixed with black the way them curves shaped," he said as he admired the beautiful white woman in front of him.

Candy stood there with a black fitted Chanel dress split down the middle showing off her huge breasts. The stilettos made her long thick legs look extra tasty. Science grabbed his dick and let her in. “C’mon in and have a seat. Make ya self comfortable.”

“I can’t stay long, I just wanted to see what you was talkin’ bout,” Candy said nervously.

Since being with Sheek she hadn’t even looked at another man for fear of getting her teeth knocked out. Sheek was very abusive and controlling. He was the type of dude who yearned for power; especially when it came to his women. Candy knew the consequences she would face if he ever found out where she’d gone.

“You can’t stay long? Shorty we kickin’ it, you stuck with a nigga tonight.” Science said with a smile. “It’s 11 o’clock now. The sun will be up before I let you go.”

Candy snickered as she sat on the bed. “I can’t do that. I told you that already.” There was something about Science that had her willing to risk everything. She smiled sexily as Science walked over to take off her shoes.

“Let them pretty toes breathe. So what’s good with you and Sheek? You ready for a real nigga, yo?”

“I don’t know what I want Science. I just know you look good as hell and that ain’t enough for me to give up what I got at home. Even though Sheek is some bullshit, he’s helped me out a lot.” Candy shook her head as she became emotional. She was confused and scared. She didn’t know why she’d showed up to see Science. But there was something special about his touch that had her hooked already.

“Helped you? How he help you out?” Science asked wondering what that lame nigga did to make her stay so loyal.

“I was dancing in Houston, that’s where I’m from. I left the foster home I was in because my foster father tried to rape me. I was in the strip club lost, young and dumb. Sheek and Gwop came through there and he ended up taking me with him. He was my first, and the only dude I’ve ever been with sexually.”

Science sat there rubbing her feet acting as if he was listening to every word.

Oh dis about to be easy. She young, fucked up background, and her nigga ain’t doing her right. Got one! Science stood up and looked into her eyes deeply and kissed her full lips.

"I gotcha baby, fuck that nigga. Don't you want to be treated like a queen? Don't you want a man to call you by your name, and not bitch this, bitch that? Don't you want to come and go as you please, and shop whenever you want?" he asked, while lying her down on the bed, and spreading her legs widely. She didn't resist as he raised her dress noticing she didn't have any panties on. Her pussy was completely shaved just like he liked it. "Don't you wanna nigga to eat your pussy like it's supposed to be eaten?" Science asked sincerely. He slowly inserted his index finger in her vagina and caressed her g-spot. Candy arched her back and moaned.

"You cool, Candy. If you want me to stop, it's okay. I don't want to rush you, Ma."

"Mmmm… I'm okay... don't stop," she said, biting down on her lip. She was damn near having convulsions from the sensual feelings her body was having from his touch.

After playing with the kitty for a while he parted her pussy lips and tasted her wetness. He took his time licking her slowly, like the tastiest lollipop he'd ever eaten. Candy had never been eaten out before and this made her body quiver with pleasure. She always asked Sheek to do it, but he complained.

A hefty groan escaped her lips as Science's tongue flickered his way up and down her vaginal walls picking up speed. He showed no mercy as Candy squirmed all over the bed cooing, shouting oooohs and aaaahs. He knew he had her when she grabbed his head, clutching it for dear life.

"Oooooooohhhhh Science! Right there, that's the spot right there!"

Candy couldn't help but scream out in passion. Science thrust his tongue into her more and more. Satisfied with the licks into her love hole, she squirted, letting Science know she wasn't going back home that night. "I'm willing to suffer the consequences," she told him.

He walked over to the nightstand and cut off the light. He opened the blinds and let the moonlight shine in. Candy lay there mesmerized, attempting to regain her strength. *That was the best feeling in the world. Oh my God, so that's what an orgasm feels like.*

"Take ya dress off," Science ordered.

She obeyed Science's order like it was the game Simon Says, but it was Science Says. She removed her dress without any extra thought while Science stripped out of his clothing. All she wanted was him inside of her. She'd been thinking of him ever since she laid eyes on his frame at the club. The anticipation was killing her. She looked at his chiseled chest and felt her pussy get even wetter. She put the pillow over face and screamed with excitement. When she uncovered her face, Science was naked putting a condom on his thick penis. Even though he was nine inches, his dick made Sheek's look like a tic-tac. He climbed on the bed and Candy invited him with open legs. Science held the base of his member and began to insert it inside her.

"Ouch, hold up Science, hold up. Do it slowly and don't put it all the way in. It hurts. Don't forget I only had lil dick ass Sheek."

Science smiled because he only had the head of his dick in her and she was already squirming. *Oh, it's a wrap. Once I put this dick on her she gonna forget who Sheek was,* he thought.

"Yo, dis pussy extra tight, I don't even think he popped ya cherry yet." They both shared a laugh and inch-by-inch Science slowly worked his way inside of her. He took his time and slowly stroked her gently. His dick was already creamy from her cum and he hadn't even started to fuck her like he wanted. He rubbed her big breasts and licked her pink nipples. When he felt like she was used to him, he picked up the pace. He pumped her harder as the sounds of her moaning and her juices made him go faster. He pulled it all the way out and slowly put it back in hearing her pussy fart. She laughed never hearing her kitty make that sound.

"Turn around, let me hit it from the back." Candy once again did as she was told and got in the doggy style position.

Her long hair came to the small of her back. Science gripped it all up with his right hand and entered her from behind. "I need for you to cum for me, Candy. If you don't cum, I won't cum. C'mon baby, bust on this dick!"

Science hit her with a hard thrust from behind hitting the back of her pussy walls. Candy threw that ass back as she gripped the sheets and let out screams of joy in the pillow. She felt Science yank her head back from the pillow and suck ferociously on her neck. He went in and out of her, faster, smacking her ass leaving a handprint.

"Ahh, I'm cummmminnnn'!" Candy squirted.

The huge orgasm made her weak causing her to fall flat on her stomach. Science lay on her back, still inside her, kissing at the back of her neck.

Damn, that feels sooooooo good. I don't think I'm ever leaving you.

The ringing of Science's cell phone interrupted the moment. Cecil had obviously wasted no time in calling his father.

"Yo," he answered.

"Yo, my ass. Nigga you owe me!" Damya shouted. "I've been thinking about this shit all night. Since you home now and got money to be all at the clubs and fuckin, bitches, then you can pay me to keep quiet. I'm thinking at least fifty grand. Come to my house this week and lets discuss, or you gon' have the police knocking at your door, nigga."

Science shook his head in disbelief. Damya was still up to no good.

# CHAPTER 8

It had been a week since Science vowed to grind his way back to the top. He'd been fucking Candy real good and selling coke out of the hotel room at the Ramada. Although they fucked at least four times a day, Science still made moves in the streets, and hooked up with Gwop a few times to re-up. Between selling his product and attempting to reconnect with his old soldiers, he hadn't had time for anything else. Surprisingly, Science found out way too often that his old crew had been killed off slowly, or had gone to jail. Candy assured him though that she knew enough of Sheek's people to make Science's job easier.

Candy never wanted to leave his side. She stayed with Science the whole time helping him count money, bag up, and sell his product. She was the one who introduced him to the main customers he supplied; even customers who'd bought mostly from Sheek. By the end of the week, Science had profited twenty grand. It wasn't nearly enough; or what he was used to making in a week. But Science knew he'd eventually get back to being boss in the streets. Finally, after prying himself away from Candy, he headed to his mother's spot to check on his son.

As soon as Science rolled up to the house, his mother's tongue-lashing began.

"Cecil, is you crazy, boy? Where have you been?"

"Taking care of business, Ma. I told you I needed a day or so."

"A day or so? You've been missing for a week. And you left your son with me. What kinda shit is that?"

Science held his head downward as his mom continued to fuss.

"You're a grown ass man with a child. After you didn't call back yesterday, I sent Lil' Cecil back to his mother."

"Damn, Ma, I wish you woulda told me first."

"Told you, for what? I didn't have time to wait. That boy is bad as shit and needs some home training. He's been ova here talking about guns, killing people, and singing all those vulgar songs. He's only nine. You need to step up and be a father, fast."

Science didn't even bother to argue because he was wrong and felt bad about leaving his lil' man behind for his mom to take care of. He realized he had to get Lil' Cecil under his wing and away from his mother. For now, he definitely didn't want to face Damya; especially now that she was on some blackmailing shit. He had to find a way to deal with her, and fast. So many options floated through his head, but going back to jail was certainly *not* an option.

"I'm sorry, Ma, I fucked up. I was wrong. But trust me…it won't happen again."

"It better not. You thirty-one years old, Cecil. Ya ass need to act like it and be a man!"

His mother sucked her teeth and placed her hand on her hip as Cecil walked up behind her and placed his hand around her wide waist. He kissed her cheek softly and gripped her tightly, wanting her to know how much he loved her. For Cecil, family was everything. Being gone all those years had changed him. He simply wanted to make her happy.

"You haven't even been here to see what Donte did for you?"

Science let loose and stared his mother in the face. "What do you mean?"

"Donte fixed up the basement. He went and bought you a bed and a television. He's in the shower, go down there and see what he did."

"Oh, snap yo, he looked out like that."

Science felt good inside knowing that if his brother spent any money he'd come across on him, then he really did have his back. He rushed to the basement and hit the light. To his surprise, a queen-sized bed with an expensive looking comforter set sat in the corner of the room. The large flat screen TV hooked up with three other electronic boxes filled the space around the area. Science noticed his wallet on the bed and a brown paper bag on the top of the TV. His mind began analyzing the situation. His wallet had been stolen? He wondered what the fuck was going on? Quickly, he scooped up his wallet realizing everything was still there, his prison ID, a couple dollars, and a picture of Lil' Cecil.

"How the fuck…?"

Science snatched the paper bag from the bed and opened it up. Inside, stacks of money wrapped in thick rubber bands filled the bag.

"Get the fuck…" Science shouted.

Science ran upstairs so fast he almost knocked his mother down on the way up to Donte's bedroom. He opened the bathroom door and pulled the shower curtain back with his wallet in his hand. Donte was washing his chest, but smiled immediately when his eyes met Science's.

Shrugging his shoulders, he said, "Yo bro, I didn't know you were going to be there."

They burst out laughing; reading each other's minds while Science shook his head repeatedly.

"We gonna talk when you done, nigga."

$$$$

Mooch strutted into Vita's condo with bags from Gucci, Victoria Secret's and Neiman's. He dropped them by the door, yelling Vita's name. "Got some goodies for you, sexy!"

Mooch walked in the kitchen and opened the refrigerator hearing Vita rush to grab the bags. There wasn't even a thank you as she picked up the items and waltzed back into her bedroom with Pepper following directly behind. Vita was selfish like that and only cared about what she wanted. Mooch knew it, but couldn't shake how Vita made him feel in the bedroom. A sex maniac, she had him by the balls. Mooch grabbed the Simply Orange Juice and drank straight from the carton, thinking about Vita until his cell vibrated.

"Yo, what up?" he answered, knowing he'd have to give the caller the bad news. "Nah, I'm out, yeah probably tomorrow," he told him, feeling the pressure.

Mooch hung his cell up and placed it on the kitchen counter. He was out of weed and his connect wouldn't be straight for a week. He just lied to his customer to stall him out. Mooch portrayed a fake image; with most thinking he was loaded with money. He stayed fresh but in all actually was hustling backwards.

Things were getting tight. Vita stayed hitting him for money to go shopping, paying her bills, and keeping her pockets filled. But being a lover boy meant there were other females on his team that he hit off regularly. With only $4,000 left to his name, he needed to save up. That money was to re-up on his haze. If he spent another dollar he would be cutting into that money. He loved Vita and he worked to supply her with the nice things she was accustomed to, but hoped like hell she wouldn't ask for even one dollar. He walked in her bedroom as she tried on the low-cut thongs, and sexy, lace bra he'd just gotten her.

"Why the hell I spend all that money on some shit I'm just gon' snatch off you? Ain't nothing sexier than ya birthday suit."

Mooch flopped down on the bed and watched as Vita sexily danced in front of him. For minutes, she played around licking her fingers, inserting them in and out of her love box. He hated the way Pepper barked whenever they were about to have sex, but Vita refused to put him out of the room. After ignoring Pepper's barks, Mooch eventually got hard and was ready to snatch her down on the bed until her phone rang.

Mooch reached over and picked it up. He heard the machine say collect call from a federal prison…Press 5 to accept or 7 to block. He quickly pressed 7 and hung up.

"I thought you cut that line off, Vita?" Mooch snapped, hopping up from the bed.

"Mooch, it's only P. He's just lonely," she exclaimed. "I can't just leave him like Damya did your brother."

"Fuck that! No wonder your house phone bill be so damn high. I ain't payin' bills so you can talk to another nigga. Cut him off!" he shouted. "You hear me?"

He saw the hesitation in Vita and decided to make his demands known. With a strong back hand slap to her face, Vita screamed, "Why the fuck would you hit me, Mooch?"

"Cause you disrespecting me. I told you before to cut that nigga off. "You still writing him, too?"

Vita didn't answer.

"Oh okay. I see how it is now. I'm gone, yo. Where the keys at?" Mooch screamed, scurrying his way toward the bedroom closet.

"Stop acting like a lil' boy. I'm with you, baby. What difference does it make if he calls every now and then?" Vita proclaimed.

"Lil' boy, oh I'm a lil' boy now. You calling and writing a nigga in jail, but you with me. I thought that nigga used to beat ya ass and you hated him, huh? What happened to you saying that nigga gave you a STD a couple times and never was faithful? He even fucked your cousin!" Mooch yelled. "Where the keys at, Vita?" He started looking around the room.

"Let's talk about this, Mooch!" Vita said with tears building in her eyes. "And don't forget, that's my car."

"Bitch, I pay for that mafucka. Besides, didn't you get enough talkin' with that lame ass nigga, P! You got me fucked up."

Mooch was hot and ready to put hands on her in the worse way. He thought about what Science had taught him about not beating on women. His brother had always said let a bitch go when they start making you put your hands on them.

"You tripping, Mooch! Baby, just calm down. I love you, I just don't want to turn my back on him," Vita pleaded.

"Oh shit, now I get it. So, you don't want to turn ya back on him, huh? You think I'm tripping. Well, watch this." Mooch walked over to Pepper, grabbed him by the neck, and opened her bedroom window.

"Mooch no! Please…baby don't do that!" she yelled out.

Mooch lifted the window as high as it would go and looked at Vita with anger in his eyes. "This muthafuckin' dog is all you care about!"

"Mooch, please don't hurt him!"

"Nah, fuck that. Do you think you gonna play me like that, bitch?"

Tears streamed down Vita's face as she held out her arms. "I'm sorry…I'm so sorry. I'll never talk to P again. I promise. Please give him back to me."

Mooch looked at her with pure hatred. "I bet you named this muthafucka Pepper cuz it started with P, huh?"

Vita quickly shook her head. "No, I didn't. I promise."

"All you love is my money! You don't give a fuck about me!"

"That's not true."

"Yes it is, and since I know you lying bitch, follow this lil' muthafucka downstairs."

Vita's screams could probably be heard a mile away as Mooch released his hand and watched deceitfully as the puppy hit the pavement.

# CHAPTER 9

Donte turned into the club's parking lot as he listened to Science fuss at Lil' Cecil. He understood why his brother tried to spit knowledge to his son. The streets of Baltimore were cruel. Young soldiers were dying every day and no one knew why there was such an increase in deaths on the streets of Charm City. The victims were becoming younger and younger, causing Science to really worry about his son.

"So, why did you leave out after I told you to stay in?" he asked him. "You hard- headed."

"Cause Damya told me to drop the nigga's package off. She said she'd give me forty dollars."

"Forty fuckin' dollars. Yo, you serious!" Science belted. "I'ma whip her ass. Yo, don't let no nigga have you carrying his shit! You understand!"

"I hear you. But yo, I gotta eat," Lil' Cecil uttered.

"Yo, that's what parents are for."

"Nah, Damya said I gotta provide. I'm almost 10."

Donte shut the car off and sat quietly hoping to calm his brother as soon as he got off the phone. He knew Science hated hearing his son speak that way. "Yo, you wanna go get 'em now?" Donte questioned.

Science waved him off and kept talking to Lil' Cecil. "And what's this I hear about you skippin' school?"

"You heard right, Dad. I ain't goin' no more."

Frustrated, Science shouted. "Yo, get yo shit packed. When I leave this club, I'm comin' to get you."

Science hung up, shouting and ranting, telling Donte how disappointed he was with his son. Donte just laughed. "Yo, bro, everything ain't what it seems."

"Yeah, just like you robbin' the gambling spot, huh?"

Donte took a few moments to fill Science in on what actually happened. He told Science they'd gotten close to one hundred thousand, but it was six of them, and most of Donte's cut was getting back his brother's money. So he really didn't hit for much, just a little over ten grand. Donte told him that he was scouting his next big hit. He was tired of the small hits. They laughed about it and ended up going inside the club to celebrate Donte's independence.

Inside, Science nodded to Gwop and Sheek who were ballin' in VIP as usual. Several half-naked chicks filled their area partying to the loud music. Instead of chopping it up with them, Science kept his distance. He still didn't feel too good about Gwop and knew that the moment Sheek found out about him and Candy shit would get ugly. They grabbed a booth and ordered a couple bottles while watching Skeek shoot nasty looks their way.

"Yo, we need to stop playin' and get that nigga, Sheek. He thinks he's untouchable or something," Donte said as he pulled a few stacks from his pocket. "I hear he sittin' on millions."

"A nigga like that you gotta sit on. If you don't do it right you'll end up in a dumpster somewhere," Science said with a smirk.

"So, what up? We gonna get that nigga or what? Cause I'm tired of being in moms' crib yo. I'm ready to get my own shit," Donte replied with passion.

"No doubt, I got my lil' shorty gettin' a condo in her name as we speak. I'm too old to be at moms' crib fo' real. But everything takes time. Good plannin'."

Science took a gulp of his drink and nodded his head. Out of the blue, Damya came through the crowd and stopped in front of Science giving him the evil look. "I thought you were in the hospital for food poisoning, Science? Why you ain't call me back, nigga?"

"I was," he lied with a straight face. "But I'm still chokin' off yo' threats. You really serious?"

"I'm real serious," she sassed. I think you owe me that. And fifty grand ain't shit to you. I coulda gone to jail as a cop killer for even being with you." She laughed.

Immediately, Science got nervous even though no one could hear them. He began looking around the club noticing Sheek eyeballing him every chance he got. "Damya, look, let me hit you off with a couple thousand, and some good dick. After that, give up the evidence and go on about your business."

She crossed her arms with a smirk.

"Nigga, you know how it goes. You gettin' money now. And I got yo son to take care of. It's expensive living in the hood."

"Yo, you not even takin' care of my boy. You got 'em wantin' to be a gangsta."

"Don't judge me, nigga," Damya shouted while eye-balling Donte. "What the fuck you lookin' at me for?" she asked Donte harshly.

Donte just shook his head. He thought about throwing his drink on her but let his brother do the talking.

"Look, Damya, I ain't got time to argue with you. Get a drink, it's on me," Science told her, knowing Damya would have to go. He didn't want his son to be motherless, but she wasn't letting up. She was dangerous as hell and would be disposed of as soon as he got the chance.

"Whatever, buy my cousin one, too," she sassed, smacking her glossy lips. "She just came here a couple weeks ago."

"Whoa, this ain't 'Free Drink Day from Science'. I'm only buyin' you one because I'm kinda drunk. But where ya cousin at so my lil brother can hit?" He gave Donte a pound before the laughter began.

"Please, she ain't about to talk to scrub ass Donte. That nigga's a hoe."

"Oh shit Damya, we got something in common," Donte joked.

"Fuck you nigga," Damya spat. "You don't want me starting with you. What if I tell your brother about yo ass?"

Silence filled the area.

Eyeballs moved from one person to the other. Everyone just kept staring.

At that very moment, Science's mouth dropped. He wasn't even listening to what Damya had just stated. He was now glaring down the throat of Damya's seductive cousin who'd walked over to their table. He couldn't believe his eyes. It was her; the woman who'd said, "If it's meant to be, we'd see each other again." He couldn't forget her diamond nose ring, or the mole just above her thick, juicy lips.

"Jasmine," Science said.

Damya looked at her cousin and then at Science.

"Her name ain't no Jasmine," Damya belted. "You got her confused with one of your lil groupies. This Genie. She a country girl, but she family. And don't try to fuck her either." Damya waited for her cousin to set Science straight, yet she didn't. She stood speechless while Damya continued.

"She living down here now."

"Oh yea," Science uttered.

As Damya gave the scoop, all Science could do was stare. He wasn't crazy even though the woman on the bus had given him the wrong name. The bus ride from prison couldn't be forgotten. Her wetness couldn't be forgotten. He played it cool though; if she wanted to play the stranger role he wasn't going to pop her bubble.

"Oh my fault, I thought you were some bitch I fucked back in the day. I'm Science and this my brother Donte," he said, extending his hand.

The woman he knew as Jasmine gave him a look that reeked, *very funny, nigga.*

"Nice to meet y'all. I'm Genie. And I heard that you were Damya's broke ass baby father," she said with a smile.

"In the flesh, shorty. You want a drink?" Science offered.

"Nah, I don't want to hurt your pockets. C'mon girl, lets go dance. I seen some money-getting niggas in VIP," she uttered slyly.

Science looked past Damya and saw Candy walk through the doors. All eyes turned her way as she strutted like a runway model in tight black jeans and a V-neck Prada shirt. She had her bag clutched in her hand as she stood frozen, out of place, looking around for a few minutes.

Science sighed. He had told Candy that coming to the club wasn't a good idea. It would be rubbing the shit in Sheek's face. It was clear Candy didn't care and decided to show up anyway.

"Look at this cracker bitch," Damya blurted.

"Why she gotta be a bitch?" Science asked, as Candy spotted him.

She smiled and headed in his direction. Meanwhile, across the room Gwop had spotted Candy, too. Little did they all know things would turn foul all too quickly.

"Hey boo, I missed you," Candy said, as she kissed Science's cheek.

Donte, Genie and Damya were at a loss for words at how Candy's whole swagger was different. She had a glow and it wasn't the make-up she had on. It was a glow like she had been getting fucked really good and had become happy and confident.

Still in VIP, although pre-occupied, Gwop had to tell Sheek what he'd seen. "Ayo, Sheek! There goes Candy right there," Gwop said with a big booty groupie on his lap.

Sheek looked over and saw Candy looking all sexy, yet different. His facial expression changed instantly. He expected her to have been in a car accident, or some type of bad situation that prevented her from calling him. But Candy looked good; hair done, nails done, and made-up to the tee.

"Where the fuck that bitch been at?" He shrieked, preparing himself to head in her direction.

His blood boiled as he clutched the bottle of Grey Goose and turned the bottle upside down on his lips. Sipping tightly, his thoughts raced as he watched her sit on Science's lap from a far.

This bitch really tryna play me. In my shit, with a nut ass broke nigga?

"What the fuck is this? Candy, you know Science is my baby daddy," Damya barked. "You better get up off his lap before Sheek drag ya cracker ass outta here by ya neck," Damya spat, looking back across the room at Sheek.

"I ain't worried about Sheek. My man's right here."

Candy once again kissed his cheek then tugged between his legs openly. Science just smiled. He could've cared less about Sheek or Damya. He was a gangsta and did what he wanted; dated who he wanted, too.

"Take a deep breath Sheek, you got this," Gwop coached, trying to keep Sheek from leaving the VIP area. "You gettin' money, nigga, so that bitch ain't worth it. But I'm tellin' you, if you beef with Science, he gonna take it to the max?"

"I ain't scared of that nigga!" Sheek roared.

"I know you not, yo. I'm just sayin'…it ain't worth it. That nigga, Science don't know how to fall back once he get started."

Sheek listened intently then stood up and told his entourage to follow. His eyes were blood shot red as he made his way through the crowd. He locked eyes with Candy who was still sitting on Science's lap fondling him.

Gwop's gut bubbled inside. He wanted to stay independent, far from the middle of Sheek and Science's drama. Science was too unpredictable, he told himself. He needed to be more careful about how he handled things with him moving forward. Science seemed to be one up on him, holding something inside, and being way too distant. As Gwop watched everything unfold from across the room, he showed out in front of his chicks, cursing, calling them names, and slapping them on the ass. The one chick who asked too many questions got champagne poured over her head as she rubbed all over his crotch.

"This bitch must be crazy coming in my spot searching for another nigga after disappearing for a week! Oh hell no!" Sheek stated, coming through the crowd rowdily.

"I see you fuckin' lil girls now, Science. You'll put ya dick in anything." Damya shook her head and looked at Science with disgust as she fired off at the mouth.

"Lil' girl? What you talkin' about?" Science was confused. That comment took him by surprise.

"Oh, Miss America ain't tell you? She only seventeen, nigga! She about to send ya horny ass back to jail for rape and child molestation. Plus that's Sheek's hoe. You really gonna beef over a white, trailer trash bitch?" Damya was throwing shots but she didn't care. She wanted Candy to say one disrespectful word. She wanted a chance to whip some ass.

Strangely, Damya's cousin stood off to the side but giving Science the eye. She attempted several times to throw signals but Science was focused on Candy. Still, she needed to get his attention. The info she had for him was important.

"Damn, Damya. You a hater like that? I'm 18 and I can fuck who I want. If you would've played your part right when you had him, this could be you and him right now." Candy licked his ear and rubbed his chest slowly. “You could be getting some of this good dick. Instead, I’m getting it all.”

“Oh, so Science gave you a heart now? Bitch, you must be stupid talkin’ crazy like that to me.”

Just as the two stood to square off, Sheek came between them.

“Cool out, chill! Ain’t nobody fighting in my shit tonight. Damya, take ya girls to my booth, drinks on me. Candy, let’s go bitch. You had ya fun, time to get punished.”

Sheek grabbed her hand but she yanked it away. “I said let’s go.” He reached for her arm and she snatched it away.

“No! Science is my man.”

She sat back on Science’s lap and put her arms around his neck.

Science just smiled.

He sat calmly without a care.

“Really?" Sheek asked with a smile. “This how we doin’ shit now?” he asked Science directly.

Science looked up at Candy then at Sheek. He shrugged his shoulders then uttered, “The pussy always knows what it wants.”

“Sheek, I'm with Science now. Move on, it's not that deep," Candy said with a smirk and kissed Science on the forehead.

Candy knew it would make Sheek angry, but he had made her shed tears for years. She felt she deserved to make him feel like shit for once.

“Oh, it’s not that deep? Bitch, are you crazy? Are you guys fuckin’ serious, or am I being punked?”

“Nigga, you are a punk, yo!” Donte interjected.

Sheek turned around in a full three-sixty beating himself in the chest like the incredible hulk as he spoke. “Where the fuck is that white muthafucka, Ashton at? I know he ‘bout to tell me that I been punked. Please come the fuck out now!” Sheek yelled getting everyone’s attention with his big bearded security and goons with guns in hand, ready to blast off.

Candy was quiet. She didn't know he would cause a scene so chaotic.

“Ohhhhhhh, so you been with this nigga all week?” he asked for clarification. “So, the whole time I’ve been calling you, this where you been?”

It seemed as if Sheek couldn't wrap his head around the fact that Candy had actually been with another man all week; and a man that had just come home from jail; a man with less money than him. It was clear he was embarrassed.

"Candy, be serious baby, I saved ya life. I took you from a life of shakin' ya stiff ass on stage. Besides with the way I got you livin' this broke ass nigga can't afford you," Sheek roared, causing more attention to be placed on them.

"Afford me? I ain't no object for sale! We done Sheek, can you hear? It's over!" Candy picked up the glass in front of her man and downed the Henny.

"Science, that's how it is, nigga? You just gonna take my bitch like that? Do you know what you gettin' ya self into, Scrap?"

Sheek looked Science deep in his eyes hoping to see fear but saw none.

"Look yo, you wasn't treatin' shorty right so she found a real nigga. No disrespect. C'mon yo, I know you ain't tryna beef over some pussy. It's plenty to go 'round. She got you that wide open, yo? You supposed to be able to say, "Fuck dat bitch!"

"Oh, nigga, somebody got to pay the price for disrespect!" Sheek took a few steps closer in their direction.

"Whoa yo, calm down," Science said, rubbing on Candy's ass.

He didn't care how loud Sheek got. He assumed Sheek knew not to cross the line with him. Most knew Science's violent ways before he went in. He figured Sheek knew he'd die before being considered weak or soft.

Sheek's blood boiled. He was being played and disrespected in his own club in front of all these females. He wanted to pull his gun out and leave Candy and Science's brains on the wall. But he knew deaths out in the open weren't a good idea.

"Fuck dat bitch!" was all Science heard before Candy was yanked abruptly off his lap and dragged to the dance floor by her hair. Science jumped up but was re-seated when three, 300 something pound, baldhead big bearded men surrounding him. With guns drawn on him by Sheek's goons there was nothing he could do. There was a silent dare in place as Candy yelled, screamed, and kicked across the floor. He couldn't see but he heard the slaps and the cries from Candy as she yelled for him to help her.

Onlookers watched as Candy's body was thrown helplessly into the ground. Sheek stomped her with his Timbs as he kicked her over and over again, in her torso and face. "Bitch, you gon pay for playing me!"

As Candy screamed, a few people shouted for him to stop.

"Yeah, I bet you won't think you cute now, huh. Know ya role bitch before you switch teams."

Science sat powerlessly knowing he'd have to retaliate on Sheek.

"Y'all better be glad I respect niggas with trigger fingers," he told Sheek's goons. "If not I would've been through y'all," Science said with frustration.

"You want ya girl?" Big Cuz the head of Sheek's Security asked. He'd seen Sheek moving and Candy in a fetal position laid out on the floor. The guns were tucked and they let Science get up. When Science saw Candy, he closed his eyes and clinched his fist. Sheek had disappeared into the crowd as she lay in a pile of piss and blood on the dance floor.

Quickly, Science helped Candy up. His blood boiled and his mind said to handle things immediately.

Out of the blue, Sheek shouted from the opposite side of the room, "You right Science, fuck that bitch! I'll buy another one like Nino say." He laughed wildly. "Science, hit me up. I'll throw you an extra ounce when you cop. Until then I guess I'll be fucking somebody's baby mom tonight." He turned to Damya, who was now by his side, tongue kissing him.

# Chapter 10

Candy winced in pain as Science attempted to clean the deep scrape on her left thigh.

"Shit Science…that hurts!" Candy yelled out. Every inch of her body throbbed and burned, especially her bottom lip that now resembled a red latex balloon.

"Sorry, yo. I'm just tryna help," Science replied.

"I told y'all dumb asses to stop and get some alcohol or peroxide from the store before we got here," Keisha added. She was Donte's old crush from high school. After running into him at the club just before Sheek turned into a mad man, Keisha offered to tag along and help once she saw Candy's condition.

"Look bitch, fall back, you ain't no nurse," Donte chimed in.

He hated girl's who acted like they knew everything. But couldn't help but stare at Keisha's apple bottom ass in the tight dress she wore. For a petite girl, she had a sexy shape that included a small waist and muscular calves. Her cinnamon complexion, chin length hair and beautiful almond shaped eyes added to her cuteness. Donte was sure that once everything with Candy was under control, he and Keisha would surely be fucking.

"Don't be calling me no bitch, nigga. I ain't one of yo little hood rat groupies. Besides, I ain't gotta be no nurse to know that peroxide is better than using water, asshole. The scrape might get infected," Keisha shot back.

Donte's dick immediately got hard. He liked her feistiness but didn't want to seem like a punk in front of his brother. "Who do…"

"Both of y'all shut the fuck up!" Science suddenly interrupted. "Y'all been goin' back and forth since we got to the room."

Candy looked down at the wound that was surely going to leave a mark on her perfect white skin. Within seconds, tears filled her eyes as she thought about the numerous bruises on her body, especially her face. She was embarrassed at what Sheek had done but most of all pissed.

"That muthafucka don't deserve to live after what he did!" Candy screamed.

"You right baby, he don't," Science agreed. "I promise you I got something for that nigga."

"Have you seen my face?"

Everybody in the room stared at Candy with pity in their eyes. Nobody wanted to make matters worse with the exception of Donte.

"Yo, you do look pretty fucked up," he had the nerve to say.

Keisha punched him in the arm as Candy's tears now raced down her cheeks.

"Don't worry, baby. Sheek's momma might as well pick out his fuckin' casket, yo," Science tried to assure her. "I'm bustin' off on him, that clown ass nigga Gwop and that shiesty bitch, Damya!"

"Yo, I can't wait to get at that nigga, Gwop," Donte agreed.

While Keisha tried to comfort Candy, Donte pulled Science to the side and passed him a piece of paper.

"What's this, yo?" Science asked, looking at the ten numbers.

"It's Genie's number. The bitch you call Jasmine," Donte responded.

Science quickly looked over at Candy to make sure she wasn't looking. "Why the fuck are you givin' it to me now, nigga?"

"Cuz she said it was important that you call her and I wanted to give you the shit before I forgot. Yo, that bitch phat as shit. Let me know if you wanna run a train, homie."

Science looked at Donte as he laughed then back at the number. He slipped the piece of paper in his pocket.

"Yo she said it's somethin' that ya must know so I suggest you call," Donte added.

Science shook his head.

"That nigga ain't shit! I should've emptied his safe before I left his ass," Candy suddenly said.

Science and Donte looked at each other at the same time and blurted out. "Safe?"

"Yeah, that nigga gave me the combination to the safe at the crib. It's in the stove. You gotta turn the oven on to 350 three times and it will open up at the bottom. Then you'll see the safe. He keeps like 500 to a couple mil in there depending on if he just knocked off some work. I used to hit it for a few stacks all the time and he never even noticed."

"And you know the combination, baby girl?" Science asked.

"I know the combination to that safe and where all the stash houses at. That nigga run his mouth and showed me all that shit, thinkin' he stuntin."

Science rubbed his short goatee and smiled inside.

The rest of the night was filled with crazy sex. Science had a lot on his mind but laid back and let Candy do her work.

$$$$

The next morning Science rolled over and felt for Candy. She wasn't there. His head was pounding from all the alcohol he, Candy, Donte, and Keisha drank the night before. They got adjoining hotel rooms. Science got up and opened the door that connected to Donte's room. He saw this dude with his mouth wide open snoring. Keisha wasn't there either so he figured they went and got some breakfast.

"Wake ya ass up, nigga!" Science screamed in his brother's ear, causing him to fall out of the bed. He looked up and saw Science in his boxers and wife beater.

"Why the fuck you playin' so early in the morning?" Donte asked, still on the floor.

"Nigga, you need to get some air freshener cause this shit smell like some old ass pussy in here," Science joked, holding his nose.

"I don't give a fuck. I like a bitch with a lil tang to the pussy. Pass me my boxers right there by ya foot."

When Science tossed him his boxers, Donte put them on and stood up.

"Yo, shorty can suck a dick! I mean fuckin pro head game. The pussy was some trash, but it was only a one-night thing. I wanted that bitch since tenth grade. She used to always be stuck up."

"Nigga, you crazy," Science replied.

Suddenly, the ladies came in the room laughing as Keisha held a bucket of ice in her hand.

"What's so funny?" Donte questioned.

"Nothing," Keisha stated giggling.

"C'mon, I want to laugh, too," he continued.

"Yo, these two Mexicans down the hall tried to talk to us. They about to check out and asked if we wanted to smoke some weed and relax. They look like they were up to no good though," Keisha responded.

Donte's expression said it all. "They got what we need baby. Let's do this!"

"Go holla at 'em!" Science and Donte commented at the same time. They both were thinking, *Two Mexicans in one hotel room. They got that work.*

"No, Science, I ain't about to holla at no Mexicans," Candy quickly replied.

"Look, y'all just go down to the room and tell them you want to smoke. We gonna come right behind y'all. It's gonna be quick," Donte stated.

When Candy continued to shake her head, Science put his puppy-dog face on.

"C'mon girl, fuck it," Keisha finally said. "Is anything in it for us?"

"A little something," Donte uttered.

Keisha pulled Candy along, knowing what the guys were up to. "Come on girl, it'll be good for us all. Easy, too."

"Get ya gun and get dressed," Donte told Science.

They both quickly got dressed and followed behind the girls as they knocked on the door of the Mexicans and stood to the sides. Donte had his gun out as the door opened.

"Ladies, I see you come back," the one Mexican said with a huge smile. He had long hair that was tied back in a ponytail.

"We changed our minds, we tryna smoke," Keisha blurted out and tapped the horny Mexican's crotch area. He let them in, watching both of their round booties. He never saw the blow to his head that knocked him out cold.

Donte came behind him with the gun pointing, he found the other short Mexican on the couch smoking a cigarette.

"Where the shit at, yo?" Science belted. He dragged the sleeping foreigner into the room with his buddy and kicked him in the stomach to wake him back up. After it didn't work he slapped him until he started to regain consciousness.

"Where the shit at, yo? Don't make me blow ya shit off." Donte put the gun to the short Mexican's head.

"Lift the mattress, lift the mattress! The money is under there, and the weed is in the closet," the long hair Mexican admitted.

Just as his friend was getting himself together, Science sent him back to La La Land. There wasn't any need for him. Science went to get the weed and money. He tossed the bed over and the stacks of money were right there for the taking. The closet had two black trash bags tied. Science lifted the bags and could smell the strong aroma from the weed.

"Oh yeah, y'all was doing big things in here!" Science smiled and opened one of the bags that revealed the green marijuana. "Dis dat good." He didn't waste any time as he quickly tossed the money inside.

"You guys really don't want to do this," the long hair Mexican uttered with his hands in the air. He looked down at his friend snoring on the floor and back at Science. Before Science could respond, Donte swung his pistol so hard at the forehead of the Mexican blood gushed out and he was out like a light.

"Shut the fuck up!"

Candy and Keisha both covered their eyes at the sight of the blood oozing from his head. Science looked at his brother and couldn't believe how much of a goon he was. Even though Science was okay with a couple of hits, he was no robber. He was a soldier in the streets who was used to grinding for his own. He hoped Donte didn't think he'd be doing this on a regular basis.

"Lets go!" Science yelled as he tied the bag up and looked down at the blood filling the carpet.

"We gotta finish these niggas off, yo!" Donte told him placing the gun to the head of the wounded Mexican.

"You bout to get us life, nigga. We in a hotel. Let's get the fuck outta here. C'mon!" Science and the girls headed for the door as Donte stood over the bodies ready to end their lives.

"Bro, this the game, yo. We need to off these wet backs!" Donte gripped his gun ready to pull the trigger.

"Let's ride," Science demanded.

Donte backed out of the room slowly still aiming his firearm.

"It was nice doing business with y'all. Word of advice though, boys. Next time some fine chicks want to give y'all some play, decline the offer, cause it's a set up."

# CHAPTER 11

Mooch skipped school for the third day in a row. He was still sick over the beef with Vita. His heart hurt from all the lies she'd told him about her ex-boyfriend. Her appetite for shopping sprees and the fast life was never satisfied. She wanted too much from him, and he was beginning to feel like she was in it just for the money. Mooch had some old school Jagged Edge blasting in his room. He sang along to the lyrics, *I Promise*. The door flew open and Science and Donte appeared. They were laughing loudly and talking shit to each other about how they'd scored and who was the brains behind what they'd accomplished. Science tossed two trash bags on his bed. Mooch sniffed hard knowing it had to be some green.

"What the fuck you got the slow jams playing for looking all sad and shit?" Donte flopped down next to Mooch and laid his head on his chest.

"What's the matter boo-boo, ya girlfriend stepped on ya heart and kicked you to the curb for a big dope boy?" Donte said playfully before Mooch pushed him off of his bed.

"I hope you ain't in here singing love songs over no bitch. We don't do lame shit like that, yo. We got you some good ass tree to sell," Science told him.

Mooch hopped up, and opened one of the bags allowing the smell to smack him in his face.

"Oh shit! Where the hell you cop this at? You put a nigga back on. This look like 10 pounds of all buds. I ain't never seen no shit like dis. It got yellow and red hairs on it and it's lime green." Mooch picked a bud up and put it to his nose.

"Don't worry about where we got it. Just bag it and sell it," Science instructed. Science walked out of the room with Donte right behind him. They both walked outside and sat on the front steps. Science felt his new cell phone vibrate that he'd gotten a couple days ago in Candy's name. The new phone would be used for strictly for Candy and business.

"Yo," he said after hearing the phone ring.

"I'm at the place right now, baby. It's perfect. I think we should get it."

"I trust you can handle that. I'm at my moms. Come scoop me when you signed all the paperwork and put that money down."

"Okay baby, I love you," Candy said.

"No doubt babe, me too." Science hung up and looked at Donte.

"What?"

"Candy got the condo. You can have fun here with moms and Mooch." He smiled.

"Ha, ha very humorous. When we split that money I'ma go get my own place, too. A nigga wanna walk around naked sometimes and fuck all around the crib. I can't do that duckin' my mother. Plus Mooch tryna get some of the bitch, too."

Science laughed loudly. "You wild boy. You gotta settle down with one chick one day."

"Nah, never that nigga. Is that why you haven't called Genie back yet?"

Science looked at him crazily. "Look, I'm with Candy and I got business to take care of for now."

"But she stressed real hard like it's mad important, yo. I think you should at least call her."

"I will," Science said nonchalantly. "Especially if I need some extra pussy. Her shit was mad good, yo."

They both shared another laugh as they sat on the steps watching the dope fiends stand in line for the testers the block was giving out. Junkies came running, praying they could taste the new package and get the monkey off their back this morning.

Bozo was the last to get in line and came up short on his free blast. He had a book bag and tried to show the young dope boy what he wanted to trade for drugs, but got kicked in the ass and sent on his way. Like every ghetto in America, it's always a drug addict you can buy something off for dirt-cheap because, nine times out of ten, it was stolen. Bozo was that drug addict and he stayed hustling anything he could get his hands on. His hands were the size of oven mitts from all the dope he shot up in the veins.

"Yo Bozo, holla at me," Science shouted.

Within seconds Bozo came running.

"What 'chu got there, yo? My son might need a book bag for school, how much?"

"Nah man, the book bag ain't for sale. It's what's in the book bag, brother. Exclusive shit, ain't nobody got this in the hood." Bozo unzipped the book bag, with his oversized hands, and pulled out a police jacket. "Check it out man, it's a one size fit all."

"Bozo, what the fuck I'm a do with a jacket with Police on the back of it? You gonna get me shot wearing some dumb ass shit like that," Donte said, grabbing the jacket.

Science had a different reaction. He wanted to know more.

"You got some more of this shit? Where you get it from?" Science asked.

"Yeah, brother. I got all types of shit. Me and Bubba hit this police truck down there on Fairmount and Gilmore. They busted a couple dope spots and we saw an opportunity. Shit, we got helmets, ski masks, police jackets, vests, some badges, and Bubba crazy ass got that big steel shield they be using. We tossed it on the back of his truck and got the hell outta there."

"You still got all that shit?" Donte asked with a devious grin on his face.

Science was confused at why he would be interested in some police equipment.

"Man we got all of it," Bozo said with a smile showing off his brown teeth.

"Let's go get it Bozo. I got a couple dollars for you." Donte stood up thinking of a master plan.

It didn't take long for Bozo to lead the guys to the equipment. Science had to hold his nose when he and Donte entered Bozo's house. It was an abandoned home that he claimed. It was now a dope house full of dope fiends shooting heroin. It smelled like a combination of the people that hadn't washed in months, plus throw up and old piss.

"C'mon Bozo, clean this shit up. It smells bad in here, yo! Ya'll got a dead body in this bitch or something?" Science said, covering his nose with his shirt.

"That's the smell of good pussy. We got Vicky upstairs if you tryna get some ass. She a old ho but that box and mouth still good. A bag of dope and she yours for one nut," Bozo told him.

"Man, I'll smack the shit outta you, Bozo. That bitch ninety years old and she got that package. I'm surprised y'all junky ass still hittin' that pussy. Take us to the merchandise before I kick ya ass." Science was getting annoyed. Just being in the house made him want to throw up.

"Okay, okay brother. It's in the basement, follow me."

Bozo led the way and the two brothers followed behind. Down in the basement, Bozo showed them all the police equipment they stole. Donte had discreetly told Science what his plans were and Science saw dollar signs. The number of people Donte wanted to hit meant major money. He knew with this move they would be good.

"Oh yeah we in the game with this, yo," Donte boasted.

Donte shook his head satisfied at the things Bozo had boosted from the police. Science tried on the Teflon vest with ATF on the back and it fit perfectly. Donte picked up the shield that the police used to storm in to protect themselves from oncoming danger.

"Yup, we need all this shit," Donte stated.

"Shit, well throw a number out there and see if I catch it," Bozo announced then ran his fat hands together.

"$150!"Donte told him.

"That was over thrown young brother."

"$250," Science said, taking off the vest.

"A lil bit more, I might've caught that. C'mon man, this is high quality shit here. You gotta come good." Bozo licked his dry lips and looked at the two brothers for another try.

"Nigga, fuck that. If it's high quality why it ain't sold yet? I'll give you $150 dollars and an ounce of crack to sell and make the rest. Take it or leave it," Donte told him with a mean mug.

"Alright, that's good with me. I'll take it."

Donte dug in his pocket and passed him his money. "I'll bring the drugs by later today. I gotta cook it up."

Science and Donte started packing up the equipment in the large black duffel bags. “I’ll come get that big shit another day, it’s too bright outside to be carryin’ some shield with ATF on it.” Science and Donte packed everything in the trunk and pulled off.

“Yo, where you get some coke from?” Science asked as Donte drove.

“I ain’t got no coke, nigga.” He laughed. I just figured after he shoot up all that raw he ain’t gonna remember about no ounce of crack. Besides fuck that dope fiend if he do, he burnt!”

Science just shook his head at how wild his brother had become.

# CHAPTER 12

When Science strutted through the doors of the hotel room, Genie's eyes lit up as she pulled on her blunt one last time.

"What's so important we had to meet here?" Science asked, taking a seat in the chair next to the bed.

"I'm tryna put you on some real shit cuz I fucks with you. You acting like you don't miss me, Science… like we ain't share something special."

Genie glared at Science seductively as she put the blunt out in the ashtray and licked her lips. She looked at her slim waist and round ass in the full-length mirror. She admired her body and she knew Science wanted her. She thought, how could he want Candy over her? She walked over to Science slowly looking at his buff chest sitting up in his button up shirt. She stood between his legs and felt his manhood stiffen.

"I thought you was faithful, why he acting up?" She moved her knees closer to his crotch.

"Chill yo!" Science said but didn't attempt to move her." I don't even know who the fuck you are…Genie, Jasmine, or who the fuck ever. You shady."

"I can explain all that," she said, bending over, sucking his neck where his B-More tattoo was located.

"That tat right there got you this pussy on the bus that day. It's sexy as shit," she uttered, dropping to her knees.

"You playing, yo. What you doing?" Science asked in a child-like voice as his stiff, erect, manhood was pulled out. "What 'chu call me here for?"

She began to suck the head slowly for a few seconds causing Science to lean back in ecstasy. She licked it and looked deeply in his eyes before speaking.

"That nigga Gwop ain't no good. He tryna set you up, so watch that nigga. He be all up in Sheek's ear telling him to move on you. Him and my cousin both want you outta here. They plotted the moment they knew you was coming home."

She then went back down to suck some more. Science wanted to hear more but the head was too good. He held the back of her head and fed her every inch of his dick as she spit on it and slurped it up. Science felt himself about to cum so he pulled out and started to jerk himself on her tongue.

"He want me outta here, huh. What else? What else you got to tell me, since you got all the information these days?" Science asked but before she could answer.

He filled her throat with semen then wiped his deflating penis on her face with a smile. Science couldn't help but laugh.

"You nasty, yo!" He said, looking at her with his nut all over her face.

"You like that shit tho. That's the shit that keep y'all niggas. Look, Science, I have a confession."

"Oh, yeah? Shoot."

"I knew who you were before you told me on the bus that day. The moment I saw you I remembered the countless pictures Damya showed me of you. That's why I told you my name was Jasmine just in case it clicked that I was Damya's cousin. She always talked about you and showed me pictures when she would visit. I had a secret crush on you."

Science just glared at her with a blank look on his face.

"So yes, my real name is Genie."

Grabbing a towel and wiping her face off, Science stood up shaking his head. He snatched the towel from her and towered over her thick 5'2 frame. "So now that you've given me the info we done, right?"

"Hell no! I believe we really had a connection on that bus. I wanna see you again."

"Nah, I can't do that. I'm taken."

"You mean that white bitch got you linked up like that?" Genie had her hands draped over her wide hips.

"Don't hate on my snow bunny." He laughed and slapped Genie on the ass making it bounce back.

"Whatever. You must attract bitches that ain't worthy. You need a down ass bitch like me by your side."

"Damya your cousin, yo."

"Who cares? The truth is the truth. Damya know you getting money. Now and she wants it," Genie said with attitude.

"Why you say that?" Science cleaned his dick off and tossed the towel on the floor. He zipped up his $300 dollar jeans and sat back down.

"She keeps saying Im'a tax that nigga Science… he know I know. That's all she keeps saying, 'He know I know. I want this and that', like talking shit. I had to tell you she really tripping."

Science listened to every word. He liked Genie but she could get him caught up with her freakish ways. He wasn't trying to mess things up with Candy.

"Science, are you listening?" Genie asked, seeing how blank his face was.

"Yeah, yo, I'm good. Just thinking. Good looking for clearing some shit up for me." Science rubbed his goatee and looked Genie in the eyes. He did have an attraction to her, but knew it wasn't a good move. He had too many things to handle at the moment; he needed to handle, Gwop, Sheek and Damya, but at the right moment.

As he remained in deep thought, Genie began taking off her clothes. Science stood up fast, shaking his head. He had to decline even though Genie was stacked.

"Nah, I'm out. Let me get outta here. Look, good looking on the info. I appreciate it."

Science made his way toward the door.

"Wait, you not gonna fuck me?" Genie asked from the bed naked.

"Nah yo, I'm going home to Candy. I can't be smelling like sex or some hotel soap. That head was love though."

Science opened the door and was about to step out.

"So what about Gwop and Damya? What you gonna do?" she asked with one hand on her nipple and the other in her wetness.

Science looked at her pussy juices dripping on the sheets. Her finger made the sound of lovemaking and Science almost went back for it. "It's cool, they my peoples," he said and closed the door behind him.

$$$$

A week went by with a lot of changes happening in that short period of time. Science and Donte both got condos in the same building. They didn't see Mooch too much since he'd already ran through the 18 pounds of weed. Science and Candy had Lil' Cecil over to the house almost every other day with Damya still complaining and threatening Science. He never let her know he knew she and Gwop had been plotting against him. He had a plan for Damya that she wouldn't see coming.

With Science having a three bedroom and Lil' Cecil having his own room, he was the happiest kid in the world with all those games and toys. Candy treated him like her own, and blessed him with shopping sprees at Toys R Us and Gameland. Science hadn't re-upped on the cocaine he got from Gwop because of two reasons. One; his mind was made up on how he would get money. Get down or lay down, you was coming up off that cash. Being a stick up kid seemed a better way to earn a living. He was only sitting on a couple stacks due to all the money he spent getting himself situated, so he needed a new lick soon.

Science also figured the drug game had gotten too foul. Now that he'd gotten word from Genie on Gwop being sneaky, he knew how to play Gwop. He didn't want to break bread with no shiesty niggas. Gwop would have to die so Science could prove a point to anyone else who thought about crossing him.

He wanted to keep the money he'd made from the robbery on the low, making sure not to buy anything flashy. He copped a 2003 Expedition and put some 22's on it. It had a vicious system. He got Candy a red Chrysler 300. They were planning on hitting Sheek's home, his safe and his stash spots but wanted to wait for the right time. He had to wait for Gwop to make his next move, before knowing how to play him.

The fellas were at Donte's crib smoking and playing PlayStation 2. Science was back to his old ways and stayed smoking some good green. He went in the kitchen to grab some water when Donte blurted out in front of Mooch.

"What the fuck we waitin' on? Let's hit dis nigga, Sheek!" He slammed the controller down.

Science peeked around the corner giving him the, *Mooch right here you dumb ass nigga*, look.

"So we plannin' on hittin' Sheek? Let's do it then, yo. I hate that fake ass nigga. He swear 'cause he from Philly that we country or something. Everybody knows B-more niggas go hard. We Body More!" Mooch cut in.

"Chill mini gangster. You ain't doing shit. Just go to school and sell ya weed. This big boy shit right here." Science dropped down on the Italian leather recliner.

"Big boy shit? When Donte become a big boy? I've been takin' care of his lazy ass for years now. I want in, fuck that! I'm tougher than ya'll think."

"Yo Science, you did say we needed another man. Who better than a nigga we can trust? Let the nigga ride," Donte commented.

"Is you crazy? If something happened to him that's on me. Moms gonna snap on me because I'm the oldest, yo. Look Mooch, just sell ya weed and do that school shit. Let us do this."

"Listen Science, you been gone for a minute. I've been the one holdin' shit down. What's wrong? You think I won't bust my gun? Too late, I been popped, nigga! Cats know how I get down. I'm a thorough ass young nigga that get money and fuck bad bitches. But don't ever get it fucked up, I'll open a nigga skull quick!"

"If you wanna get down, fuck it… Remember Mooch, when shit goes down, I warned you," Science fussed while pacing the floor. "Do not hesitate to pop a nigga, or his bitch. This shit serious, blood gonna get spilled and it might be yours. Make sure you can live with dat….or die with it. I don't wanna lose you, yo."

Science leaned down to hug his brother, Mooch. He knew what he was allowing him to do was wrong. Just then his phone rang. It was Genie. He knew he was dead wrong for giving her the number. He hit ignore and just shook his head. She wanted more of him…something he'd already told her couldn't happen.

The moment the phone stopped ringing, it rang again. Science knew it was Damya's number. He ignored the call but quickly listened to the message she left.

That's it, nigga. I gave you enough time. If I don't hear from you by noon tomorrow, I'm taking that gun to the police. "Crimes don't go unpunished, nigga."

$$$$

Every female at Kim's was eyeing Gwop when he came in the shop. He had double-parked and hopped out of his G-Wagon. All eyes were on him as he bolted through the doors looking fresh, and holding his crotch. He had his fitted hat to the back, a fresh white T-shirt and some Gucci sweatpants with the matching jacket and sneakers. The two jawbreaker sized diamonds in his ears made females put on their shades they blinged so bright.

His platinum chain with the G pieces were flawless. "Ayo Kim, where the bathroom at, Ma? A nigga gotta piss."

Kim was so shocked that Raven had to step up and say it was in the back on the right.

"Good look." All eyes still were glued to his confident walk to the bathroom. He had a swagger like no other.

"Damn Kim, open ya mouth girl. He ain't all that," Damya said, washing out one of her client's hair who almost broke her neck to check out Gwop.

"Bitch, don't hate cause he walked right by ya ass and didn't speak. That's what you get for giving up that pussy on the first night. Niggas like Gwop, who can get any bitch they want, need a challenge. They like a chase and want a female that plays hard to get. I guarantee he come back out here, look around, and speak to a female that gave him less attention, and one he didn't fuck."

"So why he say something to you if he been ran through that?"

"Maybe because my pussy taste better than all you other bitches."

All the ladies laughed and noticed every last one of them, besides Raven, had either fucked or sucked Gwop before. Raven was a new stylist that Kim hired a couple months back from D.C. She barely partied because her time was consumed with school and work. Gwop came out the bathroom drying his hands off with a paper towel. He looked around the shop at all the ladies he had been through and smiled.

"I don't know why y'all so quiet. Whose business gettin' aired out today? Don't fake 'cause I came through here." Gwop went over to the trashcan by Raven's booth and tossed it in.

"I ain't seen you around here, Ma. Where you from?"

Raven blushed and told him D.C. "I go to school and work that's probably why you don't see me on the scene."

"I guess so, 'cause I know I couldn't miss you. Look, take dis and holla at me. My number is on the back. That's an exclusive card for my club Shopz that me and my man Sheek own. Come through sometime and get at me."

Raven didn't want to seem desperate so she nonchalantly put it in her pocket and got back to her client's hair. "If I get time. I'll definitely slide through with my girls."

Gwop smiled showing his chipped tooth and started toward the door. Just as he was opening the door he heard Damya shoot a cheap shot.

"That nigga ain't shit girl, trust me I know."

Gwop backed up and looked at Damya to give her the attention that she wanted.

"So it's like that, Mya? What's with the hate, yo?"

"Oh, hi to you too, Gwop. I guess you didn't see me right here. Why you been duckin' my calls?"

"That's because every time you call, it's about some money. Ain't none of them kids mine. I did what I did for them lil ones, yo. I ain't giving out no more free checks. Plus, you ain't handle what I asked you to handle."

Damya knew he was speaking about Science but she didn't respond.

"Ayo, Raven holla at me, don't listen to the hate thou. They pocket books is light and pussy's been stretched too much." With that said, he saluted the women in the salon and exited with a laugh.

# CHAPTER 13

Over on the Westside, on McHenry and Gilmore, Science and his brothers were in a rental checking out the scenery. This was supposed to be one of Link's main corners that did major numbers; Sheek's moneymaker. The tinted windows to the blue Thunderbird allowed them to post at the end of the block and observe their target. Strangely, it was the same spot that Science once claimed before he got busted on his last bid. He tried not to hate thinking about all the money being made that used to be his.

"We been sittin' out here for almost six fuckin' hours, son," Mooch announced breaking Science's trance. "The crib in the middle of the block is where the cash at. Look, I can even see that. Them lil' runners passin' the money off the ol' boy, and every hour since we been here, he go to that same spot."

Mooch was in the back seat annoyed, but Science was ignoring him. His words fell on deaf ears. Science needed to be sure of everything and he wasn't about to risk getting jammed up. Everything was about precision. He watched as the block was set up perfectly, organized. The flaggers and runners were plain to notice as they made their moves.

He would of gotten noticed a while ago, but the lookout designated to his location had been mackin' with some young girl for almost three hours. He also noticed the Lieutenant of the block posted with his foot on the wall talking on his cell phone. Every hour the runners would pass off money and he would go to the house Mooch was talking about and come back out with the package. A few times, a blue Denali on 22's came through, and the lieutenant went in that same house and passed off a brown paper bag. Science figured that was the Capo.

"Fall back, yo! Let me handle this shit, Mooch. We got to plan this shit out, kid. We just can't go ambush shit. I bet you ain't even notice the cans falling from the roof onto that pile of trash over there." Science pointed to a small pile of chip bags, soda cans and tobacco.

"I see it and what?"

"The roof, the shit coming from the roof. Ain't nobody even standing there. They got shooters on the roof right across the street from the stash house."

"Oh shit, I just saw a hand toss a Skittle wrapper. You right, yo!" Donte stated, seeing the red plastic float to the concrete.

"So what's the plan, yo?"

"Fall back and just watch for now. This shit ain't hard, you just got to use your head."

Science subconsciously thought about the kids out on the block and how material things so easily influenced them. He saw the young runner who couldn't be no older than 13; the kid reminded him of himself in his adolescence. These young blacks in the urban community saw the dope boys and wanted to be down so bad. They never realized the consequences; they just saw the immediate gratification of a fast dollar. He was once like them. He felt sorry for the mothers who would most likely be planning their funeral before the age of 21, or visiting them in a prison with enough time to make a mom cry. He also thought about his own son, and how he'd been talking to him lately about life, and how to make it on the streets of B-More.

Just as Science cranked the car up, a black Lambo turned on the block, with the same Denali behind it.

"There go ya boy, Link, right there, yo."

Science was feeling slightly envious for the first time as he saw the foreign car slowly move up the block. He looked on the license plate and it read *Shittin'*. The car never stopped. It just cruised up the block slowly, and low to the ground, like a wild cat in the jungle about to strike its prey. Link could barely be seen, but still had that bulky figure that he remembered.

"Yeah son, we'll hit these niggas tomorrow. Let's peel out before the ill, young nigga peep we been here too long."

$$$$

Not a word was being said as Science, Donte and Mooch were all in the car driving in the pursuit of a dollar. It seemed like the next day came so fast and it was time to put in work. They all were disguised as the Baltimore Task Force. Donte pulled his ski mask over his face and cocked back the Tech-9. Science had a 9mm with the extended clip ready to put somebody down if they didn't cooperate and just hand over the money.

"Five minutes!" Mooch said from the driver's seat. Donte took a deep breath with money on his mind. Being with his brothers felt great and he was willing to do anything for his blood.

"Y'all niggas ready for dis, yo? Mooch, you hear me? We go in, cuff whoever in there, and get all the money. Leave the guns and drugs where they at."

Everyone listened as the white caravan they bought yesterday off a fiend turned on Mattenry and Gilmore at top speed. The van came to an abrupt stop and the three brothers hopped out like trained S.W.A.T.

Science went first screaming, "Police, open up!" He knocked on the door with one thunderous kick. Mooch and Donte came behind him telling the occupants in the house to get down and freeze.

"Search the house for anybody else!" Science yelled to Donte as he and Mooch proceeded to cuff the three dealers in the front room.

Donte carefully walked towards the kitchen slowly aiming his weapon. He saw a figure dart across the entrance and make his way to the back door.

"Freeze!"

The guy attempted to open the door until a flurry of bullets from the Tech-9 made Swiss cheese of his back, and he slumped over onto the floor, dropping the brown paper bag from his lifeless hand.

"I told yo muthufuckin" ass!" Donte fired with his mouth.

He was amped. Still aiming the high-powered machine gun, he walked over to the dead body and kicked him to make sure he was gone. He bent down to grab the bag and a pain in his back as he heard shots fired.

He fell to the floor, returning fire and gave his shooter the rest of the clip. The bullet ripped through the kid's flesh, jerking his body back and forth. When nothing else came out of Donte's weapon, the kid's shirt was dark burgundy and filled with holes. He fell over on his face and the blood poured from his stiff body.

"You alright?" Mooch asked through the mask muffling his voice.

Donte got on his feet and reloaded. "I'm good, check upstairs." He proceeded in the basement.

Science had the lieutenant and two runners hand cuffed and sitting on the floor in the front room. "You wanna go to jail or you wanna go home?" He copied Denzel's voice in *Training Day*. He noticed resistance from the lieutenant and walked over to him and put cold steel to his lips.

"Oh so you a gangsta, huh? You a tough guy? I asked you a fuckin' question." Science shoved the gun in his mouth forcefully seeing the fear in his eyes. He noticed urine run down his shorts and onto the wooden floors.

"Yeah I thought so. Where the money at?"

Donte came back into the front room with a huge zip lock bag of caps full of crack in small individual plastic bags. He knew that was the packs that Link gave out and grabbed it from Donte's hand. He tossed it on the pissy guy's lap.

"Ain't shit or nobody upstairs," Mooch chimed in with his gun to his side. "What's the time?" Science asked.

"Eight minutes!" Donte yelled looking at his watch.

"Look mafucka, I don't want this shit, tell me where the money is and I'll let you walk with all that's on your lap. Just tell your boss the cops took it. Now where's the money?"

"It's in the couch and in the fridge. Open the two bottom drawers in the refrigerator and it should be 50 G's in it. The couch got almost a 100 grand."

"Go get the duffel bags," Science ordered.

Mooch had emptied the refrigerator and Science was lifting the couch upside down. He pulled a small knife from his pocket and ripped the entire bottom of the cheap sofa. Stacks of money in rubber bands sat there for the taking and Science tossed every last one of them into the duffel bag.

"Listen up boys, ya boss ain't been payin' his taxes around here. We gotta eat, too. Let him know the new Flex Squad was in. Now buy yaself some new boxers youngin'…you smell like piss."

Science quickly left unnoticed with a huge Kool-Aid smile under his ski mask.

# CHAPTER 14

Damya slammed the car door to her Benz as she held the cell phone tightly to her ear. "Girl, I don't give a fuck, I'm about my money, bitch," Damya stated sassily. "I'm making these niggas pay. Shit, I got kids to feed. They want pussy, I want money; fair exchange ain't neva been no robbery."

She laughed crazily while looking around to check her surroundings. The block was empty and she was tipsy from all the free rounds of alcohol from the club. She sashayed around the trunk of the car quickly in the short Prada dress that gripped her curves and rose to her pussy line. She looked at her cellphone as Genie spoke in her ear to check the time. It was 4:22 a.m.

"Bitch, Im'a call you back. I'm going in the house to see if these kids cleaned the fuck up. If they didn't, I'm waking everybody up."

Not waiting for a response, Damya hung up, fumbling for her keys. She couldn't wait until she moved into a new neighborhood that was safe. She already had her heart set on a condo downtown where they had a doorman for the building. She just needed Science and a couple other niggas to come up off the cash they owed her. She'd been smashing Gwop, and was now fucking Sheek here and there. Money would flow soon, so she hoped.

When she reached for the doorknob, all she felt was a pain to her head. Suddenly, Damya's body hit the ground.

"Shiesty ass bitch," she heard a voice say.

She was too dazed to see a face clearly.

"Yeah, I bet ya ass won't keep blackmailing niggas now," Damya heard as she was dragged on the ground, scraping her back for several yards. Eventually she was tossed inside the trunk of a car.

"Ahhhh shit! What the fuck!" She shouted, "Pleaseeeeeeee stop let me out!" as the trunk came crashing down.

She screamed in the darkness. "Let me outta here!!!! What the fuck!!!!"

She felt the side of her face realizing she'd been hurt badly.

"Oh my god... Oh my god, please help me. I swear I won't ever do wrong again. Get me out of here, pleaseeeee!"

Damya said the first prayer of her entire life. With her eyes closed snugly she held herself fearfully and asked for forgiveness for all the wrong she'd done. Her body shivered while blood gushed from the side of her face. Damya cried out even louder as the car whipped corners and zoomed through the streets throwing Damya's body around harshly.

"I bet you wish you could take shit back now, huh? Huh, bitch? You hear me, you whore?" The voice screamed from the front.

She knew she'd heard the voice before but just couldn't make it out. She assumed Science was behind the attack since the assailant spoke of blackmailing, but she couldn't be sure. She'd blackmailed many niggas in the past.

Then she thought of each of her baby's daddy's; it could have been any of them. They all had scores to settle with her. Damya just cried, asking God to save her.

When the car came to a stop and the trunk lifted, Damya saw a man with the ski mask on.

"Science, is that you?"

He didn't answer.

"Look, you don't have to give me the money!" she cried, after seeing two other guys walk out from the old abandoned building to her left. "I'll give you the fuckin' gun! It's ova, okay?"

Strangely, one of the guys who'd just emerged from the warehouse didn't have a mask on. His scarred up face showed no remorse as he spoke to Damya like trash.

"Bitch, put this on," he demanded, tossing her a dirty, long piece of cloth to put around her eyes.

"Listen, please don't kill me. I will pay you. Just let me go!" Damya pleaded.

The stranger pulled a chrome .44 from his waist and smacked Damya forcefully, landing her back on the ground.

Damya took a moment to look at the facial features of the guy who didn't have on a ski mask. He was short, and had a face full of acne. She'd never seen him a day in her life. Who the fuck was he? Who were the other two guys? And what did they want with her?

"This not a game, bitch!" he shouted, while tying the rag around her eyes and head, landing her back in darkness. "Don't talk, just shut the fuck up. You like blackmailing motherfuckas!" he said, pulling her by the back of her neck, and dragging her into the building.

Once inside, Damya was told to stop crying so damn much. She stopped immediately.

"I got kids," she sniffled. "They need me. Just tell me what you want?"

"You," a voice sounded. "You gotta be taught a lesson, so the others can learn."

"What are you talkin' about!" she shouted.

"Bitch, stop talkin," the voice sounded."

Damya felt a hand slide up her dress and rub on her thighs. She instantly thought the worse. Rape. That's what would happen. They wanted to gang rape her. Her insides exploded. Fear filled her body as she felt someone take her shoe off.

"You got some pretty feet, yo."

Damya felt him massage her foot. "You should like this," he said, gripping her feet.

Within seconds he'd locked her legs and tied them together quickly, and securely.

"What are you doing? Pleaseeeeee.... no don't!" Damya said as she was being punched in the mouth.

The next thing she knew her arms were quickly being tied and the cloth around her eyes had been removed. Her heart skipped a beat after seeing a pair of pliers closing in on her big toe.

"Oh my God, pleaseeeeeeee no!" she shouted!

"If you move even one time, I'm going to shoot you. That's all you get. I can shoot you now or you just take this. Don't move."

Damya bit down on her lip with tears streaming from her face. She'd never experienced any type of torture before, but could tell from the goons' face, he was about to send a violent message to her. Her warned her that things would only get worse day by day.

Before Damya could respond, shout, or move, her toe nail was swiftly pulled off.

"Ahhhhhh!" Damya screamed, but didn't move one inch.

"Shhhhhhh...It's not over, bitch. This is the easy part. I'm just giving you a pedicure. But if you scream, or move this time, I'm going to chop your fuckin legs off! You hear me!"

"Shut the fuck up!" the masked man standing on the sideline shouted.

Damya took a deep breath and closed her eyes. Each toenail was ripped away forcefully. She lost consciousness from the pain and blood. And all she heard over and over was his voice saying, "You'll never see your kids again, bitch."

$$$$

A blue Denali parked on Catherine St. where Link had another one of his spots. This was basically for meeting purposes. The lieutenant from his block that got knocked yesterday, and two of his gunmen, walked in the house.

Link was a dark skinned, sort of stocky goon with some huge hands and a wide, buffed chest. He was known for smacking someone's lips off. He was brought from Philly with Sheek nine years ago to lock down the blocks Science once controlled. He only stood about 6'1" but his reddish eyes put fear in a weak man's heart. His downfall was that he stayed high all the time.

He paused the PlayStation 2 video game to greet his worker with a firm handshake. His two gunmen stood by the door in silence.

"So what happened on the block yesterday?" Link asked, pulling a cigarette from his pocket and lighting the end of it.

"Look yo, some cops came through and kicked the shit in. They shot Skinny and Max and cuffed me and the youngsters.

They said, 'Tell my boss they ain't been payin' they taxes and it's time for them to eat.'"

He prayed Link believed him because he had taken all the drugs and gave the youngsters a $100 apiece. He was about to start his own block after all this blew over.

"Oh yea son, they said they was the new Flex Squad."

Link blew the smoke in his face as he exhaled. He knew that the Flex Squad were crooked cops in Baltimore that took money and would plant drugs on you if you didn't pay up. But they never bodied nobody. "So, they took everything in the crib? Money and the drugs?"

"Yeah yo, I told 'chu they did."

"You think I'm stupid? You stole my shit!" The two goons gripped the guy up by the arms. He struggled but to no avail.

"C'mon Link, what's good yo? I ain't steal shit! C'mon, don't do this!" A loud smack echoed throughout the house as Link's heavy hand left a red imprint on the guy's face. He had already talked to the youngsters that were in the spot and their side of the story was different. They told him about the $100 dollars he gave them, and the drugs he took. Link was far from stupid and a thief in his camp wouldn't last long.

"If you woulda told the truth, young bull, I woulda let you live. But nah, you a liar and a thief." Link took his cigarette and placed it on the tip of the man's nose. "Now we gon' smoke you and feed you your own dick before you die."

"C'monnnnnnn Link, don't do this man!" he shouted as someone grabbed him and tied him tightly to a chair.

"So, you like stealin' my shit, huh?" Link roared, looking at the kid with disregard.

Link stood, smiled and rolled up his sleeves.

"You country ass niggas got the game fucked up out here!" Link said, pointing his finger in his face.

"I'm sorry man, I swear to God! Just don't kill me!" The kid pleaded. Link just shook his head and pulled his gun from his waistband.

"Y'all niggas watch me closely. This how you set examples out here." Link looked at his goons and slapped the kid across the face with the gun. A tooth flew out his mouth and Link repeated the blow over and over.

The blood from the kid's face was everywhere and you couldn't recognize him from the lumps and gashes on his face.

"He dead Link, it's over," one of Link's men said, after watching Link zone out.

"I know." Link stopped then let off a shot with the bloody gun, forcing the kid's brains to explode from his skull.

"Now that's how you kill a nigga," he said to his goons, passing the gun off.

# CHAPTER 15

Science and Mooch walked into Aldo's in Little Italy with Candy and Vita on their arms. The waitress gave them a booth in the back and Science could sense the hate from the women and men as he cuffed Candy's ass all the way to their table.

It wasn't common to see a black guy with a white woman, but Science couldn't care less and neither could Candy. Ever since they were together, she had been playing her part, and Science couldn't knock that she was a dime piece with the best pussy he'd ever had. He wasn't ready to introduce her to mom yet until he tested her loyalty a few more times. But she was straight with him so far.

"I'll be back to take your order, if you figure it out earlier, just call me. My name is Rudy and I'll be your waitress this evening. Would you like some refreshments while you make your decision?" Rudy asked politely.

"Yes…ahhhh Rudy, I'll have a Long Island Iced Tea," Vita chimed in.

After everyone ordered their drinks, Science whispered something in Candy's ear. She giggled and placed her hand underneath the table. "I love it when you talk nasty," she responded.

"So Science, I told mom that I'm movin' out. I can't be up there like that son. I'm 17 now and I gots to be a man, you feel me," Mooch interjected.

"Nah yo, finish school and then move out. I keep tellin' you don't be fast to grow up. I'm 31 and it feels like yesterday I was 17, yo. That shit go quick."

"I'm just tired of moms actin' like I'm still 8. I'm movin' with Vita."

Science looked at Vita who was sipping on her drink with a funny grin on her face. She dropped her keys on the floor and went to pick them up. She noticed Science had his dick out and Candy was nonchalantly caressing his thick member. When she sat up she licked her lips and gave Science a smile.

"Yeah, don't trip Science. He's coming…with me," Vita hissed. "I know how to take good care of a man," she said sexily. "And he'll still go to school. I'll be sure he do his homework," she laughed, before tongue kissing Mooch in front of everyone.

"Yeah whatever yo, I think you should fall back until you finish school. But do you."

"I will. I got this," he told his brother proudly. "Plus, with all the moves we making, I can't be in mom's house anymore."

"I told him he's gotta watch his back," Vita chimed in. "The games ya'll playing are for the big boys."

Science gave Mooch the evil eye. He knew he'd have to get him straight later. He didn't trust Vita at all and didn't want her to know about anything they were involved in. Before long they all got up with Vita making sure she clutched Science's dick when no one was looking. Science just shook his head wondering why Mooch had chosen such a roller.

$$$$

Shopz was popping as usual and Gwop was already tipsy from the bottles he had consumed. Gwop was fresh in a white T-shirt, Gucci jacket and matching hat, some eight hundred dollar jeans and Gucci sneakers. He had a customized charm that ran him 300 thousand. It was a million dollar bill with Gwop in the middle of it set in green diamonds that glistened under the dim lights of the club. He gripped up a bottle from the bucket of ice on his table and walked out of the VIP section. He ran into Link who had two of his goons with him mean muggin'.

"What up, yo?"

"Ain't shit, where Sheek at? I got some shit to talk to him about."

"I'll go get him for you. He in the back. Have a seat in my section and get them fake ass looks off ya mans' grill. It's too much pussy in here to be gangsta right now."

Link slightly chuckled and him and his boys proceeded behind the red velvet ropes.

Gwop made his way through the thick crowd and was met by Raven and Kim coming out of the bathroom.

"Hey Gwop," the girls said in unison.

"Damn yo, y'all lookin' sexy as hell. C'mon, let ya boy get a complete spin."

Raven and Kim both did a 360 showing off their sexy new outfits. Raven had a short, red, fitted Versace dress that was strapless with the back out. Kim was in a blue Gucci dress that gave more than enough cleavage and hugged her wide voluptuous hips. He licked his lips at Raven's curvaceous body and took a peep at her cute toes in those Versace sandals.

"Look yo, y'all go to VIP, pop a bottle and I'll be there in a minute."

Gwop gave Kim the, *you know what it is* look. The only reason he hadn't cut Kim off completely was because of her bisexual ways. He would get a girl that's willing to try and call Kim to seal the deal. She went hard when another female was involved. So she knew that the look Gwop gave her and Raven would mean a great night full of sex.

He walked up the stairs to holla at Sheek in the office and could hear him conversing with somebody as the door was ajar. He was just about to open it completely when he heard his name.

"So what about Gwop? I thought he was your partner?" the mysterious voice said. Gwop couldn't see the guy's face.

"Yeah, he my silent partner as in 'don't say shit and shut the fuck up'. Man, fuck the bull for real. Ain't none of dis here in his name," Sheek boasted. "That country ass nigga went off my word that he was a partner. This 100% Sheek right here. He a good dude and all but his cocky lil ass be gettin' on my nerves. He ain't built for this big boy shit. It's cool though, because I was like that at his age. The nigga only 26. He ain't never had shit."

Gwop felt like pulling his Ruger from his waistband and putting a hole in Sheek's head for playin' him like that. All this time he was loyal, he never shorted the money and always kept it real. Now Sheek showed his true colors and was caught.

"Look Rome, these country ass B-more niggas green fo 'real, Cannon. These bulls is suckers out here. Us Philly boys can run this city! But fuck all that. What's good with my cousin, Cash?"

Now Gwop realized just who the mystery man was. He was Rome, from Philly, who was down with them W.T.O. niggas. He was known for being notorious and had killed hundreds of niggas with no regrets. Link and Sheek used to always say how Cash and Rome had things on lock in Philly, so that's why they came to B-more to eat. Gwop didn't want to hear any more of this fake ass nigga talk. He sipped his Cris and knocked on the door softly.

"Who the fuck is it?"

"It's Gwop, nigga."

"Come on in, nigga."

Gwop came in acting like he was still tipsy, but that feeling had disappeared when he heard Sheek talk that bullshit. "Yo ya boy Link downstairs waitin' on you." Gwop tried to keep his composure and remain calm as he sipped the bottle of champagne and glared at Sheek.

"Ayo fam, dis my mans' right here, Rome. You know my cousin, Cash's right hand. He came through to see how shit jump in B-more."

Rome gave Gwop a head nod checking out his jewels which definitely impressed him. It wasn't nothing country about that chain and piece. At the same time Gwop noticed the tattoo on Rome's hand that said Cash. He often wondered why Cash was that boss that could get another man to put a tattoo of his name on his body.

I'ma let y'all get on homeboy time," Gwop stated. "I'm about to fuck these hoes down here. They love an official B-more nigga."

"Oh, it's like that?" Rome questioned, looking like he could bench press four hundred pounds.

With those words Gwop downed the last of the Cristal, ignoring Rome. He got ready to leave but Sheek stopped him to be fake for a minute. "This my nigga, here," Sheek lied, grabbing Gwop by the shoulder. "We own this fuckin' city!"

Gwop pulled away and walked out closing the door behind him. He knew he'd have to move forward with his plan.

$$$$

The redness in his eyes and his slurred speech showed how the drugs and liquor was taking a toll on Gwop. He sat on the leather seats in the booth between Raven and Kim. He was eyeing Sheek, Link, and Rome chat it up only a few feet from him. All he could do was think about how they were over there clowning him and his city. He had a devious grin on his face as Kim licked his earlobe, talking about what she was going to do, simultaneously rubbing his penis through his pants.

"Ya better not hold back Gwop. I got Raven down to do whatever and I want you to fuck me from the back," Kim seductively stated, as Gwop exhaled the hydro he was smoking. He loved the way he didn't have to struggle for girl-on-girl action. It seemed like every chick in B-more was on pussy. Kim was an old freak that still had a vicious body. At 41, she still could hang with females in their twenties. The only thing was she had been around the block a few times and her pussy definitely felt like it.

"We out!" Gwop stood up and snapped.

Neither Rome, Link or Sheek paid him any attention. The girls got up as Gwop wrapped his arms around their necks and they practically held him up as they made their way out of the club. They got to the parking lot still holding Gwop as they approached his Benz truck.

"Go in my left pocket and grab my keys."

Gwop's weight was beginning to hurt Raven's arm. She reached in his pocket feeling a nice wad of cash and thought for a brief second about getting him for it. She scooped up the keys and Kim stood him up against the Benz. As Gwop talked some drunk fly shit to Kim, Raven opened the driver door and got in. She smelled the scent of Sean Combs Unforgiveable through the interior. She unlocked the doors with a push of a button and when Kim put Gwop in the back she noticed his Benz had a lockbox on the floor when the light came on. She wondered what was inside.

"Where we going, Gwop?" Raven chimed in as she cranked up the luxury G-Wagon.

"Out the county, y'all going to be the first bitches to see the bachelor pad of the century. My shit exclusive. I dropped a few tickets on that joint, yo."

With those words, Raven pulled off. She could barely drive as Gwop played with her pussy the entire ride to his house. It was a good thing the road was empty because she swerved a few times climaxing to his circular motions on her clit. Kim just watched envious as Raven got all the attention during the ride. When they pulled up to his home it was as if Gwop found a slight bit of energy. He hopped out of the seat and exited his vehicle.

"Damn!" Raven said, looking up at the mansion where Gwop resided. There were two foreign rides out front that Kim had never seen Gwop in; a black on black Maserati and a Black on Black Bentley GT.

They watched as he hit the security code to his alarm system and the door automatically unlocked. They followed Gwop through the Grenada mahogany custom made doors in awe. They passed the foyer and Gwop hit the light to his lavish living room. Raven looked to the left and could see the curve of the stairway.

"Have a seat, ladies," Gwop announced as he picked up a huge remote from the glass and crystal coffee table that controlled almost everything in the house. He pushed a button and the fireplace came alive.

Kim was impressed especially with the chinchilla material of the living room's furniture. She kicked off her shoes and ran her toes through the expensive soft fur. Just being in a multi-million dollar home made Kim's pussy moist. She waltzed over to Raven whose jaw was on the floor. She kissed her neck as her hands ran up her thigh and tickled her clit.

"Mmmmmmm...." Raven exhaled as Gwop took off his shirt and began to unbuckle his pants.

"Gwop, baby, you good?" a voice sounded.

Raven and Kim both were caught off guard at the beautiful female that turned the corner. She appeared to be a mixture of Asian and Black and stood at 5'2 with a curvy frame and silky long black hair.

"What's good, baby? I'ma entertain these two tonight. Ya wanna join us?"

The exotic bombshell looked at Kim and Raven and back at Gwop.

"I'm alright, are they staying the night?"

"Yeah, this gonna take a minute." She nodded her head and walked over to Gwop and kissed his lips. She then disappeared upstairs.

"Gwop, who was that?" Raven asked curiously.

"That's wifey, but don't trip, she cool. She just seeing if I got something for her, that's all."

Kim shrugged her shoulders wishing she could get a taste of that gorgeous female. Gwop hit another button on the remote and the lights went out. The ceiling opened and a nice size fish tank hung down with a blue light showing the small hammerhead shark swimming about. The blue light from the fish tank was the only light that illuminated the room.

$$$$

Shopz had finally let out and Sheek, Rome, and Link were in Sheek's elegantly designed office. He sat behind his cherry wood desk in his oversized recliner smoking a black.

"I called my connect at the BPD and he told a nigga he ain't hear shit or know nothing about no raid on ya side," Sheek announced to Link. He gave him an unsuspecting look as he spoke. "Usually he gives me the heads up but I pay my taxes so I don't have that problem."

"Look Sheek, the cops that come through my strips, said they ain't heard shit either. Plus I pay my taxes, too. I make sure them pigs get they lil 20 grand a month. This shit fishy, Cannon."

"Let me make some calls and get some more info on this shit. For now, we can't sweat it. You paid ya taxes so hopefully them pigs good for a minute. Just be on point and spread the money out. Don't have more than 50k in a spot at a time," Sheek ordered.

"Bet dat," Link agreed.

"Yo Rome, you like these B-more bitches?"

"For sho!"

"I got a good one for ya ass," he said, thinking of Damya.

# Chapter 16

They say brothers think alike because Donte had already bought a new car despite Science telling them not to buy anything flashy. The streets were still talking about Link and Sheek's spot getting robbed. All eyes and ears were open but Mooch and Vita were now at the Lexus dealership going over the paper work for the new GS. Mooch was putting it in Vita's name for safety measures and her talk game was vicious. She had a nice relationship with Michael, the salesman. She stroked his ego and flirted just enough for him to pull some strings and change some numbers, making it happen.

"Oh, Michael, you're so funny. I love the way that suit fits you. Have you been working out?" The beer belly white guy with the Homer Simpson hairstyle blushed as she signed the papers and Mooch handed him the cash. "Baby give Michael a tip, he's doing us a favor, sweetie."

Mooch wanted to laugh the way Vita was laying it on for this guy, he couldn't believe he was falling for it. She really had a way with the fellas.

"No Vita, that's okay. I'll be fine but please come back anytime and I'll be happy to be of service."

"Well Mike thanks for the hook up. V, let's ride, baby." Mooch gave Michael a look like, *Yeah mafucka dis my bitch.* Vita stood up and Mooch gripped up her ass and walked out with keys to a brand new Lexus GS.

$$$$

Leakin Park was where B-more's finest pulled out the best for this traditional Sunday car show. Nothing but dirt bikes, four wheelers, and something from another country could get play this day. The ladies were out and about, riding on the back of dirt bikes in skimpy outfits almost like it was bike week in Myrtle Beach.

Science was the first of his brothers to get there. He found a good spot to park. He had a good view at the whole scene and couldn't miss anything. He opened all the doors to the Expedition and let his system thump. He was in a pair of shorts, a white T-shirt, and a light blue fitted hat that complemented his shorts and matching Jordan's. The Rolex watch on his wrist was flooded in diamonds. When the sun hit it, it glimmered. Candy was in a pair of really short shorts that exposed her red G-string. She had a wife beater that was hugging her huge breasts that cut just under her D cups. Her flat stomach made her diamond naval ring look so sexy as she sat on the hood of Science's truck.

The ladies were dressed so scantily that Science couldn't keep his eyes off them. Nothing but big asses and breasts walked by him giving him the sexy eyes. He picked up his cell and leaned on his truck to figure out where his brothers were.

"Yo, where you at, Donte?" The sound of almost 50 dirt bikes echoed throughout the park as Science held one ear to get a better listen.

"What? I can't hear you."

When the noise subsided he heard Donte say he was pulling up. Science looked around but couldn't spot Donte anywhere. He pulled up next to the Expedition, and Donte hopped out in a fresh Gucci sweat suit with the matching shades.

"I like that, Donte. You shittin' on these dudes out here." Science ignored Candy's remark and pulled him to the side by his arm as he was eyeing a groupie under a tree.

"Yo, what the fuck is wrong with you? What is this shit?" He asked with a firm grip on his brother's arm.

"It's a Benz, nigga." Donte laughed and yanked his arm away.

"I know it's a Benz. Why are you drivin' it, dumb-ass?" Science smacked him in the back of the head.

"Ouch! Nigga, chill! I copped it and I'm tryna show these clowns we eatin', too. Fuck you so uptight for?"

"No, no no you didn't! You hot right now. We just robbed a nigga for almost 200 grand not even two weeks ago and ya broke ass pull up in a Benz? You must be stupid." Just as Science was schoolin' Donte, Mooch pulled up in a blood colored brand new Lexus with Vita riding shotgun.

Science's eyes widened at the sight of another expensive ass car that the streets knew Mooch couldn't afford. Mooch stepped out in some black Dickie shorts, a white T-shirt, a black fitted hat and some black suede Timbs.

"You like, yo?" Mooch announced, pointing to his whip. Science shook his head in disappointment.

Mooch was thinking about how he was flossing in the streets. His demeanor had changed ever since his first robbery with his brothers. He once was a laid back dude with a pretty boy swagger. Now, he had become slightly arrogant and cocky, feeling like certain people were beneath him.

"Both of y'all niggas in my truck, right now. Candy go talk to Vita." Candy hopped off the hood quick and ran over to Vita. Science closed the doors but kept the music at a high level where his brothers could hear, but all ear hustlers would be out of luck.

"What the fuck is wrong with y'all niggas? We just hit these niggas! And you both have brand new cars, over 50 thousand. Think what dis shit look like after Link just got hit." Science looked at both of them with hard stares.

"Fuck them niggas and whoever got a problem with it. They think the police hit 'em, not no stick-up niggas. I'm tryna enjoy this paper and stunt on these niggas. Fuck what a nigga think." Donte added with confidence ready to open a nigga skull if they jumped out there.

"I'm with Donte, Science. Chill yo, they think the cops hit 'em. Let's just do us. We still hittin' that other spot tomorrow on Fairmont and Gilmore?" Mooch asked and Science shook his head but couldn't help to laugh. His little brothers were all the way in the game. It wasn't no turning back now. They were turned out.

"Besides, look who talkin' with a house on his wrist." Mooch said, pointing at the pricey Rolex on his brother's wrist. Science looked down at his watch and couldn't say anything.

"Fuck it, let's get this paper." He gave his brothers a pound and turned the music up louder blasting *Hustlin'* by Rick Ross.

Everyone was posted on their rides smoking and drinking. Horns beeped loudly as all heads turned to see who it was.

Everyone was shocked at the black and platinum two-toned Maybach. Science noticed it coming his way and couldn't see who was inside because of the dark tint on the windows. It parked on the left side of Science's truck and the back window rolled down.

"I got bottles!" Gwop said, with conceit, holding up two bottles of Cristal. All the doors opened and four females in tight skirts, short shorts, and bikini tops hopped out with him.

"When you cop that, yo?" Mooch asked, while Vita grinded on his dick to the music.

"I got dis wit old money. I ain't even start spending that millennium money yet. Dis still '99 money. Ya boy had a nice run so it's only right I stunt like dis here. Science told me before he got locked up, 'Save that money. Don't worry about stuntin' today. Be the one that can do it whenever and forever.' Remember that Science?" Gwop put his hand out for Science to shake it.

Science declined.

Gwop sneered, then passed Science a bottle.

Science jerked his body backwards. When he didn't reach for a bottle, Gwop frowned. "Yo, what's up?"

"Ain't shit. But we need to talk, yo. I'm hearing some foul shit about you, yo." Science's scowl made it clear that there was a problem.

"C'mon yo, my new car got that green eyed monster on ya back?"

"Nah, that shit tight Gwop, fo 'real yo, that joint official," Science said with his face bawled up. "But you got some answering to do."

"Shoot nigga. I got bitches to get at," Gwop said arrogantly.

They walked slightly to the side away from everyone. Donte stood by angry that Science had given Gwop any conversation. He felt Science was getting too soft. He wondered why Science was waiting to kill him. They'd agreed days ago, it would be done.

"So what's got ya dick so hard, playa?"

"Nah, this ain't the place or the time. Later," Science uttered, letting Gwop know he wasn't feeling him at all.

Gwop tried to make light of the situation by grabbing a chick and telling her to show Science her tits. But the show was taken away when the Philly guys came through. It was like a music video how Sheek, Rome, and Link pulled up side by side in the red, white and black Phantoms all on 26-inch rims. The driver side doors all opened at the same time as beautiful ladies in chauffeur uniforms hopped out. The uniforms were altered to short shorts. Their jackets were unbuttoned and they had nothing under it. They had on knee high boots and matching hats. They all opened the passenger door of their assigned vehicles and Sheek, Rome, and Link came out fresh from top to bottom.

Sheek posted up against his cocaine white Phantom rubbing his hands together like Bird Man from Cash Money. He was showing off a huge diamond pinky ring, an iced-out Jacob watch, and some Gazelle shades.

"I see niggas is doing it up all crazy," Sheek said, looking over at Science and his brothers.

"Okay, the infamous Sheek. What's the deal, baby?" Donte boasted with two fine sistas from the clique, Prissy Pack. All the female crews were out today getting at a dollar. The Curvy Crew, Thick Sisters, and many more. Sheek lowered his shades to look at Donte on his new ride.

"When we start gettin' Joe with each other? I never said a word to you, Cannon. Let's not start nothing new. I see you and ya brothers put ya lil money together and rented some nice cars. Did you move out momma's house yet, lil nigga?" he asked, followed by major laughter.

Donte's temper rose all too quickly. Science could see it in Donte's eyes. He hoped he would chill.

"Chill Sheek, you out of line," Candy stated.

"Naw fuck dat! I'll say what the fuck I want. Hey Candy, you ain't get tired of this scrub yet, Ma? I still got a spot for you at the crib. I got a 'Candy' sign over the dog house in the back yard."

Link and Rome laughed but Donte was boiling inside. He wanted Science to go back to his old ways.

"You got jokes, huh? I like that," Donte sneered. He walked closer to Sheek who was on his super cool gangsta lean. "Rumor going around you can't even pop a bitch cherry ya shit so small."

"Oooohhhhhhh," the surrounding listeners and nosey groupies said in unison.

"What?" Sheek stepped up.

Donte hit him with an overhand right to the chin and followed with a left hook to the jaw knocking him to the ground.

That was the cue to pull out guns. Mooch pulled out two pistols from his waist and Rome and Link followed suit. Rome pointed his gun at Donte and Link pointed his at Mooch. Mooch had his at Rome and Sheek who was struggling to get on his feet. Gwop couldn't help but laugh seeing the commotion.

"Ya'll niggas chill, yo," Gwop chuckled, and tried to keep a straight face. "Put them shits away before the police lock all our asses up."

Sheek finally got to his feet picking up his frames from the ground. He placed them on his face nonchalantly like he didn't just get put on his ass. All eyes were on Sheek. Everyone was wondering how he would handle this bubbling conflict. He spit some blood on the ground next to Donte's foot.

"Put them guns away, yo. This was just a misunderstandin'. That lil nigga don't know what he just did. Donte….if I see you anywhere consider ya self dead."

"Nah nigga we can handle dis now yo!" Mooch stated with fire in his eyes ready to make World War III at Leakin Park in front of everybody.

Science stepped in between Mooch and Link who still were aiming their guns.

"Look yo, just chill! Dis ain't the time or place. Just dead dat shit right here and now yo. Sheek, you still trippin' over Candy ass? It's over. She's with me now. C'mon yo, you got too many hoes on ya heels now to start a war over some petty shit that ain't gonna get nobody no paper. Mooch, put them pistols away."

"What Science? These niggas still holdin' and I ain't about to let shit pop off and not be ready to clap one of these clowns!" Mooch yelled.

"Put it away!" Science yelled back, knowing this wasn't the time. Plus he saw a few dudes playing the cut ready to blast for Sheek that wasn't in the conflict. Rome looked at everybody and shook his head.

"All this over a bitch, Cannon. C'mon pimp, we makin' too much cash to beef over some broad. Wait til I tell Cash you out here sprung over a snow bunny. This ya problem, but I ain't about to lay my life on the line over no bitch. You trippin'!" Rome tucked his chrome .45 in the small of his back and posted on his car.

"I'm about a dollar and I came out here to fall back from the bullshit. I could of stayed In Philly for dis ya'mean, Scrap. I'm about to grip up one of these party jawns real quick. Y'all can shoot each other up all crazy. I'ma get my dick wet. Ayo ma, let me holla." Rome strolled over to a light skinned girl with some boy shorts on with a butterfly tattoo on her butt cheek.

"I ain't fuckin' with these penny pinchin' ass hustlers. Rome's right." Link placed his gun back under his shirt in his waistband and Mooch did the same. Science grabbed Candy and she started to grind on his dick while he leaned on his truck. Candy stared Sheek in the eyes and he got in the back of the Phantom with some chocolate vixen. Before he closed the door he heard Science yell.

"Don't ever threaten my family again, my nigga. If anything happens to mine, shit wont be a fight. Believe that."

Sheek waited for him to finish his statement before he told Gwop to get in his car. He closed the door not about to beef over a female. It just bruised his ego that someone could take anything from him.

Inside, he began telling Gwop that his boy Science had used two strikes already. "Three strikes and that nigga's out," he told Gwop.

Gwop took the opportunity and ran with it. The lies began to roll off his tongue effortlessly. "Yo, I didn't wanna say nothing until I new for sure, but I think Science either hitting ya spots or putting the cops onto you."

Sheek's gruesome looking face twisted into a tight knot. His nose spread as anger spread quickly through his veins. "What the fuck you say, nigga?"

"Yo, I'm just saying. I'm still investigatin' this shit, just listenin' to what the homies tellin' me in the streets. He tryna do you in, yo…take over your blocks. He wanna get shit back to the way it was before he left eight years ago."

"That nigga is done. Washed the fuck up!" Sheek yelled. "And his family about to be done, too," he roared.

Gwop beamed inside. His plan had always been to turn Sheek against Science. Mission accomplished. None of them had a clue about what was to come.

# CHAPTER 17

The masked man entered the room slowly, trying not to wake Damya. He wanted to make sure his boys had been following his orders and treating their prisoner like pure garbage. The rules were clear: NO food, no water, just dick.

It had been four days since she'd been kidnapped and Donte was losing patience. As he walked in circles around Damya's naked body that lay on the cold concrete, he wondered how long she would last. He hoped that she would've died by now so that he didn't have to be responsible for killing Cecil's mother. If she died on her own without food and water, he could later blame it on the other guys. Who knew if Lil' Cecil would want to avenge her death later in life.

After watching her closely, Donte decided to lift her head and remove his mask. He didn't care if she knew anymore. The gruesome scene made him want to punk. She stank badly and had deep, purplish bruises covering her body. Her face proved that his goons had done as he'd instructed. She'd been beat badly, with both eyes completely black, and one that wouldn't even open.

"Donte?" she asked weakly.

"Yeah, bitch, it's me!" he snapped.

"Why? Why are you here? Help me!" she said, attempting to reach for him.

Donte jumped back.

"Hell no!" he spat. "Bitch, I put you here. My brother was taking too long to take care of yo deceitful ass. I wasn't 'bout to let you send my brother back to jail, yo."

"I'm sorry, Donte," she cried out. "I won't do a thing, I swear."

"I guess not, trick! 'cause you ain't never leaving here. Nobody comes back here to these abandoned buildings. You gon' die here!"

"Noooooo, Donte, Noooooooooo. I'll tell you where the gun is. I'm the only one with proof!"

Damya fell back on her back. She didn't even have the strength to sit up and plead for her life. Her throat was so dry she began to choke. She hoped Donte would feel some sort of remorse. He didn't.

"Backstabbin' bitches like you can never be trusted."

"I swear I've changed. I swear."

Donte kicked her in her side. "Lies, bitch. Lies."

He took out his dick ready to piss on Damya when she closed her eyes abruptly.

"Damya, wake up, bitch," he shouted.

No movement.

"Damya," I said wake up.

Still no movement.

$$$$

The door came crashing down at Link's other stash house on Fairmount and Gilmore. Mooch busted through with the steel shield that could stop any bullet made by man. Donte and Science followed behind in full police gear screaming, "Freeze! Police! Get down!"

Being as though the last altercation with one of Link's spots had ended up with two dead, the two hustlers who were inside didn't attempt to pull out their guns, they just got on their knees and were cuffed.

"We ain't got shit!" One of the two young brothers screamed.

Donte and Science searched the rest of the house for any more people and the money. Mooch set the shield up against the wall and pulled the talkative one's braids. "Where the money at? Tell me where it's at and you won't have to worry about the crack I'm going to put on you if you don't!"

"I'on know," he belted.

"You know how much time a key of crack is in the federal system? Life plus some, tough guy! You ready for life?" Mooch asked him as he yanked his braids.

"Ahhhhh c'mon, yo! Let my hair go." Mooch pushed his face into the wood floor forcefully busting his lip open and drawing blood.

"Ain't no paper here. Y'all bitch ass police late. Link moved all the cash out the stash spots the day y'all hit the last one. Ain't shit here so you can just uncuff me," the other kid said with confidence.

Science emerged from the basement and Donte came from upstairs.

Mooch shrugged his shoulders. "Nothing, yo."

"Me, too. Where the cash at?" Science kicked the guy, who wasn't bleeding so hard in his ribs he began to choke and cough. He gripped him up off his feet and slammed him against the wall.

"Listen muthafucka, you don't want to fuck with me today. I'm having a very stressful week and I'm ready to really hurt somebody."

He had the kid up on the wall with his feet dangling. He dropped him on his ass and slapped him across the face.

Science placed his gun on the man's lips and the guy could see the death in his eyes through the ski mask. His pride wouldn't let him fold so easy because a gun was in his face. His life had been hard for years dealing with the police so this was something he was used to. He grew up in the game dodging and ducking cops.

"Well then I got some information for you that might be helpful," the guy with the gun in his face said.

"Oh, is that right? What is it?" Science asked.

"Suck my dick, pussy! Find another nigga to ask."

"Oh really." Science smacked him across his face with the gun. Both the guy's eyes were shut, and his head swelled up like a pumpkin.

"So you got something to tell me now, nigga?" Science stated, with his trembling hand holding the bloody gun over his victim's unconscious body. He looked over at the other kid and before he could speak he gave it up.

"The toilet upstairs in the bathroom. Just lift it up and it's a small space open in the floor. All the money is in there," he said quickly not wanting to be the next pumpkin head.

"Go check that!" Science ordered.

Donte put his gun in his holster and ran upstairs with the black duffel bag around his shoulder. When Donte went into the urine infested bathroom he walked over to the dirty toilet. He attempted to pick it up realizing it wasn't stuck to the floor. He moved it to the side and the built in wooden space was filled with cash.

"Bingo!" Donte began to fill his bag up with the individual stacks of money.

By the time he made it back downstairs, everyone was silent, wondering what happened upstairs. Donte looked at the guy on the floor who was mean mugging him as if he wanted to do something.

"Wassup yo, you got a fuckin problem?" Donte fired. "We being real nice letting you mafuckas live and you eye ballin' me like you wanna do something!" Donte gripped his gun tighter and aimed it at the head of the now weeping man.

"Nah yo nah yo! I swear to God I wasn't looking like that!" He put up his hands.

to cover his face. "I told you what you wanted to know! The money was there, wasn't it!"

Donte stood over his body and clutched his weapon. He looked over at Science.

"Do it or don't but we gotta go!" Science roared.

"Say no more!"

Donte let his bullets rip through the body of his victim. He let out a devious laugh as they made their way out of the door.

# CHAPTER 18

Sheek was at his ranch out the county smoking a perfectly rolled Dutch Master observing his horses as Link vented.

"What the fuck is the verdict, Sheek? I'm getting' hit back to back like I'm soft or somethin'! Like my gun don't go off! What's good with ya people down at BPD? I need to know who the pigs are that keep hittin' my spots. Dis shit crazy, Scrap! These police drawin' like shit on my blocks. My shit hot, fiends actin' like that monkey ain't scratchin' no more."

Link stood there waiting for a response as Sheek continued to exhale and inhale the exotic weed. He watched over his thirteen horses as he sat on the wooden fence.

"What the fuck you want me to say? We dealin' with the police. We can't just body bag these suckers and keep it movin'. This shit apart of the game right here, crooked cops, snitches, snakes, jackers, and a bunch of bullshit. Take dat shit on the chin. It ain't like they hit you for no mills," Sheek said as he blew smoke in Link's direction.

"Fuck dat! I wanna know who hittin' my corners! Them my stash houses gettin' raided. Make some calls, nigga!"

Sheek plucked the ash from his Dutch in the grass nonchalantly and looked at Link with a smile.

"Who the fuck you screamin' on like that? Them my fuckin' spots. I put you in position. Before you came down here you was serving packs on the dirty block in Philly. I got the weight pushin', nigga. Calm the fuck down before I calm you down!"

The look in Sheek's eyes showed he was dead serious and even though Link was far from soft, Sheek was the cause of Link's mom getting that big house. He turned him from a 1-ounce flipper to a brick pusher. He wasn't about to let his pride get in the way of that.

"You right, Cannon. You got that. I just don't like a nigga takin' shit from me like I'm soft. Police or not!" Link said, ready to lay somebody down.

"Look, when I tell you this, you gotta lay on this shit, I mean it. We gotta plan before we react, ya feel me?"

Link looked at Sheek crazily. He wondered what in the hell he was talking about.

"Gwop told me he thinks Science is behind the police coming at us. It might even be his folks. I don't know. He might be payin' the police. I just don't know everything yet."

"What the fuck!" Link exploded.

After Sheek went on to explain that Gwop said Science intended on taking their business down, they plotted on how to handle Science. Link decided he wanted to react faster than Sheek wanted.

"Hold tight, yo. Timing is everything," Sheek reiterated.

"Yeah, but if that nigga keeps hittin' our spots, I won't have no loot. He need two to the chest and one to the head, this week!" he ended.

"I feel that and I respect that, but you gotta chill. I told you to start puttin' yo money in a business and investments like me. Look at this ranch I got; twenty acres for my horses. These ain't any old horses. These is Asil Arabian, million dollar horses man. See that brown one by himself to the left with the metal brace on his leg?" Sheek pointed.

"Yeah, he looks sick though," Link commented, calming down slightly. "He ain't as big as the rest," Link said looking at the horse.

"That's my best one. He's a Scottsdale Champion Wester Pleasure, 2000 U.S. National Reserve Champion Western Pleasure. He's just been isolating himself since he's hurt. He shattered his right hind leg so he stopped being around his peoples. He's lonely and miserable, losing weight and shit. Take a look at that. He took a loss and didn't know how to handle it and folded. Real niggas don't fold, my nigga. Fuck that petty cash, we on that real money."

Link nodded, understanding where his friend and boss was coming from. Sheek pulled out a 9mm glock and cocked it.

"Science's days are numbered, yo."

$$$$

Donte was just getting up from his king size waterbed. Two Puerto Rican females still were asleep under his silk sheets. He had hit the jackpot last night when he went to DC with his homie, Tarik who'd been monitoring Damya and Donte's flunkie over at the abandoned building. He needed a break so they partied at Dreams and Donte brought two exclusive dime pieces back. Puerto Ricans were rare in B-more so he had a blast smoking and enjoying another ménage-a-trios.

He grabbed the half blunt out of the ashtray on the nightstand and lit it as he walked into the living room. His place was messy, clothes and sneakers everywhere. There was two empty boxes of pizza on the kitchen counter and two bottles of half empty Belvedere on the coffee table with several plastic cups. He took a seat on the couch as he exhaled the hydro. Life was good and to him it could only get better. His cell phone was full of pretty females. He had his own spot, cash in his safe, two cars, and plenty of clothes.

"This the life right here, yo!" He said aloud.

He did as he always did every morning and turned on the news. The 52" inch flat screen on the wall had the best picture on the market money could buy. He had his PlayStation 2 hooked up to it with a bookshelf with nothing but games.

"You got a light?" Donte was watching the report on all the bodies being dumped in Leakin Park and the high murder rate in B-more. He thought he recognized the last victim but his naked associate broke his train of thought with her seductive stance. She had a joint in her hand that looked to be rolled in top paper.

"I got the smoke right here, ma. C'mere and blow this." He told her.

"Nah, I really don't mess with weed like that. It ain't got shit on the water." She sat down next to Donte and held the joint to her lips and he lit it as she puffed.

"Water? What the hell is that?" He asked with his face screwed up.

"You know water, wet, love boat, you never heard of it? It's way better than weed. The high is amazin' papi you gotta try it."

Donte looked at her, bitch ain't nothing better than some good dro. He finished his blunt and put the roach in a plastic cup with a little liquor in it.

"Let me see that shit. I blow, so this shit better be some fire." Donte took the small joint and pulled hard trying to seem like it was nothing. After about five long hard drags of the joint, he passed it.

"You feel it yet?" The naked beauty stated calmly, inhaling the strong drug that her body had grown accustomed to. Donte sat there on the couch stuck. He couldn't speak as the TV began to stretch and colorful dots came in front of his eyes. He thought he was talking but his lips were moving slow with nothing coming out. He heard the girl talking but he could barely understand her. He attempted to stand, feeling like he was floating on air, but that thought vanished when the pain of his face came upon him as he hit the floor. He heard the girl by his side speaking, her voice screwed up, and all he remembered was her saying, 'Call 911!'

# CHAPTER 19

Mooch got the call from his mom that Donte was at Johns Hopkins Bayview Medical Center. He was trying to figure out what happened but all his mom was doing was crying and yelling on the phone. So his Saturday morning was spent throwing some clothes on and speeding down East to find out what happened.

He left Vita in bed, running lights, hoping and praying Sheek didn't cash in that threat a few weeks ago. He promised himself that Sheek and everybody who loved him would feel the wrath of a scorned brother if his ass was behind Donte being in the hospital. He quickly hopped out in front of the emergency entry and ran to the front desk.

"Donte Walters! My brother where is he at? Tell me where my brother at!" Mooch screamed on the lady at the front desk with the crooked wig.

"Room 312 on the 3rd floor. He can't have any—"

Mooch didn't hear anything after 312 on the 3rd floor. He didn't even take the elevator as he hopped up three steps at a time on the staircase. He got to the 3rd floor and burst through looking to his left and then to his right. He saw his mom, Science, Candy and two sexy Spanish girls in the hallway. He ran to his mom and hugged her tightly.

"What happened, moms?" he asked with fire in his eyes.

"These fast ass bitches gave Donte P.C.P. and it fucked him up. I told 'em about these hot in the ass girls he been dealin' with," his mom said, as she started to cry.

"The nigga fell on his head and slipped into a coma," Science stated with his hand on Mooch's shoulder.

Mooched walked over to the Spanish girls and calmly asked, "Which one of you gave my brother some boat?"

"I didn't mean to, it was just a lil bit, I'm so sor—"

The beautiful girl didn't get to apologize as the force from Mooch's punch landed on her nose and knocked her back two feet down the hall. Candy jumped on the helpless female like a lion on a wounded zebra in the jungle. Seeing her friend getting double-teamed by Mooch and Candy, the other girl slid down the hall and onto the elevator away from any bodily harm.

The security came moments later and pulled Candy and Mooch off the girl whose face had several cuts on it from a box cutter that Candy kept in her purse. Blood was everywhere as the security and doctors helped the unconscious female on a stretcher to get some medical attention.

Science sat in the corner watching everything unfold. He couldn't believe how crazy life had gotten. He'd been plotting on taking out Damya for almost ten days, but couldn't locate her. His brother was now in the hospital, and Lil' Cecil was acting up in school. Science sent Candy to resolve the school issues. So while Science spent the rest of the evening watching over Donte in the hospital, Mooch and his glock went out searching for info on anyone wanting to harm his family.

$$$$

While Donte lay in a hospital bed with his life on the line, Candy and Vita were walking through the doors of Club Choices later that night. Candy wanted to get her party on without seeing Sheek eye balling her from the other side of the room. Even though this atmosphere wasn't like Shopz it still had fine brothers with money and the music was good. Candy loved the way Science gave her space, he trusted her not to creep. Besides, the way he was laying the pipe, Candy wasn't about to mess that up. She was in love and never felt that way about anybody.

"Gurrrl, look at these fine ass niggas in here. C'mon let's get a drink and go to the dance floor." Vita said. She had her hair in a bun. Her Chanel dress clung to her body letting her natural curves show. She had a diamond necklace and matching earrings that Mooch got her for her birthday. The Prada pumps made her legs shine from the baby oil she took almost an hour massaging over her smooth peanut butter skin.

They walked through the crowd and finally made it to the bar ordering some cranberry and Grey Goose. It wasn't long before somebody was tapping on Candy's shoulder with a weak pick up line from the 70's.

"Hey baby, God must have broke the mold with you because he can't come no closer to perfect." An older man said in a tailored black suit, with grey around his thick sideburns. Candy almost laughed in his face but kept it clam.

"I'm a lesbian, this is my wife," she lied, pointing to Vita who was downing another drink.

"Oh, is that so? If you're interested, I'll be willing to pay top dollar for both your services."

Candy couldn't believe he offered to trick like she was some high priced hoe. She scooted over and whispered in his ear. "Since you acting like that, let me see it Big Daddy. Pull it out right here and now. Let me see what you're working with."

The man's eyes lit up like a Christmas tree and he quickly unzipped his pants and pulled out his uncircumcised penis from his boxers. Candy looked at him and then at his penis.

"Close your eyes, boy. I want you to enjoy this."

The man couldn't believe what was about to go down. Never had he lucked up and found a freak like this. He closed his eyes and heard Candy say don't peek. He felt her grab his dick and he instantly was fully erect from her touch.

"Open them, Daddy."

The guy opened his eyes and his heart almost skipped a beat. He saw Candy holding a box cutter to the head of his dick.

"Now, how should I do this? How about an inch? Or two inches maybe? I don't think you can afford to lose two inches," she said, gripping his penis, which was shrinking in her hand.

"Please don't do this. I'm sorry if I offended you," the man stated with beads of sweat on his forehead.

"No, you ain't sorry but you'll be, once half ya shit on the floor. I ain't no fuckin' hooker, get ya old crusty ass out of here."

Candy kept the box cutter gripped tightly just in case he tried her. He wasted no time putting his penis away and quickly disappearing in the crowd. Vita and Candy laughed hysterically until Vita's cell phone rang. Candy watched as Vita's demeanor changed quickly. She rushed off to the side saying she needed to go to the bathroom.

Candy told her to go ahead and that she'd wait for her to come back. But it didn't take long for Candy to secretly follow behind her. She'd heard Vita saying, "Hello, hello, hello," as if she couldn't hear.

Once she got near the bathroom, Vita became annoyed after hearing her ex's voice.

"Yo yo... You get that cash up for me yet?" he asked boldly.

"No, P. I will soon though…" she huffed. "I need more time," Vita stated with an attitude.

Candy stood nearby as tons of women entered and exited the bathroom. Vita had no idea Candy was watching and listening closely as Vita held the phone tightly to her ear, talking loudly so that P could hear her.

"Bitch, stop playing with me. I know all about ya lil' boyfriend out there cuz you told me. I know he gettin' money with his brothers. Get my money, bitch, unless you want ya lil' secret to come out."

"P, I need more time. Mooch doesn't keep a lot of money around and I can't get close to his brothers."

"Get my money! Or you know what it is!" he shouted.

"I can't find out where they keep the money that fast!"

Vita heard him hang up in her ear. All she could do was cry before turning to see Candy standing behind her with her hands crossed over her chest.

# CHAPTER 20

The plan was in and out. Get the money and exit safely within ten minutes. The unsuspecting van pulled up on Sinclair over East at one of Sheek's major spots that pumped dope. Science had been watching the block for about five days and figured out which house was the stash spot. They were fully dressed in their police disguise. Science had the automatic pump shotgun with the extra shells placed in the slots on the side of the high-powered weapon. Mooch had a .45 caliber handgun in his left hand with the black duffel bag over his shoulder.

"You ready, yo?" Science asked. You seem like you got something on ya mind."

"Just thinkin' 'bout Donte still in a coma, yo."

Mooch had been in shambles, praying for his recovery. It had been seven days and Donte hadn't shown any sign of getting better. Vita had not shown up at the hospital once since his brother had been there. He was really upset about her not showing up to show support for the family.

"Look-a-here, bro. He gon' come outta this. I know he will. And when he wakes up he'll be happy 'bout what we about to do."

Science reached over and gave his brother some dap.

"Let's get it poppin', big bro."

The van stopped in front of the house and they both hopped out aiming. Mooch kicked the door and it came crashing down.

"What the fuck?" The kid said as he sat on the chair getting some head from a young freak on her knees. He reached for his gun on the floor but Science swung the pump to his nose and he put his hands up.

"Don't move! Is there anyone else in the house?" He aimed his weapon.

"Nah yo, just me and shorty. Can I pull up my pants before y'all take a nigga out with his dick swingin'?" The guy asked, before pulling his pants up from his ankles.

"It depends, where's the money at? It's tax time for Sheek and it's pay day." Science cocked the shotgun and touched the tip of the kid's nose with it.

"Upstairs, backroom in the mattress. Flip it and you'll see the cut. Look man, I just got out of jail last week." Mooch quickly hit the stairs and to the backroom.

Science listened to the kid talk but the girl still on her knees began to move.

"No, no, Miss Lady. Don't try nothing stupid. Put your hands up and slowly lay flat on ya stomach," he instructed.

She followed his demands reluctantly.

"Got it, let's go," Mooch stated as he rushed down the stairs with a bulky duffel bag. Science turned his head slightly in Mooch's direction and heard a loud gunshot. He saw that the bullet just missed Mooch's head by an inch and turned to look at the girl who was aiming the gun. She pulled the trigger again but gun jammed. Science had his shotgun right at her forehead.

"Put the gun down before I put ya face on the wall."

The girl dropped the gun as quickly as she picked it up.

"That lil' bitch almost blew my fuckin' head off! You stupid slut!" Mooch ran over and kicked her in the face. She fell back onto the floor.

"Stupid bitch, let's ride."

He spit on her body and they turned to leave.

Science and Mooch came outside but saw a police car coming up the block.

"Oh shit yo, what we going to do?" Mooch asked.

"Chill, yo. Just stay calm, I got this," Science said as they hurried down the five steps to the concrete.

The police car came to an abrupt stop and two officers took cover behind the doors of the car aiming their guns.

"Freeze! Put the guns down, now!"

Science looked at Mooch and his eyes said, '*Chill lil' bro I got dis.*'

"Officers calm down, this is a routine drug bust, all you got to do is call it in. This is a known drug house and we're just doing our job."

"Bullshit, put the guns down!" the one officer screamed.

"We police, you asshole. Put your guns down!" Mooch yelled back ready to let the pigs have it.

The officer let off two shots and one caught Mooch in the leg.

"Ahhh shit! You mother…fucker!" Science raised the shotgun letting off two rounds at the police car.

The hood of the squad car lifted and Science and Mooch went for cover. The officer continued firing back as Mooch and Science ducked behind parked cars.

"Nah, this ain't about to end like this. Fuck that!"

Mooch crawled on his knees down the block about four or five cars behind the police car as the shooting continued. His leg was leaking badly but his adrenaline was pumping so he couldn't feel a thing. He gave Science the signal and he came from his hiding spot with two more rounds from the pump. The officers ducked down grabbing the radio calling for back up.

Mooch let his bullets rip through the backs of both officers as they fell to the ground. He hopped over to their slumped bodies with the heavy bag still over his shoulder.

"Ya back up right here, yo!"

He put one in each of the cop's head to make sure they were in a permanent slumber.

"Let's go!" Mooch yelled, after seeing Science pop up, running toward the car in the middle of the street.

"That was some movie shit, bro. What the fuck? You bleeding bad as shit," Science said, looking at Mooch's leg that was leaking all over the seat.

"Nigga, fuck my leg! We out."

They pulled off leaving smoke behind them from the screeching tires.

# Chapter 21

The two brothers sat in Donte's condo counting the money from the last lick. Mooch had his leg wrapped up from the bullet he took. Luckily, it had gone straight through. He couldn't go to the hospital or he would be in jail. The TV was on and the squad car camera showed the entire shootout from when they stepped out the house. It never showed Mooch coming from behind laying the police down but you could hear the shots, and Mooch saying, "Let's go," and them getting in the van. The shootout was almost on every channel and the Mayor of Baltimore wanted justice for the slain officers. The words search for COP KILLER filled the screen causing Mooch to have a blank look on his face.

Science sat in deep thought making sure he'd covered their tracks. He'd ditched the van knowing it was hot and every van that fit that description would get pulled over. He thought about how they'd worn gloves, so no prints. He just wished they'd left no witnesses.

"You good, Mooch?" Science asked his little brother.

"I'm straight yo, that shit went straight through. A leg shot not stopping nothing over here. I'm a gangsta, and if I go out, niggas is coming with me. Not just one, a lot."

Mooch threw a stack of money at the TV as he watched the van pulled off on the television.

"Yo, my boy got a nurse he know who gon' come check you out. Stitch you up and shit. Or whatever, you need."

"Whateva. I'm gangsta, nigga."

Science laughed at how his brother tried to be tough.

"Let's count this money, yo. We gotta get Donte in some new hot shit when he wakes up. Probably down Big Boy Whips or something. Let him stunt like he supposed to."

Science looked at his brother and smiled even though on the inside he wanted out. Things had gotten too crazy. Still, he began counting, feeling good about the heist. By the time they'd finished counting, $400,890 was the total amount of cash. They put $75,000 in Donte's safe and took enough for his wake up gift.

They sat back and passed a blunt back and forth while watching B.E.T and waiting for the nurse to come.

"These corny ass hood movies is wack, yo. This shit fake as hell. We need to show' em how to make a real blackbuster movie. *Charm City* style ya'mean, take 'em through the streets of Baltimore," Mooch added as he exhaled the weed smoke from his nose.

"So you tryna direct movies and shit, yo?" Science laughed.

"Fuck it, this bullshit that's out, I know I can put together something better than this garbage. Get official street niggas to play some gangstas cause they ain't got to act, that's they life. We gonna sell millions of DVDs. Real shit!"

Science felt his cell phone vibrate and picked it up.

"Yo. Fo 'real? Oh shit! I'm on my way right now."

Science looked at Mooch who was dumb high with the chinky red eyes.

"Donte opened his eyes!" Science said with a smile.

"Let's go then yo, what we still sittin' here for? Help me up, nigga." Mooch reached for Science to help him up.

"Nah stay here, yo. You hit, and the cops prolly gonna be at the hospital waiting for a nigga with a leg shot to come in there. Just chill bro, trust me. Plus, the girl coming by to get you right."

"You right…tell that nigga I love him. And he dumb as hell for smoking that wet!"

When Science got to the hospital, Candy and their mother was right beside his bed. Science hugged Candy and thanked her for being there for him. He looked at Donte who was lying there with his eyes open trying to speak. Science got close to hear what Donte was trying to say.

"Y'all…went…without me," he exhaled weakly.

Science started laughing and asked for his mom and Candy to leave so they could talk.

"You and Mooch getting a lil' too grown, boy. That boy came out of me. I went in labor for eighteen hours with his big head ass. Now hurry up and talk because I need to speak with my son," his mother said, and kissed Donte on the forehead, happy to see him awake.

When the females left, Science pushed the button to raise the bed up.

"So what's good, sleepy head? I bet you won't smoke that shit no more." Science joked and they both laughed.

"Yo, where them Rican girls at? Dog, them hoes fucked a nigga so good it wasn't even funny," Donte said with a half of smile.

"Fuck them bitches. Candy cut one of 'em up bad, and Mooch knocked a tooth out. The other one got ghost," Science told him.

"Well fuck all that, how much y'all get?" Donte asked full of energy all of a sudden.

"What?" Science asked.

"Man, moms had the news on, and I could hear all that shit. Man disguised as police shoot it out on a city block over drug money. Where my cut, nigga?" Donte smiled, and put his hand out.

"Same old Donte, all about his. You should be glad ya crazy ass still alive. You been out for a minute."

Science grabbed his hand and squeezed it. "I love you, bro." He hugged him and kissed his cheek.

"C'mon wit all that, bro. So I guess we gon' hit Sheek's crib when I get outta here?" Donte asked with a serious look.

"C'mon yo, you trippin. It's all over the news about the fake cops knockin' off drug houses in the city. We hit!" Science told him.

"Man fuck that, Candy said he got mills! We on that bitch ass nigga. A.S.A.P.!"

"You crazy Donte, fo 'real yo. You just got out a coma and you thinkin' about robbin' a nigga?" He smiled and sat by his side to give him the scoop on the police shooting.

$$$$

"Get the fuck outta here! These mafuckers ain't even police. Gwop was right! I guarantee you it's the nigga Science and his crew," Sheek commented aloud.

He sat behind his huge oak desk at his club, watching the news on his flat screen, trembling with rage. He listened to the news reporter say the two men disguised as Baltimore City Task Force went into a known drug house and recovered an undisclosed amount of drug money.

"I'll tell you how much they took! $400 thousand dollars of my fuckin' money!" Sheek yelled to the TV and threw the remote across the room, breaking it into pieces.

He looked around his office at his top enforcers, and of course, Gwop. Sheek looked at Link who had the, *I told you so* expression on his face.

"I told you that nigga was foul," Gwop announced.

"Nigga, you brought him around," Sheek shot back.

"Mannnn, how was I supposed to know he'd come home and be on some weak, robbin' shit. He wasn't like that before. That nigga used to be official," he said with confidence.

Sheek stood up and began pacing the room, throwing anything in sight.

"I want everybody in our spots to know that if we get any visits from these nut ass niggas to shoot on contact. No hesitation. And I mean shoot to kill!"

Gwop sat unbothered by Sheek's rant. He began playing around with his phone until he said, "I bet his brothers behind this shit too, yo."

"Kill 'em all!" Sheek raved. "And double up my fuckin muscle at all stash spots! Make sure our guys know these bulls ain't police so tell them to keep they fuckin eyes open, and guns loaded and cocked. These niggas want to play gangsta and steal my shit, huh? We can play."

He slammed his fist on his desk. Sheek couldn't quite put his finger on the way Gwop was acting. He was quiet and laid back. He didn't look at Sheek not once since he'd made his last comment.

"All y'all got that? Am I fuckin clear?"

He looked at Link then at Gwop.

"You good, cannon?"

Link nodded.

"Gwop, what's poppin?" he asked him. "You actin' kinda strange."

"Ain't shit yo, just thinking. This shit fuckin' crazy, that's all," Gwop responded.

"Think about findin' out where Science and his whole family lay their heads."

"Oh, I know the answer to that," Gwop responded without delay.

"Oh really," Sheek stated with a malicious grin. "Let's talk then, Cannon. The rest of you fuckas get the fuck out my office. All of you!"

Sheek lit a cigarette and took a long hard drag, and waited for Gwop to give up the info.

$$$$

The streets were calm as Lil' Cecil walked home from school slowly, playing with his handheld game. The clouds became dreary signaling a strong rain was coming. With the exception of three other kids on the block, no one seemed to be out. Lil' Cecil looked up from his game and crossed the street. He never noticed the Black Denali creeping from a short distance.

"What's the move Sheek, is we laying the youngbull or what?" Link asked cocking his .45.

He clutched it tightly from the passenger seat while watching Lil' Cecil continue to play his game. Sheek remained silent in the backseat, rubbing his chin. He'd been contemplating for hours just how to get back at Science. He wasn't hell bent on killing kids but Science had crossed the line. Gwop had given him all the information he needed on where Science's mother stayed and where Lil' Cecil went to school.

Rubbing his beard, he said, "I got this... Big Cuz, roll up on youngbull," Sheek told Big Cuz who was driving.

"Fuck all that! Is we killin this lil nigga, or what?" Link asked with frustration. "You got us out here playin' when we need to be hittin' Science and his brothers. Fuck you think we down here for to play with niggas!"

Link was yelling loudly and wildly, not recognizing the spit flying from his dry lips. Sheek watched Link's temper tantrum and just shook his hand. Still, Link put his hand on the trigger of the gun.

Sheek rose up in his seat. "Chill nigga, this my show."

Sheek rolled the window down as Big Cuz pulled up on Lil' Cecil who was still walking the block slowly with his head downward.

"Fuck dat! I'm hittin this lil nigga!" Link roared and aimed his gun across Big

Cuz ready to squeeze.

Big Cuz's eyes grew wide. The butt of the gun ended up right in front of his nose. He had sons of his own and definitely didn't want Link to fire on the kid. He had been in the gang banging business for years and had seen it all. But killing a kid wasn't what he wanted to see. He felt sorry for him and wanted to pull off. But Sheek was his boss.

Finally, Sheek spoke up, shouting from the back. "Nigga, is you fuckin' crazy! Chill, I said I got this!" Sheek snapped.

"If you think that nigga Science behind this shit what the fuck you stopping me for? Cash sent goons down here—not fuckin pussies. You need to chill, Sheek. Let me do what needs to be done," Link said seriously, placing his gun back on his lap.

"Yeah, I thought so," Sheek boasted, leaning toward the front seat. "Calm down, nigga. This my operation down here. Remember, you work for me, nigga. And don't lift that fuckin gun again unless I tell you to."

Big Cuz breathed a heavy sigh.

Link grimaced and balled his fist to the sides.

"Fuck you think shooting this lil nigga right here and now gon' get us dickhead!" Sheek mushed his gun in Link's face and waited for him to act gangster. "Life in prison, nut!"

Link seemed to be in deep thought after listening to Sheek's comment.

"Oh ok... That's what I thought. Don't make me fuck ya check up and send you back to Philly broke!"

Sheek sucked his teeth and turned his attention back to Lil' Cecil, who had now spotted the car following him.

"Pull up, pull up," Sheek told Big Cuz.

“Yo lil man!" He yelled from the car tryna get his attention since Lil’ Cecil had picked up the pace. He was now totally focused on what was going on up the block.

“Hurry up and pull up on youngin,” Sheek ordered, causing Big Cuz to speed up and make the sounds of a car skidding as he got right up on Lil’ Cecil.

“Yo Lil’ Man,” Sheek began.” I need to holla at you for a minute.

“I don't know you, yo,” Lil’ Cecil said as he looked Sheek in his with a frown, and chest poked out.”

“Lil’ Man. No worries, yo. You good with me. Something came up with ya pops. I'm his friend so he asked me to get you. Get in, it's no time to waste.”

The apprehension on his young face made his mean mug wash away. He slowed his paced and thought for several seconds. He’d never seen the guy before but made mention of his father.

“What’s my father’s name?” he asked quickly.

“Science,” Sheek laughed. “You a smart lil’ nigg. I like that. I know ya uncle Donte and ya Daddy’s woman, Candy. We all cool.”

Lil’ Cecil warmed up and allowed a slight smile to slip through the side of his mouth. He clutched his backpack and stopped completely. So did Sheek’s car. At that moment, Sheek tried again.

“Yo, come on. Hop in. I’ma take you to your father.”

Lil’ Cecil raced over to the car. Once inside he took his backpack off, then looked at the other two guys in the front seat. The moment he saw Link’s grimace and unfriendly glare he looked back at Sheek.

Then back at Link again.

That’s when he saw the gun.

# Chapter 22

Science went to go pick up his brothers' gift while he recovered with the family. He dropped Mooch off at the hospital in D.C. after the nurse who'd helped Mooch suggested it. It wasn't safe to go in Baltimore. The cops were on everything coming in with a leg wound. Mooch gave the doctors some bullshit story about getting robbed and someone shooting at him. He ended up having to concoct a story to give the police a report, but not once did he flinch. Mooch tried to call Vita, but he kept getting her machine. Her lack of concern for his family was really bothering him and he was on the verge of dismissing her for good.

Science on the other hand had been worried about Lil' Cecil for hours. He didn't call once he got home from school like he normally did. He vowed that he'd punish him, teaching him a lesson. Science walked in and saw Donte looking unhappy to see him.

"What's good, you ready to go or what? I got a surprise out front for you, yo," he said to Donte.

"I keep tellin' these doctors I'm good and ready to go. They saying wait a few more days. Look yo, get a nigga outta here, Science," Donte demanded.

"Let me go holla at the doc and see what's good. I'll be right back."

It only took a few words from Science. The doctor gave him some papers, and Science, Donte, Candy and his mom exited the hospital.

"Oh shit!" Donte was in awe at the sight of the convertible Mercedes Benz SL, all black with grey interior, and the butterfly doors. Donte stared at the car ready to hop in.

"That's you Donte, from me and Mooch. We know how you like to stunt, so we thought this would do you just right." Science held up the keys and Donte snatched them quick.

"Boy where'd you get the money to buy this car? I hope you ain't selling them drugs, Cecil. Please baby, didn't you learn ya lesson?" his mother asked suspiciously. She wasn't ready to lose her eldest son to the street life again.

"Chill mom, it ain't from me selling drugs. I promise." He hugged her and kissed her cheek.

"I ain't going back to jail." He promised her.

"I hope not," she said, hugging him tightly. "I can't lose my boys. My heart isn't strong enough to take that."

"Candy, drive with Donte, I'll take mommy home in my truck."

"Let's ride then!" Donte said hype to get back on the streets and stunt. As he watched Science and his mother walk away, he shouted, "I love ya'll."

They laughed from a distance with his mother blowing kisses.

Candy couldn't wait to help Donte into the car. She'd had the Vita incident on her mind and didn't know when she'd be able to settle Science down to tell him. She knew Donte would have the best answer. As she paid the parking attendant and exited the garage, she asked Donte how well he knew Vita.

"I'on really know the hoe," he joked. "That's Mooch's bitch."

Candy turned onto the main highway with a blank look on her face. Donte sensed something was wrong. "What? You caught her with a nigga?"

"No," Candy blurted. "But I did overhear a conversation that has me worried."

"Go 'head. Tell me," he urged.

"She was talking to some guy named P. I'm not sure what he was saying to her, but the way she responded, it seemed liked she needed to come up with some money from Mooch, and possibly you and Science, too."

"What the fuck?"

Donte immediately picked up his cell and called Science. He told him the moment he dropped their mother off, he needed to meet him at his spot. He also told Science that he'd done some shit he wouldn't like.

$$$$

As soon as Science dropped his mother off, he jetted over to Donte's. The sound of his voice made Science think it was important. On his way over he tried Lil' Cecil again. He hadn't gotten home yet, and it was after 6 o'clock. Science was worried and thought about going to check on his son first, but decided against it. He figured meeting up with Donte would be quick.

As soon as Science walked in the door, Donte jumped up like he hadn't just got out of the hospital. He was extra hyper. "Yo, I told you that bitch, Vita was no good."

"Whoa, what are you talkin' about, yo?" Science questioned, while looking at Candy's glare.

"Candy overheard that bitch tellin' the nigga she used to mess with that she needs more time to come up with the money. Candy said the bitch mentioned Mooch's name and said his brothers. Now what the fuck would she say his brothers for?"

While Donte paced the floor like a mad man, Science twisted his mouth, thinking. "Candy, you think she up to no good?"

Candy nodded her head sadly. She hated to say it, but she didn't trust Vita anymore. Donte completely flipped out and went on a rampage. "I swear, Mooch's soft ass betta murk her. Nigga's don't ever wanna take care of business when it comes to chicks."

"Calm down, Donte. Let me think."

"Man, by the time you finish thinking, Vita and her dude gon' try to blast us. I'ma kill the bitch….just like I hope I did to Damya."

Science's eyeballs bulged. "Damya? What did you do Donte?" he asked with crazy emotion. "You know I've been lookin' for her!"

Donte turned away from his brother and placed his hands on top of his head in frustration. "Shit!" he shouted.

"Donte, what did you do?" Science repeated.

Candy ran around to the front of Donte's face. "Tell us, Donte."

"I kidnapped the bitch and left her for dead!"

"Aweeeee no, Donte! Whyyyyy, yo?" Science shouted. "That's my son's mother."

"Yo, you got soft. I was tryna protect you too. First she was gon' blackmail you and send yo' black ass back to jail. Who knows what was next?"

"You left her for dead, where?" Science said, feeling empty inside. He'd plotted on doing Damya in himself but hearing Donte rattle off all he'd done to her made him sick on the stomach.

"Take me to where you left the body," Science ordered.

Candy tried to place her hand on Science's back but he pulled away, rushing out the door. "Go look for Lil' Cecil," he told Candy before shutting the door.

# CHAPTER 23

The entire ride over to the West Side of Baltimore Donte pled his case about why he didn't tell Science he'd kidnapped Damya. None of what he said made any sense. He told Donte that he'd gotten too wild and crazy; he was out of control. Science also told Donte not to touch Vita. They agreed that they'd tell Mooch what Candy told Donte and they could decide what to do from there.

"Call ya boy again, Donte. Ask them did they kill her. I wanna know did she die 'cause you didn't feed her. This is bullshit, yo."

"I called already, dog. You want me to stalk a nigga?"

"Yes," Science emitted as Donte turned off the exit. He was so angry with his brother for what he'd done.

Science looked around observing the area as Donte pulled into a desolate industrial area. He couldn't believe the condition of the run down buildings. It reminded him of the abandoned houses off Monroe street. Once out of the car, Donte jetted toward the unit where he'd taken Damya.

"Look, yo, they mighta moved her body by now. Last, I saw her, she was alive, just beat up badly. So don't blame shit on me."

Science just shook his head in disgust as he listened to his brother talk.

"You gave the order, nigga," Science shot as they entered the building.

"Yeah, but for you, bro," Donte said sincerely.

The building was cold, moist and filled with; mice running around, massive bugs, dust, dirt and shit flying across the ceiling. Science felt dirty just being in the place. As he walked the sound of his voice echoed. All he wanted to do was give Damya a proper burial if Donte's boys hadn't taken her somewhere already.

"Where to now, Donte?" he asked, wanting Donte to take the lead.

Donte took a quick left, and walked up a pair of shaky steps. A few steps down the hall, he opened the door where he'd last seen Damya. Donte frowned at the jug of water and the candy wrappers he saw. He instantly felt disrespected. He'd told Tarik not to feed her or give her water.

"Oh Shit! Damya!" Science called out as he saw her frail body bawled up into a knot on the nasty, cold, concrete floor.

The fact that Damya didn't move didn't surprise Donte. He assumed she was dead. Science ran toward her body at top speed. When he reached her, he pulled her close and wrapped his arms around her bruised, purplish looking body. The color seemed to be absent from her face. And everything about her appeared flushed and dead. Science's facial expression made Donte think he wanted to cry.

"C'mon man, when we get here? The bitch was tryna extort you, and send you to jail for life. Remember that, yo. Now you wanna bring her back?"

Science ignored his brother's comments because he realized Damya was breathing. He leaned down to put his ear closer to her mouth. She seemed to be unconscious, or simply unable to speak. Instantly, Science reached over, pouring water over her mouth from the jug, allowing drops to seep through her lips. When Damya began choking it surprised them both.

"Aweeee shit! She's alive!" Donte shouted in amazement.

Science spent the next few minutes smacking Damya trying to wake her up, and cleaning her face with his shirt. By the time she woke up and was able to speak, Science and Donte couldn't believe their eyes. Damya wailed constantly as she cried out to Science.

"Oh my God, Scienceeeee! She wailed. "Thank you for saving meeeeeee!"

"It's okay Damya, just relax. I'ma get you some help," he told her.

"It hurt soooooooo bad. But you came!" Her tears wouldn't stop flowing and her expression showed remorse for the way she'd treated him.

"I'm soooooooo sorry. I shoulda never listened to Gwop," she continued to cry. "That's the only reason why I tried to blackmail you."

"Damya, it's okay. Stop talking. Donte, call the ambulance," Science instructed.

"Hell no!" Donte shouted. "Let her talk, then we can take her. She might tell 'em I had something to do with this."

Science thought about what Donte said as Damya kept mumbling.

"He had those goons waiting for you when you got off the bus, Science. And he paid me to keep tryna ask you for money. I'm soooooooo sorry," she kept repeating.

"Pleasssssseeeeeeee, forgive me. He wanted me to give him that gun so he could frame you, but I didn't." She began sobbing again.

"Damn," Science said thinking about Gwop.

"Why, Damya?" Donte interrupted. "Why is the nigga Gwop doing all this?" He leaned in expecting an answer.

"He wants to turn Sheek against Science and Science against Sheek. He wants to take over everybody's territory. He's killed so many people in the city and wants people to think it's Science. He said he's gon' rule all of Baltimore. Charm City is his," he said.

"Shhhh," Science told her, putting his finger to her dry lips. "Rest. Save your energy, yo."

"He knew when you was coming home Science. He wanted you to take the fall for everything. It would all be blamed on you. His whole plan."

"Let's go, Damya," Science said, lifting her into his arms. He knew he needed to get her to a hospital. He didn't care about the consequences. Or what other info she had on Gwop. He'd heard enough.

"Pleaseeeeee take Cecil…show him a good life. I'm not gonna make it!"

What had been done to Damya angered Science to the core. He briefed her and everything to say once he got her to the hospital. He knew the staff would call the police in to take a report. Damya vowed not to turn Donte in, or his boys Tarik and Smack. Tarik was actually the person who saved her life. He'd been giving her food and water, helping her to survive. She had no idea why, but was thankful.

Hours had gone by with Science remaining by Damya's side. She'd been given a healthy dose of drugs to calm her nerves while the doctors accessed the damage. He was in no mood to deal with the drama that was about to kick off when his cell rang. He hoped it wasn't Candy calling to fuss again about him being with Damya. She wanted someone else to watch over her.

Science answered and then nodded his head as he listened intently. Then he began screaming, shouting into the phone as Lil' Cecil told him what Sheek had done. Luckily, Sheek let him go, and his son was safely at home. But Sheek had sent a message through Lil' Cecil that if his father didn't call him, the next time wouldn't go so easy.

"You gon' fuck him up, right Dad? Mail that nigga's head to his momma?"

The comment threw Science for a loop. He was thinking the same thing but didn't want his son to know it. "That's not how we handle things, son. But I'll take care of Sheek. Don't you worry."

"But you a ganster, right?"

"Most gangsters end up dead, son." He paused before saying his last words. "But I swear I'ma protect you. Sheek will never mess with you again."

Science hung up and dialed the only number he had for Sheek. As soon as he answered, Science fired like a cannon. "You touched my fuckin" son! Are you crazy, nigga?"

"You touched my money, nigga! So I touched ya son! You think I'on know you and ya crew been hittin my real estate in these streets?"

Science figured Sheek didn't really know it was him, he was just fishing. He kept his composure and put on his best acting skills.

"Nigga, that ain't on me. All my niggas done. I'm solo out here. But you crossing the line like a mufucka touching my seed."

"You better not play with me, Science. If I find out you had anything to do with my shit being hit you a dead man walking."

"And if you ever touch my son again, you a dead man walking," he fired back.

Just like that the phone line went dead.

# CHAPTER 24

Shopz was packed like any other Friday night. Sheek had his homie, Reed Dollaz from Philly perform his new single that was a smash on the airwaves. He was getting crazy love from the B-more crowd. He snatched off his T-shirt exposing his inked up chest and stomach. His diamonds were flawless as his VVS's sparkled like they had just been cleaned. Sheek sat in VIP with a bottle of Dom P. All his goons stood by guarding him with their hands on their weapons just in case anybody tried to get too close. Sheek almost choked on his drink when he saw a fine hoochie in some boy shorts, stilettos, and a tight black fitted shirt that exposed her breasts.

"Ayo Ma, ayo shorty, holla at me," Sheek yelled from behind the ropes as she walked toward the bathroom. She stopped when she saw Sheek.

She knew he had big bank. Her motive was to get his attention. It was every woman's dream in the club to snag Sheek. She had an ulterior motive. He greeted her at the purple rope and unhooked it to let her pass as everyone cheered for Reed Dollaz as he rocked the stage.

Sheek never paid attention to the blue eyes across the room at the bar watching his every move. Within seconds the female asked for a drink and accidentally spilled it on Sheek. He hopped up, upset about ruining his expensive shirt. When he left the VIP to go to the bathroom the eyes locked in on him and followed behind.

Inside the bathroom, Sheek cleaned himself up and checked himself over in the mirror. The black Armani button up fit him perfectly and the 5 ct. cufflinks he sported blended just right with his attire. He had a bracelet and watch that both were the price of the average American home. No chain or earrings tonight, he kept it simple as he knew how. He looked down at his Gucci sneakers, that didn't have a single mark on them. He was good to go.

As Sheek stepped out of the men's room he saw Candy coming out the ladies restroom. Her ass seemed to have gotten bigger and her hips had spread even more. He licked his lips remembering how good her pussy was.

"So you can't speak because we ain't sleeping together no more, shorty? It's like that now? That's how you treat a nigga you used to love so crazy?"

Candy looked in his eyes with a hint of sadness.

"You okay?" Sheek asked her.

She ran into his arms and began to cry. "I'm sorry I left you like that, Sheek. I shoulda done things differently," she wailed.

Sheek took the opportunity to caress her tits as he held her. He didn't know what was going on with Candy. "The nigga hit you?" he asked, as if he hadn't been overly violent towards Candy in the past.

"No, it's not that," she stated after a few sniffles. "Sheek, I just need somebody to talk to. Science cheated on me and he tried to lie when I walked in on him fucking some chick."

Sheek held her tightly with a devilish grin.

"See? I told you, and look at 'chu now. You shoulda stayed with me. It's all good though. Let's go have a drink," Sheek said, as he cuffed her butt gently.

"No! I don't want to be around all these people. Can we just go in your office and talk? Maybe have a drink up there? All these people just irk me, Sheek." Candy looked him in his eyes and he smiled before kissing his lips gently.

"Hell yeah. The club's letting out at two o'clock anyway. Just fifteen more minutes," he told her.

It didn't take long for the club to shut down. As the staff closed up as quickly as possible, Sheek took his private party to his office upstairs with Candy on his arm. When they got inside she kicked off her shoes and sat down on the plush leather love seat by his tropical aquarium that held two coral snakes. Sheek brought her over a glass of champagne and set the mood with some Luther Vandross playing quietly in the background.

"So what's been up, Candy? You been thinking about me?" Sheek asked, sipping his drink and sitting on his large oak desk.

Candy glared over the six security screens that showed each exit of the club, every floor and hallway and even the ladies room. "Of course I think about you, Sheek. I think about the trips, the shopping sprees, the sex, money and drugs. I also think about the lonely nights, the lies, the cheating, the abuse, and the neglect. It just seemed like you used me for sex and your trophy case. Like I was nothing important to you."

Her words hurt and he couldn't realize why he never treated her like she should have been treated. Since she had been gone, he thought of her every night.

"I love you, Candy. I did and still do. Baby, you were the only female I gave all the keys and security codes to. You was my down ass bitch and you broke my heart leaving me for my homie. That shit hurt a nigga bad."

Sheek looked at Candy's smooth legs and his dick got hard. Candy walked over to Sheek and hugged him, apologizing over and over again about the Science situation. When he licked her ear she cringed at his wet tongue, but held it together. She kissed his lips and let his hands travel over her body as their tongues wrestled.

"Sheek…wait, stop baby, hold up. I can't do this. I need to officially end things with Science before I do this. Two wrongs don't make a right," she said, holding him back.

"Yeah, but two wrongs will definitely have that nigga pissed off. Fuck that sucka ass nigga anyway. This is my damn city! These nut ass niggas down here answer to me. He better be glad he still breathin' after playin' me like a clown." He balled up his fist wishing he could just blow Science's head off for all the disrespect.

"Sheek relax, I just want it to be me and you tonight. Tell the goons to go get some pussy, and let's hold each other like old times in the back room. Remember how we used to do. Huh baby, remember?" she asked him with those pretty blue eyes looking up at him.

"You better be glad I still love ya ass, girl. I'll be right back."

Sheek kissed her lips again and gave her soft ass another squeeze before he left to dismiss the unwanted company. Candy watched the security screens as she ran to her clutch purse and picked up her cell.

"Yeah, he about to do it now. Just stay in your positions and come up in like a half hour. I know, I know. It's behind the picture of John Gotti behind his desk. 2-16-86. Make sure you play it off, though. Alright, alright, I love you, too."

$$$$

Sheek took the elevator down to the first floor to his club, signaling his team.

"Boss, what's going on?" one of Sheek's security guards asked.

"Don't worry bout that, just make you get all the workers out and y'all post up outside. I got business to handle upstairs and I don't want to be disturbed." He patted the 6-foot-4 bouncer on his shoulder, and made his way back upstairs. "Handle that now."

They locked up and set the alarm as three of his closest goons posted in front of the club and two in the back. Sheek watched from his six screens. "You see what I do for you?" He walked over to Candy. He held out his hand and she took it. She rose to her feet and he guided her behind his desk. He opened the right hand drawer and pressed the red button that was hidden in the back corner.

Candy watched as the wall opened up to reveal his secret room. The room had a pool table, Jacuzzi, and a king size bed with mirrors on the ceiling. He had a connecting bathroom and walk-in closet that held some of his best suits and shoes. Candy had been inside plenty of times, but she noticed he added a huge flat screen, and a white tiger rug on the floor.

"Ooohh Sheek, I forgot how comfortable this bed was, baby," she said with a smile as she took a seat on it.

"You probably forgot how this ma'fucka feel too," Sheek stated, grabbing his crotch. *I don't remember me ever feeling it*, Candy thought to herself. She smiled and turned around for him to unzip her Gucci dress.

$$$$

The vent in the men's bathroom came crashing down onto the tile floor. Science hopped down dressed in all black, ski masked up, with a duffel bag strapped around his chest. Donte hopped down right after him. They both pulled their guns from their shoulder holsters. Donte had two glock .40 handguns with silencers and Science had one 9mm also equipped with a silencer. They took the stairs slowly and cautiously to the main office on the top floor. Each looked like Ninjas where not even their eyes were exposed.

Science and Donte walked down the hallway to the sounds of Luther floating through the air. Science opened the door to Sheek's office and Donte came behind him to enter. Science fumbled around trying to see in the dark, and from behind the light fabric that covered his eyes. He could hear moans coming from the other side of the wall. He hoped Candy hadn't gone all the way with Sheek. He'd told her to do whatever she had to do to make it work, but now he regretted it.

He stood outside of Sheek's office trying to turn on the portable voice box that would change the sound of his voice. It was something Bozo had given them that would have them sounding like they were talking under water, or hiding out in a cave. Donte had already turned his on but Science was having trouble. Once he finally figured it out, he gave Donte the signal. When Sheek's office opened up like something in a movie, Science grinned. But as they got closer, it was clear that Sheek was sexing Candy in the missionary position and she was moaning like it was the best dick she ever had. Science felt jealousy overcome his insides and his blood boiled. He gripped the gun tighter as he and Donte observed from the front of the bed.

"Hop out the pussy real quick, yo!" Science said with his voice distorted, sounding extremely weird.

Science smacked Sheek in the back of the head with his gun causing him to roll over on his back. When Sheek's instincts kicked in, he quickly grabbed for his gun on the nightstand but had two guns pointed in his face. He dropped it to the floor as he felt the blood dripping from the back of his head.

"Ahhh! Ahhhh!" Candy screamed like she didn't know what was going on. She held her hands up as her big breast were exposed with red marks from Sheek sucking them roughly.

"Shut the fuck up, bitch!"

Donte gripped Candy by the hair and tossed her to the floor. He really did this to get a whole body shot of her nakedness. Now he realized why Science's nose was wide open for this female. She was an all around dime piece, for real.

"You a trifling ass freak," Donte shouted, loving how the voice box made him sound.

"What the fuck y'all nut ass niggas want?" Sheek blasted. "Don't you know all my security outside? It ain't no way out of here without taking some slugs. So get the fuck out of my office so I can finish gettin' my nut off," Sheek said arrogantly.

"Where the fuck the money at, yo? Give it up and you might see tomorrow," Science said with his gun in Sheek's face.

"I ain't got shit in here, and if I did, you wouldn't get a penny. What the fuck I look like? A pussy nigga? Fuck y'all! C'mon, who the fuck y'all niggas think you is?"

"Sheek, no games, yo," Science said in a more serious tone.

"Yo, when I find out who you niggas is, shit gon' be bad!"

"Just tell us where the money at before it get ugly." Donte mushed one of the guns in Sheek's face.

"It's already ugly, cause I'ma mark everybody in ya family from your momma to your granny after this."

"Fuck all this yappin', nigga!" Donte swung his gun at Sheek's face causing a cut under his eye. His cheek instantly began to swell. Donte began to stomp his chest and Sheek curled up in a fetal position.

"Sheek, just give them the money, baby. Please, Sheek please!" Candy yelled from the corner of the room with her knees up to her chest.

"The drawer! The drawer! The money's in the bottom left drawer of my desk. It's 50 thousand in a box. The key is under the chair. Take it and roll the fuck out. Ahhhhhhhhh shit!"

Sheek held his swollen face as it throbbed with pain from the powerful blow. Science quickly checked under the chair and went into the drawer. The box was there with the cash and Science dumped all of its contents in his duffel bag.

"You must really think I'm stupid. Thanks for the extra cash, but where the safe at, nigga? We know it's a safe in here somewhere. Where it at, yo?" Donte badgered.

Now Sheek was getting a little worried. How did these dudes know what he had? For a minute he thought about saying fuck them to see where their heart was at. Then his thoughts were cut short when he felt two burning slugs enter his legs.

"Ahhhhh! Fuck! C'mon, don't do this," Sheek cried out.

"I want that money, you bitch ass nigga. Unless you want an extra hole in ya head. I suggest you come up off that bread."

Donte stood over Sheek's body.

"Behind the John Gotti painting, the safe in the wall. It's a digital code….ahh shit, shhhiit…2, 16, 86." It almost crushed his spirit to give up the codes to his safe but these guys weren't rookies and he wasn't about to take another bullet, even though it was almost five million in the safe. His legs were numb as he listened to the laughs from behind the wall. Candy's crying was annoying and he promised he would smack the shit outta her for causing him to be vulnerable like this. He blamed her for being caught slipping.

The taller of the masked men came back to get the other duffel bag from his partner. They switched and he looked closer at the guy holding the two guns in his face.

"How much you want to live? I should kill ya clown ass right now. Look at 'chu sittin' there ass naked with ya lil' dick shriveled up like you just got out the pool."

Donte kicked him in the injured leg. Sheek yelled out in agony.

"Let's ride," Science said, realizing his voice box had stopped working. It didn't add an effect on Science's voice for some reason.

The voice from the taller masked man instantly rang a bell for Sheek. He couldn't believe his ears then he listened to the other one and it really clicked. Now he really was about to trip because he knew Candy was a part of this. All this wasn't just a coincidence. She would definitely pay the price because he lived by the code: death before dishonor.

"I'll holla, big spender. I hope you can get it up after taking two in the leg," Donte said, taking Sheek's mind away from what he'd just discovered.

Donte saluted Sheek and he and Science left like thieves in the night with Candy screaming, and shouting like crazy, "Help us!"

"Candy, shut the fuck up and call 9-1-1."

Candy quickly dialed 911 and helped Sheek put on some boxers. He called for his security who was a day late and a dollar short. They checked the entire building and there was no sign of the two mystery men in ski masks. The ambulance and police came to the scene. The paramedics put Sheek in the back of the ambulance and the police asked Candy and the security team what happened. Candy gave her statement and the police let her go.

Around six in the morning the next day Science got the call in from his cell phone that it was clear to go. The vent to the men's bathroom came crashing down at Shopz. The first duffel bag hit the floor and then the second. Science and Donte climbed down.

"Mooch, we good, yo?" Science asked with his cell phone to his ear. Science picked up one of the bags and Donte picked up the other. They both removed their masks and started toward the back exit. Science punched in the security code and the door unlocked. Mooch was right there in his Lexus as his brother's tossed the bags in the trunk and hopped in.

"We did dat shit, yo! I know we got a few mil!" Donte stated as Mooch pulled off. They had one more stop and this would all be over with.

# CHAPTER 25

Sheek wasn't with sitting in the hospital all day, so around ten o'clock in the morning he signed out, and got one of his security men to roll him out of in a wheelchair. His security put him in the back of his Phantom and put the wheelchair in the trunk. Sheek picked up his phone and called Gwop.

"Yo," Gwop answered.

"Listen, Gwop. Meet me at the club in the next hour. We got to talk, Cannon, so be there." Sheek hung up and looked out the window.

"Boss, you don't know who did this shit to you? You didn't recognize a voice or nothing?" Sheek's right hand security, Big Cuz, asked from the front seat.

"Listen, Scrap. I told you I didn't recognize shit. Let me do the thinkin' because I don't want you to hurt yourself. Now just drive me to the club."

Once Sheek arrived in his club, he felt uneasy. He immediately headed to the rooftop. He didn't know if the spot was tapped or what. Nothing seemed to be clear anymore. He couldn't believe someone was able to get inside his compound and run off with his loot. He paid to much money monthly for his security, and entire team. When Gwop got in the club he took the elevator to the roof. Big Cuz was at the door with a Mac 10 in his hand.

"What's good, yo?" he asked as he stepped through the door.

"Ain't shit, Gwop. Good lookin' out the other night with the strippers. They came through and did it real big wit ya boy." Big Cuz laughed and gave Gwop a handshake. Gwop saw Sheek with his back towards him. He could tell he was smoking from the clouds of smoke ascending in the air.

"Big C, you can keep it movin', go beat ya dick or somethin'. You wasn't nowhere to be found last night, so what the fuck I need you for now? Kick rocks and let me holla at Gwop," Sheek said.

Big Cuz looked at Gwop and was about to go smack that cocky son of a bitch out his wheelchair. Gwop stopped him and said he would take care of everything. Big Cuz shook his head and calmly left.

"So, what's the verdict Sheek? What we going to do about this shit?" Gwop strolled over to the edge of the roof and took a seat. "Whatever you need just give the word," Gwop stated.

"That snake nigga Science and Donte robbed me last night. And I know they responsible for the spots bein' raided. You handle them niggas and bring me Candy. I'll body that bitch myself. They won't see it coming if you put the bullet in them. Do this and you set."

"I got chu."

Gwop couldn't believe Science had pulled off robbing Sheek's personal stash. He wanted that money from Science and would do whatever it took to get it. He nodded his head and stood up.

"You want these niggas dead, it's done. I just need a favor and we good," Gwop stated with a stern look.

"Anything, name it."

Gwop went in his pocket and pulled out some papers and a pen. He placed it in Sheek's lap and sat back on the edge of the roof with a smile. Sheek read the paper and was confused.

"What's this, Scrap? I don't get it."

"That's a contract my lawyer drew up. Basically, it's stating that you giving me complete ownership of Shopz." Gwop picked up the pen and held it out for Sheek to sign.

"Why the fuck would I do that shit? Are you fuckin stupid? This my shit!" He laughed.

"Cause you ain't gonna need it where you goin'."

Gwop lifted his shirt and pulled out his chrome Desert Eagle. He pointed it at Sheek's chest.

"You country ass nigga. Dis how you do a nigga that took you from an ounce to a brick? Nigga, I made you! I gave you that swag and fed you the game. Get that fuckin' gun out my face!" Sheek yelled.

"You talk big shit for a nigga who's about see if he can fly. Sign the paper before I fill you up with these hot balls." Gwop clutched his gun tighter and cocked it.

"I can't believe ya country ass think you gonna get away with this," Sheek stated as he signed the contract.

Gwop snatched the papers and tucked it in his back pocket. "Good lookin' dickhead. Now let's get down to business. Where the money you got stashed at the crib? I know it's crazy cash there, so tell me where you got it stashed." He pushed the gun in his cheekbone.

"Fuck you nigga! You know how many Philly niggas gonna bleed this city to find you? Bald head niggas with big beards gonna hit every nigga that ever looked at me funny until they find out who killed a nigga. You won't be able to sleep!" Sheek screamed at him.

"I'll take care of that, Cannon." Gwop nodded his head for him to turn around. Sheek turned his wheelchair around and almost shit his pants when he saw Link standing at the roof's entrance with his gun out.

"Link….what the fuck you doing? Blast dis country ass nigga!" Sheek demanded.

"Nah, Cannon, the only nigga getting blasted is you, ya'mean. Niggas is tired of getting screwed and jerked, talked to like a bitch. Like we pussy, it's time for a new nigga to step up." Link cocked his gun back.

"Who the fuck gonna take my spot? Can't nobody hold shit down like me, you niggas ain't shit without me."

He felt a hand touch his shoulder and Gwop whispered in his ear.

"I'll take ya place like a real boss. Make sure everybody eat proper and ain't treated like a boy."

Gwop rubbed Sheek's head and laughed. All Sheek's security came out to the roof with guns drawn. Twelve of his goons flooded the rooftop of his club.

"That's what I'm talking bout! When a nigga really need y'all lazy asses, you finally here. Put a bullet in both these nut ass niggas heads." He yelled as spit flew from his mouth.

Gwop walked over next to Link. They looked at each other with a smirk.

"What y'all niggas waitin' on? Pop these clowns! Big C, gimme the gun. I'll do it myself!" All the security men simultaneously turned to Sheek's direction with their guns pointed at him.

"Ya time's over Sheek, holla at 'chu," Link said with a smile.

"You mafuckas is dead! Every last one of you bitches will be dead by the morning. I'm fuckin' Sheek, this my city—"

Sheek's words were cut short as a wave of bullets ripped through his flesh. The gunfire had the top of the roof looking like the Fourth of July. Everyone squeezed off slug after slug as Sheek's body opened up and his insides spilled out. His arms departed from his body as one flew off the rooftop and the other ended up in the corner somewhere. The gunshots came to an end as everyone looked at Sheek's lifeless body slumped over, disfigured. Blood was everywhere. It was time for a new king.

"We out yo, leave this bitch ass nigga for the birds," Gwop announced, spitting in Sheek's direction as he headed for the exit.

$$$$

All three of the brothers stood in amazement at all the stacks of money on Donte's living room floor. Every inch was covered with dead presidents. It took almost three and a half hours to count it all, but the subtotal of their heist was 10.6 million.

"My fuckin' hands hurt yo! We been countin' stacks since 8 this morning," Mooch stated as he flopped on the couch.

"It's the good hurt though, son! The first thing we going to do is put moms in a big ass crib out the county and give her a maid, a cook, and a chauffeur," Donte boasted with excitement.

"Y'all know mommy love that raggedy ass house she got. I tried to buy her a house before I went in. Y'all Daddy's spirit is in that house, she ain't going to leave him," Science said.

The ringing of Science's cell phone interrupted the conversation. Science sighed at the fact that it was Gwop. He told Science to meet him at some mom and pop store near Leakin Park. Science agreed but strapped up and had his brothers follow him. None of them trusted Gwop.

By the time Science stepped into the afternoon sun he saw Sheek's Phantom out front and a female chauffeur standing with the back door open. Science called out to Gwop after seeing his face. "Should I tell my boys to join the party," he asked, shifting his eyes to the car across the street, letting Gwop know his brothers were nearby.

"Nah, we good. Tell 'em to stay put, yo. We just need a few minutes."

Science took a deep breath and stepped inside. Gwop was sipping some Cristal from the bottle. He had two more on ice in a bucket sitting on the tray in front of him.

"This Sheek's whip, right?" he asked.

"Sheek dead," he said without remorse.

"How the fuck that shit happen?" Science said with a confused look. He knew a couple leg shots didn't end his life.

"He was on the roof of the club and some niggas blasted him; body parts everywhere. It's all over the news. What ya'll niggas been doing all day, yo?"

Science took a moment of silence as the news Gwop just disclosed sunk in.

When I rolled to his house them same stick-up niggas hit his house too, but left every one of his rides. You know I had the boys come through and get all of them joints. Ya'mean?" he gloated. "He ain't gonna need 'em where he at."

Gwop took another sip.

"I'm confused, yo."

"No need to be. Look yo, now that Sheek gone me and Link came together on some partner shit to take over this whole organization. I came through to see if you wanted a piece of that partnership. I know you got the funds from all the work you been puttin' in. You tryna get down or what playa?"

"Nah, I'm good, that drug shit ain't me no more."

Science popped one of the bottles of Cristal.

"It ain't 'chu! What the fuck you mean, nigga? So this stick-up shit is ya new occupation, huh? Yeah, don't look crazy nigga. I know you hit Sheek's crib, club, and the spots. You and ya brothers, but I don't give a fuck. I came to give you a seat in a multi-million dollar company."

"Yo, what you talking about?"

"Nigga please. I know. But I see you a positive person now. Look, find another place to make licks cause Baltimore off limits. That's my money you fuckin' wit now if you hit them stash spots. So take that shit to D.C. or something. I don't want us beefin' over no cash flow, ya dig."

Gwop was serious and since he was in power he couldn't look weak by getting his shit taken.

"You tellin' me I can't rob niggas in my city because you in position now? That's what you sayin?" Science laughed.

"Dis my city! Yeah, if you hit one of these major niggas you fuckin' with my bread. I supply these niggas now. So out of respect to ya man, hit them D.C. niggas. Fo 'real though, you should be good after hittin' Sheek. I know he had crazy cake stashed."

Science just sat there not knowing how to take his comments. He listened to Gwop's side of the story but he didn't feel how he was coming at him. He felt like he was giving him an order and an indirect threat. He just nodded his head.

"So is we good, yo? You over there in deep thought."

"How'd you know I did the stick-ups?" Science didn't want to beef and after the licks he'd just made, he was done robbing. His family was set. He was just curious how Gwop knew his moves.

"Sheek recognized ya voice. He wanted me to off you and ya brothers. But you know we like family son, you my brother. Besides that nigga Sheek was a coward with power. That's the worst kind of nigga to be in position."

Science knew by the way Gwop was acting that he either killed Sheek or had something to do with it. His vibe gave him away. Plus he had been planting that seed ever since he got out of prison. The only problem Gwop had that Science could see was his arrogance and his flamboyant lifestyle. In the book *48 Laws of Power* Science picked up a lot of jewels. One of the rules he saw Gwop break consistently was never out shine the master. It was like he was in competition with Sheek. He wanted the best ice; the most expensive car. He came to this realization at the car show that Sunday when Gwop pulled up in the Maybach. When Sheek came through in that Phantom, Gwop's whole face went sour, like he was mad, his facial expression and non-verbal's gave him away.

"Yo, I gotta go handle some things," Science told him with a cold look on his face.

"I got 'chu yo, and that offer still on the table. You can cash it in whenever you choose."

$$$$

Science sat out front telling his brothers everything Gwop told him. Donte was fired up and had decided he wanted them to join forces with Gwop even though he wasn't to be trusted. Science hated the idea, but didn't have time to discuss it. Candy had been calling him, saying come home immediately. When Science walked in his condo and heard the shower running, he grinned widely. He needed a good dick sucking to relieve his stress. He went into the bedroom and kicked off his shoes and laid back on the bed. Candy came out with a towel wrapped around her slightly wet body. She sat on the bed and pulled out some strawberry vanilla body lotion.

"Mmmm... I missed you baby," he told her.

Science touched her thigh and she knocked his hand away.

"Did you have something to do with Sheek's death, Science?"

"Nah, yo, why you say some shit like that?"

"I'm just making sure. It's all over the news."

Science still hadn't gotten a chance to watch it. "Well don't trip cause that wasn't my work. Now, gimme a hug."

Science went to grab Candy but she stopped him and crossed her arms over her chest.

"I can't believe I fell for your shit! You used me, Science. You don't love me. You just wanted Sheek's money and you knew I could get you in!" she yelled. "When I agreed to lure him to his office you didn't tell me everything that would happen. I had no idea he'd get shot. And now his crew probably knows I had something to do with it!"

"What the fuck you talkin' bout, yo? I do love you, you wifey." He went to grab her again and she smacked his hand away.

"Wifey? Nigga please, you don't get wifey to fuck niggas and jeopardize herself. What man let's another man fuck his chick so he can rob him, huh? What if he knew what we were up to and blew my head off, huh? Did you think about my well being? No! You thought about your pockets. Fuck you, Science!" Candy stormed in the bathroom, slamming the door behind her.

Science flopped backwards on the bed and let out a loud sigh. "Women!"

$$$$

Mooch came through the doors of Vita's apartment and saw her lying on the couch watching television under a blanket. Her hair was in a scarf and he could tell she'd just gotten up a little while ago.

"Vita I'm outta here, yo. This ain't gonna work out," he said, standing in front of the TV.

"What? Here we go again, Mooch with this sensitive shit you be on. I'm the one that bleeds e'ry month. Damn you be actin' like a bitch sometimes."

Mooch ran over to her and gripped her up by the neck.

"What bitch? Watch ya fuckin' mouth! You just after a nigga's paper. I was blind by the pussy at first but I can see clearly now. I know about your conversation with that nigga P. So forget about getting' any of my paper!"

"Oh my God, Mooch!" she yelled. "Let me explain, baby."

"Hell no! Have fun with the bills cause I ain't payin none of this shit no more."

He threw her back down on the couch and walked in the bedroom. Vita jumped up and chased him, beggin' for him to stay. She was pulling on his clothes, crying and yelling.

"Get the fuck off me!" He pushed her back on the bed with enough force to give her whiplash.

"Mooch, P's family has custody of my son. He told me the only way I could get him back was to send him money. Lot's of it. So every time I'd get money from you, I'd send it to his family! They've been blackmailing me. I swear!"

"Tell that shit to somebody who's gonna believe it! You fucked up shorty 'cause you had a good nigga. My brother was in the hospital for damn near a month with his life on the line. Not once did you show up, not once! Candy was there every day, but my so-called girl was a no show. I'm out and I suggest, you find a job because everything in this bitch, I bought!" he warned her.

"Nooooo Mooch! Please don't leave me! I love you! I thought you said we were soul mates. Gimme another chance," Vita cried out on the bed.

Mooch looked at Vita crying and rolling around on the floor. He thought about what she said her reasons were for doing what she did. He still didn't believe her. But strangely he still loved her. Donte had instructed him to get their cousins to whip her ass, take everything he'd ever given her, and land her in the hospital. But Mooch just couldn't do it. He just watched her for minutes on the bedroom floor, weeping like a baby. He had no remorse for her. She was a gold digger who got what was coming to her in his eyes.

"Fuck that bitch," was his last words as he left her life for good this time.

# Chapter 26

Two weeks had gone by with Science moping around day in and day out. Candy left abruptly, leaving a note that she wanted out. She wouldn't even return his phone calls. He crawled out the bed and picked up his cell phone like he did every morning since she left hoping to get a response. He'd left her thirty different messages apologizing for the way he treated her and how much he wanted her back. When he didn't get an answer he slammed the phone down to the floor. When it started to ring he jumped out of bed to quickly answer.

"Hello, what's good, Ma. I'm sorry. C'mon let a nigga back in. I'll never play games again," he pleaded.

"Science what the hell you talkin' bout?"

"Huh?…ummm…Damya is that you?"

"Yeah and it sounds like you pussy whipped over that white trash lil' heifer. You pickin' up ya son today? You know I gotta go to school."

Science knew he would say yes. He was proud of how Damya was trying to turn her life around. She was still healing from all the torture Donte had put her through, but she was excited about her first day of college.

"Let me get dressed and I'll be there in like 30 minutes. I got my lil' man for the weekend."

Science hung up and went into the bathroom. He yawned slightly and looked in the mirror. He needed a shape up because his beard was growing in. "Oh hell nah, I gots to get a cut, yo." He looked at himself and realized he was really out of line for lying around depressed over a female. He really loved her and wished he could change how things went down.

After washing up and getting dressed he was good to go. He hopped in his truck and headed over to get his son. He pulled up to Damya's house about 10 minutes late because of the afternoon traffic. He got out noticing the block flooded with dope fiends searching for their next dollar to get their afternoon fix. He had forgot it was the 1st of the month and this was when the ghetto had frequent traffic due to the checks the addicts got in the mail.

"It's hot as shit out here," he stated aloud as he walked the steps and right in Damya's house.

For a change it was clean, no toys or trash scattered about. His son was waiting on the couch with his book bag on. His face glowed when he saw Science walk in.

"Daddy! Where you been at?" he asked, when Science hugged him tightly.

"Ya daddy been working. We got Grandma a house. You want to come and surprise Grandma with me and ya uncles?"

"Yeahhhh!" he screamed.

Science saw Damya come from the kitchen with some tight jeans on and a fitted shirt. Her weave was gone, with her hair cut into a short bob. She slowly walked toward Science swinging her hips from side to side, carrying a yellow H & M bag.

"Get out Lil' Cecil. Me and your dad gotta talk for a sec."

"I almost forgot how good you look," Science complimented. That's what got me hooked, ya dress game and that ass. Plus you could suck a mean dick."

Damya punched his chest playfully and gripped up the new Chanel bag he'd brought her. "You play too much, Science. Look, this is serious. Here," she said extending the bag in his direction.

"What's this?"

"It's what you need to make sure you never go back to jail again."

Science opened the bag and realized it was the gun he'd used to kill the cop over nine years ago. He pulled Damya close and thanked her. It was weird being able to hold and respect her again. He dug in his pocket and peeled off several hundred-dollar bills from his wad of cash. He extended his hand and Damya gladly accepted with deep appreciation. Her gratitude showed when she kissed his cheek and wiped the leftover lip-gloss from his face.

"Get some groceries and whatever you need for your other kids. I know it's tough being a single mom. I'll break you off whenever I can."

She smiled for a brief moment then her expression changed. Sadness seemed to fill her quickly. Science lifted her chin, asking her what was wrong.

"I just gotta be honest. There's one more thing I gotta tell you?"

"What's that?" he asked, hoping it wasn't nothing too crazy.

"Remember when you first got locked up and called my house collect?"

"Of course, yo. A nigga answered."

"It was Gwop," she told him, with her head downward. "I'm sorry for what I did, but I was young and dumb. I was used to a lifestyle you provided and before I knew it, the money was gone. Gwop was right there in my ear and filling my pockets with cash. If I could turn back the hands of time I would have held you down. I hope you can forgive me."

Science turned to walk towards the door. "We all make mistakes, Damya. It's not how you play the game, it's how you end it. And trust when I say Gwop's ending won't be good. But me and you straight though…don't worry. "

# Chapter 27

Science and Lil' Cecil waited in the parking lot for his mother to get off of work. The moment she got in the car she kissed him on the cheek and leaned in the back to hiss her grandson.

Now what's this surprise you say you got for me?" she asked eagerly.

"I hit the lottery mom!" He lied.

"The lottery, when did this happen?"

"What's with the questions? I hit the lottery for a million dollars. Me and Lil' Cecil want to show you what we got you," he said with a huge smile.

"Ummmm huh," she mumbled.

The drive to Ellicott City, MD took almost forty-five minutes. As Science took route 103 to Lynn Lane, his mother broke the news to him.

"You know Candy's been coming over the house lately. She mad as hell at what you made her do."

At first Science was steaming with anger at Candy telling his mother his business. He gripped the steering wheel firmly and gritted his teeth. He took a deep breath and just stayed calm.

"So, when you start calling her Candy?" he asked.

"Since we really got to know each other. You know she's a nice girl. Maybe a little too young for you, but still she's a sweetheart. I don't know what you did, but I hope you can get her back. I know why you ain't bring her around before Cecil. You thought I would trip because she's white. But if you love that girl like I think you do, then she can be blue and I'll accept her for her. I gave her my Mary J. Blige CD and told her to soak it in relax. That *My Life* album got me through some tough times." She laughed.

"C'mon Ma, what you know about Mary?"

"Mary helped me with ya low down ass Daddy and when ya step daddy was acting a fool. I'm still a lil' hip Cecil. I ain't that old, remember?" They both shared a laugh as Science pulled up to Simpkins Court where Donte and Mooch sat in Donte's new SL Benz.

Science, Lil' Cecil and his mother stepped out the truck. His mother looked up at the $800,000 dollar home in amazement. It was a four bedroom, two and a half bathroom, sitting on one acre of flat land in a community setting. There was a brand new Lincoln Town car in the driveway. It had 'We love you', on the back window. Donte and Mooch walked up to their mother and hugged her close.

"Surprise mommy, we love you so much. All this is for you. Say hi to ya new home and car," Mooch whispered in her ear. She was so shocked that her eyes watered up. She called her boys in for a family hug.

"I love y'all asses so much. Thank you! Now, how did you pay for this? I don't want nothing to do with that drug money. As soon as I get settled, them police gonna snatch me out of it. That's one of the main reasons I didn't take the house Cecil tried to buy me before."

"Look mom, I bought this with the lottery money. We spent every dollar on you. We hate to see you in the hood in that lil' house working all them jobs. Go sit in your new car, it's paid for just like the home," Science told her.

"Oooh baby, thank you so much."

She opened the car door and inhaled the new car smell like it was a Sunday dinner.

"Open the glove box, mom," Donte stated from the window.

When she popped the glove compartment she couldn't believe her eyes at the stacks of cash stuffed in the small space that began to fall on the floor.

"What's all this boys?" she asked, grabbing the money.

"That's for you to enjoy life. Start your own business, go on a trip, go shopping or whatever. Go out and let your hair down," Donte said.

"Thank you again, boys. C'mon Lil' Cecil let's take this for a spin around the corner. Get in!" she told him.

As the car pulled out of the driveway the unmarked police car started its engine. They had no intention on following Science's mother. They were more concerned with her sons. The investigation had been going on for weeks, and Science putting his mother into a luxurious home didn't help the situation. The murders going on in Baltimore and the increase in the drug trade around the city had the Baltimore PD, FBI and DEA all working together. Sheek, Donte, Gwop and Science were all at the top of the list.

$$$$

After getting their mother settled in her new home and letting Lil' Cecil spend the night, Science and his brothers thought they would end the night at the strip club. They piled up in Science's truck and headed to Foxy Ladies. When the trio stepped in the spot, fresh from head to toe, the ladies smelled money and swarmed them for dances.

"Chill, yo, not right now shorty," Science said as he pulled out a wad of cash and handed 4 strippers in G-strings a hundred dollar bill each.

"Nah, I'll handle these ladies myself. C'mon, I need to get shown a good time. Who tryna get rained on?" Mooch added real cocky, with stacks of money in rubber bands in each hand. He took about six females to the private rooms leaving Science and Donte to talk amongst themselves.

Donte ordered a bottle of Patron and two shot glasses for him and his brother. They went to a table to discuss what was on each other's minds.

"What's the deal, yo?" Donte chimed in downing a shot of the liquor.

"What 'chu mean?"

I keep trying to talk to you about Gwop. I know you said we was waiting on the right time to get revenge on the nigga. Then you said, let it go 'cause yo'on want no more killin'. I need to know what's up 'cause he offered me a position on the team."

Science looked at his brother like he had four heads sitting on his neck.

"You can't be serious, yo. You either gon' be dead or in jail if you fuck with Gwop."

"I feel you. I just can't turn that down, yo. Ya boy got crazy cake and I need to eat like them starvin' kids in Ethiopia. Fuck what you heard. That nigga got the city on lock. Cats ain't been moving units like him since the 80's. I gotta get it, son." Donte said and downed two more shots and lit a Black & Mild. "And you need to join us," he added.

" No more drugs or that stick-up shit for me. I'm done. I'm tryna to be out here with my kid. He need a daddy, not a nigga running the streets. Plus, Gwop turning into an animal. He don't care about nothin' or no one. You ain't no different."

Donte started laughing thinking abut how cocky Gwop had gotten. He'd condescendingly changed Sheek's club name to Gwop's. He made a few changes in the club, adding four poles inside, with strippers rotating on the hour to put in work. He didn't discriminate; one pole had a male dancer who stripped from his tight speedos for the ladies down to nothing. Then of course he had the baddest bitches in town, with the bodies to match. The cash flow from the club alone had Gwop set for retirement. He wasn't having it though, the city was his for the taking and he utilized his opportunity to be a true boss.

"Listen bro, Gwop got the city on lock, and enough coke and dope to supply a small country. I'ma roll with the nigga."

"That's a dumb move, yo. You got mills, why the fuck don't you clean that up and get out while you still can? The feds givin' out numbers that ball players puttin' on scoreboards. You ready to do 30 to life?" Science asked.

"It won't come down to that, but if I have to I will. I'm livin' life and if I go down I can say I balled fo 'real." Donte looked at his brother and he saw the sincerity in his eyes.

"That shit sound stupid, yo. This shit ain't ballin' and what Gwop doin' ain't either. Them niggas gettin' money are the ones that got b-ball teams, stocks, record labels, and endorsements. This just hood rich, nigga!"

"Well, let me be hood rich. You can retire. I got more mills to make. Ain't no more to be said. Let's just celebrate that we finally got moms out the hood." Donte raised his shot glass and blew smoke from his nose with a smile.

"Laugh now lil' bro, but cry later, cause this game ain't no movie. Niggas die and do numbers, yo," Science warned him.

"Niggas die every day, bro. Pull ya skirt down, son. I'm good." Donte raised his glass and downed it.

Science let it go because he knew Donte had to learn on his own but he didn't want death or 100 years to be his lesson. He had seen it all before but he could tell by Donte's eyes and words that his mind was made up. He had tunnel vision and at the end of the day that would be his downfall.

For the rest of the night the three brothers smoked, popped bottles, and tossed dollars at strippers. Donte walked off to a private room with two big booty females in stilettos. Mooch had five large stacks of bills in front of him as he cheered on the ladies. Science just looked from his table doing shots of Patron chased with Red Bull.

"Can I get a dance?" A seductive whisper purred in Science's ear. He felt a warm wet tongue caress his earlobe as the DJ dropped Disco Inferno by 50 Cent. Science looked at his admirer and chuckled when he saw Genie.

"Okay, stranger I see you finally found your way. You doin' it real big with ya titties out and ass showin'. You still stackin' for school, yo?" he asked.

"Very funny, Science. You want a dance or what?" She snapped with her hand on her hip as her nose flared.

"Do you Ma, I ain't stoppin' you."

Genie bent over quickly touching her toes with her round ass in Science's face. She spread her cheeks giving him a good view of her pussy from the back. She slid her G-string down slowly and stepped out of them. She straddled Science, ass-naked with only her stilettos on. She grinded on him fast with her erect nipples touching his face. She took his hands and placed them on her ass. He took them away and placed them behind his head nonchalantly. Genie ignored his arrogance and pulled his face closer to her chest as she bounced on his lap. She felt him stiffen and slowly rode the complete length of his dick through his Gucci Velour sweats.

She bit his ear gently and whispered, "Gimme a G right now and we can go to the private room, or your place to really get it in. I know you miss this good pussy. You want it daddy."

Her words didn't turn him on at all. Baltimore had really changed her personality. The confident, independent, sexy female he met on the bus was now just a hoe. He knew that strip clubs could change the weak-minded but he thought she was stronger. Plus, he knew she was Damya's family and he wasn't going out like that anymore. For some strange reason he felt like there was always that possibility that he and Damya could get back together.

He whispered back in her ear, "I don't trick and if I did for a G, I could get a busload of you low budget bitches. Get the fuck off my lap!"

Genie stood up quickly taken off guard at the complete disrespect.

"Nigga, you ain't all that."

She picked up her panties and walked off. Little did Genie know, Science had a plan that would change her life forever.

# CHAPTER 28

Months passed.

Money flowed.

Gwop had no problems spending major cash.

The way the sun made the paint on Donte's new Lambo shine was like magic. Being down with Gwop's organization had his pussy magnet attraction through the roof. His money had doubled and the condo he used to stay in on N. Charles St. was just the jumpoff spot. He barely went through there. He had a house out in the county that was big enough to be on MTV cribs. He still was the number #1 bachelor in the city because he did his thing in bed.

He saw the jealous looks from the haters as he drove through the hood. Every time he got a new ride he made sure the hood saw it first, just to feel the hate and envy. Donte saw the crowd on the corner and pulled up like a boss. He let the doors flip up and he stepped out letting his fresh Gucci's get the attention first. His sweat suit complemented his hat and shoes. He zipped the jacket up to conceal the two .45's in his shoulder holster.

"Okay Donte you shittin' son, we see you. What's really good though, yo? You don't ever kick it no more," his homie Smack stated as he approached him with a stack of bills clenched in his hand from the dice game.

"You know what it is baby. I'm bout a dollar. Being around the snakes in the hood gonna leave me broke." Donte unzipped his Gucci jacket to let Smack see the heat he was carrying.

"You was ridin' my dick when you needed help kidnapping that bitch, Damya," he said rubbing his baldhead. "Now you too good for a nigga, wit' ya high dollar shoes and shit. What they run you?" Smack asked.

"Oh the new Gucci's? These shits like 700, you know small change. I got all colors, stop playin' with these haters and I might put you on. You know I'm down with Gwop and 'em," Donte boasted.

"Nah yo, y'all niggas went Hollywood. Look at 'chu yo, check ya swag. Who the fuck you think you is, Dame Dash? You still Donte that play video games and freeload. Get the fuck outta here before one of these snakes take ya ride and them boys off ya feet!"

Smack turned his attention back to the dice game. He was sweating profusely and his pants kept falling further down his bony frame. He rubbed his head again.

"That's how you feel, Smack? You hatin' like these niggas. I thought you were my homie, yo?" Donte felt salty for a second. He didn't feel like he was Hollywood. He was just living life.

"I ain't hatin', I'm keepin' it hood. I'm a get my own like a G and I'll come through in that same Lambo, but with 10 behind me filled with my niggas," Smack said with his back still turned toward Donte.

"Good luck on that, yo. I'm bout to cop that Phantom coupe next week on you niggas. I won't even stop but you can get the horn one time. Tell any of them bitch ass niggas to try me. I wish they would!"

Smack just nodded, knowing Donte was a mark. He smiled as Donte stepped in his vehicle and peeled off leaving smoke and tire tracks in the street.

$$$$

Damya answered her phone on the first ring when Science called. The information she had given him about Candy weighed heavy on his mind. Even though he had a healthy roster of jump offs and dime pieces that occasionally shared his bed at night, he missed Candy.

"What up, Science?"

"Yo, where you say the house is?" Science asked Damya.

"She stay over on Scott Street in them fly ass new townhouses."

Science was getting anxious. He was less than two minutes away but wanted to make sure he was in the right area. It had been a couple months, but he always thought Candy would've been back by now. She'd taken 50 grand out his safe but he didn't sweat it because he knew it was nothing, and she deserved it. But now she was in a fly ass townhouse on his paper and ducking his phone calls. Shit was about to get ugly and fast.

"Did you get the house number?" he asked.

"4235," Damya rattled off. "Don't go in there beggin' and shit like a bitch," Damya joked, before hanging up.

Science turned into the neighborhood and found the exact address. He parked in the driveway like he owned the spot and rushed up to the door, ringing the doorbell in a frenzy. Someone was covering the peephole so Candy couldn't see.

"Who is it?" she shouted.

No response.

She swung the door open and Science stood there in a wife beater, jeans and Timbs. She went to close the door in his face but he pushed it back open and forced his way in.

"Get out, Science! Get out!" She yelled.

"Bitch, is you crazy? Calm the fuck down, we need to talk!" Science slammed the door and walked right by Candy into the living room. Just as he expected, some young kid about twenty-two was sprawled out on the couch with his feet kicked up like he was the man.

"Ayo, homie I need for you to step so I can talk to my girl. She'll call you later, yo." Science said politely, but if youngin got outta line he would surely show him he wasn't playing.

"Ya girl? That's me, son. Candy been my chick for a month now." The kid laughed.

"Science, I ain't ya girl no more. Go call them hoes you had at the house at all times of the night."

"What? Look yo, just step before I have to take it to another level." The kid jumped up on his feet and out of nowhere had a big .357 magnum pointed at Science.

"Lil' man, you don't want to do this, yo. Put this gun away and just leave. You disrespectin' me right now. Don't make me try you," Science said with his arms up and no fear at all.

"Put it away, Jeff! Don't shoot him. He's about to leave," Candy insisted.

"No, I ain't!" Science yelled.

"Fuck that, y'all old niggas come home and think the world still like y'all left it. Nah old head, that's my bitch and you need to step!"

Science could read people well and this kid was just a pretty boy with a big gun. He wouldn't kill nothing. Out of the blue, Science grabbed the gun, twisting it and yanked it from the kid's light grip. The force from Science right hook landed on his chin knocking the kid to the floor. Science raised the gun to give him a pistol-whipping' from hell.

"Noooo! Don't do it Science, let's talk. Let him go, baby," Candy shouted.

Science gripped him up off the floor and escorted him out the door. He emptied the bullets from the gun and passed him back his weapon. "You got a pass this time, youngster. Don't come back and lose Candy's number."

Science slammed the door and tossed the bullets in the trashcan. Science turned to Candy with a mean glare.

"We gonna talk, but first, take ya clothes off."

"Why?"

"'Cause I love ya, girl. And I miss the shit outta you."

Science's words made Candy feel so good. It wasn't long before they were both ass naked and Science was thrusting all ten inches inside Candy. He grabbed both of Candy's legs and spread them so far apart she didn't know how to react. He'd always been good in bed but since they'd been apart it seemed like his love making skills had gotten even better.

"Got damn, Science, I'm sooooo sorry I left baby," she moaned wildly.

Science continued to pound her like he was about to commit murder. Candy loved every minute of it as he picked her up and carried her as he fucked her all around the room.

"This my pussy?" he asked her, seeing Candy's eyes roll up into her head.

"Yes! Yes! Yes!" she screamed. "Don't stop, Science. Don't stop. Ahhhhhhhhhhhh!" she shouted.

Before long, Science busted the nuts and Candy had four orgasms. They both lay in bed with beads of sweat sat on their foreheads and chest, the aftermath of wonderful make-up sex. Candy couldn't help the way Science's touch made her tremble with pleasure. He still had that effect on her even though they had been apart for a couple months.

"So, I guess you forgive me," he said with a smile.

"Just because that was the best sex I ever had don't mean I forgive you. You hurt me Science. I thought we had something special and you passed me off to Sheek like I was a video game he could borrow." Candy turned her back to him in bed.

"I'm sorry, yo. I was thinking about our future. Plus, I was hurt when you left. You had a nigga, not eatin' and sleepin' all damn day," Science said, pulling her closer.

"You didn't seem hurt when I walked in the house last month and you were cuddled up with some bitch. Yeah I came over like three o'clock in the morning to talk things out. I walked in the bedroom and you was holding some nappy-headed skank. So I left the hotel I was livin' in and moved in here. Then I met Jeff and—"

"You fucked him, yo?" he asked, cutting her off.

"No Science! I didn't fuck him! I don't just fuck anybody. I wanted to get to know him first. He did eat the pussy though. You got some competition in that area." She laughed and turned back around.

"What about this area?" Science grabbed his semi erect penis.

"You still hold the crown though in that department."

They hugged each other and Candy felt his dick stiffen as their tongues met. It was time for another round and her kitty was purring for that daddy dick to explore her walls again and again.

$$$$

"Ay moe, this shit some fire. I had all them niggas hatin'. Fo' real Joe, this dat fish scale."

Donte laughed a little hearing his homie, Tarik from DC talk. His slang and accent was funny to him, and much more pleasant than his acne filled face. But Tarik always had his back whenever he called. That's 15 kilos he was picking up go for 20 grand. He knew probably get a price like that in DC, but it wouldn't be the scale Donte got from Gwop. His coke was the best in the city and a few out of town people came through. That was Donte's job, to supply the DC customers.

He took the duffel bag full of five thousand stacks and handed Tarik his product in a duffel bag. Tarik swung it around his shoulder and gave Donte some dap.

"Aight Moe, get at me. Next time you come through have 20 fo' me slim. I'm steppin' my game up."

"No doubt yo, you got the number, let a nigga know what's good," Donte said, giving him dap.

"No question, Slim."

Tarik left and Donte went to counting every stack to make sure it was right. Gwop was selling each brick for 17k and Donte would make a few stacks off each kilo. Sometimes he would sell them for 22k, 23k, or 24k, but it depended on his customer. Afterward he would distribute Gwop's work, but he would compress the product, lessening it's quality and sell his for the same price as Gwop's.

Donte had his own corner over East that would go through ten kilos like it was nothing. Money was pouring in, and clientele growing fast. No one knew about his shady dealings. All Donte could see was the money and lime light but what lurked in the shadows was on his blind side.

# PTER 29

Gwo acked it was a fire hazard. He had a raffle going on and t ky winner tonight would receive a brand new, navy blue Chrysler 300 on 22-inch spinners. It was parked in front of the entrance causing all the ladies to get hyped. The numbers Gwop made off the door was crazy. The income surpassed the cost of the car and all its features. Gwop had been making fifty grand every month just from the proceeds of the club.

The VIP area was filled with all the hood stars; Gwop, Link, Science, Mooch, Donte, and the top ranking bosses in Gwop's organization. Donte had to work on Science for hours convincing him to come down to the club. Science still hated Gwop but tried to keep the peace since his brother was now working with him so closely. Science watched Candy on the dance floor shaking her ass with some of her girlfriends. Damya was a few feet away looking ghetto fabulous. He and Damya had gone out on several occasions with Lil' Cecil, making the co-parenting thing work. Science smiled to himself thinking how life seemed so perfect. He was once the kid searching the refrigerator for something to eat and now he had millions that he didn't know what to do with.

"Go out there and get ya two step on, son," Gwop told Science who sat with a bottle of Cristal in one hand and a blunt in the other.

"Nah yo, I'm good. I don't do the dancin' unless I'm drunk. Plus I'd rather watch Candy do her thing," he stated dryly. He despised Gwop.

"Yeah a'ight! When a nigga jump on her ass and grind all crazy you gonna snap, yo."

I'm good," Science ended.

Science noticed Genie talking to Damya as they began walking towards him.

"Oh shit yo, here come Sweet P I was tellin' you about. Shorty got that bomb ass head and the pussy drip for ya boy."

There were so many females in the club Science couldn't tell who he was talking about. When Damya and Genie stepped into the VIP area, and Genie sat on Gwop's lap, he knew exactly who Sweet P was.

"Hey baby, miss me?" he heard Genie say to Gwop as she licked his earlobe, and gave Science a nasty look.

"No doubt, Ma. Ayo, this my man Science but you with Damya so I guess you probably already know him. Ayo, Science this is Sweet P, shorty a rider fo'real," Gwop bragged.

"I wouldn't brag if I was you," Science uttered.

"Science, leave her alone. C'mon let's dance. I hope ya girl don't get mad at me," Damya belted. Before Science could respond, Damya was pulling him out his seat and onto the dance floor.

"What was all that about?" Gwop asked Genie.

"He a hater, don't trip. Is we chillin' tonight? Cause I really need to talk to you. Some shit's going down that you might not know about."

"Later," Gwop told her, pushing her off his lap.

The club was so packed and crowded people could barely walk. The bar on the first level occupied two Mexicans who loved Baltimore and had a fetish for its ghetto, curvy Black females.

"I like the one in the red, look, look right there." One pointed to a pretty brown skinned female backing it up on some guy with a blunt in his hand.

The other Mexican remained focused. He'd spotted the gorgeous white devil that helped get him and his cousin robbed by Science and Donte. His eyes widened and his heart raged as he instantly pulled out the .38 caliber handgun that Gwop's security allowed him to enter with. He walked toward her, moving people out of his way as he neared. He raised his gun and pointed his weapon at the blue-eyed devil. She locked eyes with him feeling someone staring at her. He smiled and squeezed.

"Nooooooo!!" Science shouted as shots rang out in Candy's direction.

Candy screamed and fell to the floor as the chaos erupted in the club. He was just a couple feet behind her when he felt the warm blood splash on his face. Damya leaned on his shoulder and he moved her to the side to get to Candy's aid. He ran over to her quickly as people ran and ducked for cover from the still echoing gunshots. He crawled over to her and picked her up in his arms.

"Candy! Candy!" He shook her body, praying that she was still alive. Her eyes slowly opened when she saw tears streaming down his face.

"The Mexican from the hotel," she whispered.

"What? Baby, are you alright? I need to get you to a hospital." He panicked.

"I'm fine, baby. Did you catch him?"

Science knew the blood came from somewhere so he checked her body again. She was fine. Then it came to him. He turned around and Damya was laid out on the dance floor.

"Oh shit! I'll be back!"

The gunshots had stopped but Science still stayed low as he jetted over to Damya who was lying on her stomach. He turned her around seeing the single hole in her forehead. Blood was leaking from her head and everywhere on the floor around him. He clutched her in his arms and rocked her like a baby being put to sleep. He knew she was gone. Guilt filled him instantly. His bad decisions had ended his baby mother's life.

"I'm sorry, baby! I'm sorry, I'm so sorry," he cried as he cradled her in his arms.

He cried with tears running down his face and blood all over him. Someone had obviously called the police. Sirens could be heard in the distance. The club's security gripped up the two Mexicans and escorted them over to Gwop. He saw Science on the floor cradling Damya and his brothers helping Candy off the floor. At that moment, he ordered security to take the Mexicans to his office, in the secret room.

The club emptied out as the ambulance and the police stormed in. They took Damya away and a few others who got hit by the crazed Mexican's gunshots. After all the questions were asked, and the wounded were treated, Gwop told his security to leave. Gwop, Mooch, Science, and Donte all went back in the club up to Gwop's office on the 3rd floor. The security had tied and gagged the two Mexicans and they were on the floor of his luxurious office. Science still had tears falling from his face as he rushed over to them, stomping both of them with all his might.

"Bitch ass motherfuckas, fuck you!" he screamed. They all stood back as Science let out his frustration.

Gwop noticed one of the bloody and bruised men giving him a pleading look. Gwop knew exactly what the look meant. Thankfully, the Mexicans were gagged, or Gwop would have to explain why he told them where and how to kill Candy and Science. That had been Gwop's goal. Yet, now he was allowing Science to batter them. Gwop had not only told them to come to the club to seek revenge, but gave them access to get in with their weapons.

They learned the hard way that Gwop was sneaky, trifling, and didn't care about anyone. Minutes passed before Gwop realized the Mexicans were no longer moving. He passed Science the gun to end their walk on this Earth. He gripped the rubber grip glock and pressed it against the head of Damya's alleged shooter. His hand shook as he re-lived the blood splatter on his face and Damya leaning on his shoulder, then pushing her off, and going to help Candy.

Science raised the gun high over his head and repeatedly beat both their skulls in. He heard the skull crack and then saw the dents in their faces from his mighty blows.

"They dead yo, c'mon we got to get rid of the bodies," Mooch said, with his hand on Science's shoulder.

"He right yo, let's get these wet back bitches to the bottom of the river," Gwop stated with a wide smirk.

$$$$

"Where you at, yo?" Donte asked.

"I'm clearin' my head, just reading. I'm tired of this shit."

Mooch was reading *Bleeding the Block* by C. Flores as he sat in the parking lot waiting for Donte to pull up. He had been working on his movie script and was reading a lot of urban fiction books. This would give him the insight he needed for his script. Since Donte was down with Gwop, and Science was doing the daddy thing, Mooch was finding himself. He wanted a new life. He'd gotten back into selling weed but his time was consumed in reading and writing. He wanted to direct the perfect gangster flick independently. That was his focus.

"I'm around the corner so I'll be there in a minute. Just chill, yo." Donte told Mooch over the phone. When he turned the corner he saw Mooch's Lexus parked in front of the old house. Ever since their mother moved, Mooch would sit in his car in front of the old house to gather his thoughts. The block wasn't that crowded, only a few smokers and old timers on the steps puffing cigarettes. It was only 11:30 am so the traffic wouldn't pick up for another hour or two.

Donte pulled up beside his brother and gave Mooch a head nod and put his hands in the air.

"That Lexus is last year's model, lil' brother. Look no hands!" Donte stated as he parked the big body Hummer he drove behind Mooch. Donte hopped out and got in the passenger side of Mooch's car.

"C'mon yo why the long face?" Mooch had a blunt of haze burning in the ashtray and Donte reached down to fill his lungs with the strong exotic marijuana.

"You trippin', yo. Science's baby momma got killed last week and you buying new whips. Have you been to go see him? You didn't even go to the funeral, yo. That's fucked up!" Mooch yelled.

"Why? Nah, fuck that shit. It's fucked up that bitch was fuckin' every nigga in the hood with a dollar. She died. And I feel for the man, but I ain't about to stop my life of ballin' for her. Shiittt, the bitch had five kids when he got locked, took his money, and fucked Gwop. I'ma keep it movin' like a G, my nigga. Fuck that bitch fo 'real, fo 'real!" he said with no remorse.

"You really lettin' that cash get to ya head. Yo fo 'real son, you changed Donte. You ain't never supposed to switch because ya pockets get bigger. Look at me, I come through the hood as I choose, no beef or hate. But you, I heard about you talkin' reckless to Smack, shittin' on a nigga that always had ya back when you were the king of NBA Live. Now you get some money you think you better than niggas. That shit ain't real, it's fake," Mooch told him.

"Please nigga, you don't know shit. Sell ya lil' weed and let me do me. I run this city! Keep lettin' these peons fill ya head with that bullshit!"

Donte quickly got out with the blunt in his hand slamming the door behind him. Mooch saw something or someone in Donte that wasn't him. He was trying too hard to be someone else, his swagger and mentality was a mirror of Gwop's. Besides, little did Mooch know that Donte had smoked Vita, killing her dead, even after Science and Mooch told him to just let her go on about her business.

Donte had been doing many things that the brothers knew nothing about.

# Chapter 30

Gwop awoke with a vicious hangover. He brought Genie over to his house and introduced her to his wifey. They three of them drank Belvedere, Dom P, and Cristal all night with many blunts in rotation. His wifey, Maliza, was pleased with Genie's looks so she agreed to the ménage-a-trois. This wasn't her first with Gwop, but she only did it with top of the line gorgeous females, and she liked Genie.

He was in the middle of two official dimes but his head was pounding. He got up and went straight to the bathroom. He splashed some water on his face a few times and looked in the mirror. He opened the medicine cabinet and popped two Advil to help his headache. He stood over the toilet still naked and let his bladder drain the champagne that made him feel a few pounds heavier.

When Gwop walked back into the master bedroom, Maliza was waking Genie up with her head between her legs. Genie moaned and rubbed her nipples as she looked at Gwop who was enjoying the show. She mouthed the words, *Join us, Daddy*.

Gwop quickly entered Maliza from behind filling her insides up with his strong hard cock. *This bitch want wifey spot fo 'real*, Gwop thought as Genie sucked on her finger, staring at Gwop getting her pussy ate. He thought back on last night. When he was fucking wifey she would keep her eyes on him trying to do something freakier or better. She sucked his dick harder and swallowed everything; moaned his name and stroked his ego so good like he was King Ding-A-Ling. She wouldn't take Maliza's spot because they had been together for five years and she played her position like a soldier. They never fought or argued about him being out or messing around. She realized he was a hustler and a man like that wasn't about to be faithful. As long as he took care of home and didn't bring her any diseases, she was fine. He was definitely thinking about moving shorty in and getting this treatment on the regular. One thing about Gwop, he was known to be Captain Save-A-Hoe. He couldn't care less as long as he got what he wanted in the end.

$$$$

The haze smoke was thick in the hotel room as Donte waited for Tarik to come cop the thirty bricks he had in a duffel bag. Fifteen of them were Gwop's and the other half was his. He already told Tarik over the phone in Pig Latin how much each was going for. Donte felt like 16 apiece was a good look, and he only did it because he had been dealing with Tarik for a while. They partied, sexed females, smoked and drank together.

He was on the phone speaking to some new jump off that he met last week at the club from Boston. Her accent turned him on and he loved an up top bitch.

"Oh fo 'real yo, aight keep talkin' like that, I might have to stop my business and come scoop you. What whip you want to fuck in? The Lambo or the Lex? Ha, ha, ha, yeah, you know I can get head and let the joint park itself."

The knock on the door made his full erection in his jeans begin to deflate.

"Ayo ma, that's my moms. I'ma call you back in like fifteen minutes. I might introduce you to my other friends."

Donte hung up and tossed his phone on the queen size bed in the small hotel room. He pulled his sagging jeans on his waist and opened the door. He couldn't believe his eyes at the two masked men aiming their weapons at him. One had a gun to Tarik's head. The other man had a duffel bag around his chest with a chrome Desert Eagle pointed directly at Donte's face. Donte thought about reaching in the small of his back for his .45 but knew he would be dead before he even pulled it out.

"Back the fuck up, nigga! I wish you would move so I can put a bullet in that big ass mouth you got, yo," the masked man said.

"It's all good yo, this lil' shit I got is nothin'. I shit bricks so you can take these shits back to ya lil' projects," Donte said, as he backed up into the room with his hands up in the air.

The door closed behind the two masked men as they calmly walked inside. The one man threw Tarik to the floor and the other began to search the room.

"Sit dat ass down next to ya homie."

The one that had his gun on Tarik was now aimed at Donte while his accomplice lifted the bed to find anything of value.

"You got it, yo. I ain't got shit but the thirty bricks in the duffel bag. I hope y'all know what you doing. I'm connected, and my team won't accept a hit like this. Niggas will hunt ya ass down. But do you, gangsta." Donte sat next to Tarik who was quiet as a church mouse. He was showing no emotion as he stared at the floor. To Donte, he appeared to be calm, considering they both might be dead and dumped in Leakin Park like so many before them.

*So this is what Science was tryna warn me about. Shit, I hope these niggas just take the coke and ride. Damn, I ain't even get no pussy today. I knew I shoulda been more careful.*

Donte thought long and hard for about five minutes as the masked men got the work and brought him back to reality with a blow from hell with the Desert Eagle across his face. He fell over and blood poured from his mouth.

"See all that cocky shit out the window now. Go ahead and say some funny shit now, yo. C'mon, you fake P. Diddy mafucka!" Donte heard the masked man's voice and it clicked instantly.

"Broke ass, Smack! Oh shit, this for us, yo? This shit ill, my nigga?" Donte sat up holding his lip. The masked man pulled his ski mask to his forehead and it was Smack. Even though Donte talked greasy to him he was really playing. He never thought he would stab him in the back like this. With Smack being revealed, he wondered who was under the other mask.

"Yeah nigga, and it's my time to eat. So do me a big favor and say more funny shit before I murk ya nut ass."

Smack's eyes were red as he gripped the big gun with two hands and aimed it at Donte who showed no fear, just confusion.

"Did you think selling extra work behind Gwop's back would last forever?"

Donte let out a slight laugh but was silenced as the bullets pierced his chest one after the other. His life flashed before his eyes. He saw Science, Mooch, his mother, and all the females he had sex with over the years. Before he began to walk toward the light, he saw Smack helping Tarik off the floor.

Then he heard someone say, "His phone on the bed yo, let 'em know it's handled."

Donte saw his father and reached out to grab his hand. His father told him to come home as they embraced in a long awaited hug.

# CHAPTER 31

Genie wanted Gwop all to herself so she asked him to go to a hotel for a full day of sex and more sex. Gwop rolled over after getting his second nut off inside Genie. She was a beast in the bed and aggressive. She scratched, yelled and screamed and was down for whatever. He reached over on the nightstand to the half of blunt in the ashtray. He lit and inhaled as Genie snuggled up close to him. Usually he would check a bitch quick for all this affectionate shit but Genie was official so he let it go. Even though his wifey looked better, he only wished her personality and sex drive was a percentage of Genie's. He cuffed her naked ass with one hand as he puffed on the blunt.

"Pass that shit, nigga," Genie said, with her hand on his sweaty chest.

"You a lil' feisty somethin'. You better be glad I like you because I don't share my haze." He passed her the blunt and his cell phone vibrated on the nightstand.

"Don't answer it, please baby, this our day. It's probably Maliza hatin' cause we alone." Genie said, with an attitude.

"Nah, I doubt it. Shorty only call if it's a 911. Other than that, she just chill," Gwop told her.

"I guess you got her trained, huh?" Genie smirked.

"Nah, she like that number one spot. She knows how to hold it down so she won't get dismissed. She like those ten thousand dollar minks and shopping sprees with no limit. This money shorty, I gots to get it." Gwop picked up the phone seeing the familiar number.

"Yo…what?"

"It's done. Seventy grand you owe, nigga."

"That's a high ass price, homie. Even for Donte. Come down on that price and I got you."

"That's what we agreed on, you bitch ass nigga!" Tarik shouted.

"Things change, nigga. This my world. You just livin' in it. I'll give you twenty." Gwop shook his head and hung up.

"Who was that?" Genie asked.

"Mind ya business. You think about what I asked you with movin' in the spot with me and shorty?" Genie kissed the middle of his chest then licked his left nipple and over to his right nipple. She got on top of him and smiled.

"I'm not really big on somebody havin' a leash on me. Plus isolatin' in the crib is really some vampire shit. Did you think about what I asked you? I know a lil' hundred something thousand won't hurt ya pockets, Daddy. I love that GT Bentley. I want one in pink. I'm tryna shit on them bitches when I come through." Genie said as she caressed his member.

"Yeah whatever yo, just suck this dick."

Just like that, Genie obeyed his commands.

$$$$

It had been almost two weeks since Donte's funeral. The streets weren't giving up any information on the death of Donte. Mooch had hit the streets hard trying to find out about his brother. At the funeral, he made a list of people who didn't cry or show any emotion, and the ones that didn't walk up to see the body in the casket. He was determined, as well as Science, to get down to the bottom of this no matter what.

Mooch sat in his car in front of their old house thinking about how his mother broke down at the funeral and hadn't been sleeping at all since losing her son. He thought back to how she wailed at the funeral pitifully.

"Oh Jesus, why? Why my baby? He didn't deserve this, God! Why? Why my baby? Please don't take him, nooooo!!"

Her tears fell continually with Science attempting to be strong for her. But he was still mourning over Damya and now had to take another blow to his heart. "My baby dead," he remembered his mother shouting. "They took my baby from me!"

Right after the funeral, their mother made an announcement that shocked them both.

"You find out who did this to your brother. You find out and you bury they ass alive. I want them suffer ten times worse then my baby, Donte. And I'm dead serious," she ended with pain in her eyes.

Never in his life did Mooch think his mom would say something like that. She put a hit out on the mystery man and Science was definitely going to take the job free of charge. Mooch had gone through several packs of blunts over the last hour while sitting outside reminiscing. Loud music behind his disturbed his thinking. He looked in his rearview mirror and it was a black Bentley Azzure blasting Jay-Z's *99 Problems*. He looked at the driver and it was Smack. He stopped and rolled down the passenger side window.

"What up, yo. You good, son? You know Donte was my nigga and I feel for you dog. Make sure you stay up. It ain't too many real niggas left out here, ya dig," Smack said, leaning from the Bentley.

"Yeah, I know. What's good though, I see you in the Bent like a boss," Mooch said.

"This is what I do."

Mooch felt alarms going off in his head. Just a couple weeks ago Smack was in a Tahoe. He was only on about 9 ½ ounces so he definitely couldn't afford a Bentley.

"I'ma get back to my thoughts, yo. I'll holla at you."

"Fo'sho, Mooch."

Smack rolled the window back up and pulled off. He was hoping he didn't give off any bad vibes like he was the one who put Donte to rest. Mooch instantly begin to put everything together. Donte played smack a while ago. He was jealous and hating because Donte was getting more money than him and he had been hustling for over ten years. Then the funeral stats kicked in. Smack was in the back of the church. He didn't view the body, cry or show any emotion toward Donte's death. *If he didn't pull the trigger he had something to do with it*, Mooch thought. One thing for sure and two things for certain, he was definitely about to find out the truth.

# Chapter 32

The undercover agents had been working around the clock gathering information. Although Link had been lying low, staying out of the spotlight, he was the one who had gotten caught on tape the most. The officers often shook their head at his stupidity. Of course now that someone had killed Donte, his potential indictment didn't matter.

Gwop was flashy, incompetent and it was just a matter of time before they would bring him in. Science on the other hand, turned up squeaky clean, other than no explanation as to how he made his income. Drumming up some hard-core evidence on him was the goal.

Meanwhile, the plan was set and it was time for Science to go back to his old ways. The streets needed to know that if you fucked with the Walter family there were consequences. When Smack heard the yells that it was the police he knew it was over. It was four a.m. when he woke up to flashlights shining in his eyes, guns, and the ski masked police officers. He thought they were S.W.A.T. the way they were dressed. He knew he would be going to prison for a long time. He had crack, guns, and money in the house.

"Put your hands up! Put em up!"

"Now, slowly get down on the ground. I swear if you make one false move I'll blow half ya face off." Smack knew the policemen were serious so he did as he was told and got on the floor and was cuffed.

"Damn, yo. Can you loosen these shits a little, sir?" Smack asked in his most polite voice. He felt steel hit the back of his head and he blacked out.

When Smack woke up his head was aching and his wrists and ankles were cuffed. He was in the back of a car on the highway. He remembered the cops coming in his apartment and telling him to get down on the floor. He smelled marijuana in the air as he tried to shake his headache.

"What kind of police smoke weed? Where the fuck y'all takin' me?" The policeman on the passenger side turned around and Smack almost shit himself when he saw Science with a blunt hanging from his lip.

"The kind that ain't really police. Now shut the fuck up and enjoy the ride." Science ordered.

"Whoa Science! What's the deal, yo? Why the fuck y'all doin a nigga like dis? We homies." Smack said, trying his best to loosen from the cuffs.

"Nah nigga, we ain't homies. You killed that when you killed my brother. Yeah, mafucka, you thought I wouldn't find out?" Science's face showed no emotion.

"Ayo, you got the wrong nigga. I fucks with you. I ain't do that shit. Let me go, dog." Science aimed his gun at him with a serious look that made Smack shut up.

Mooch pulled up into a wooded area in Annapolis, Maryland, a spot they left the day before in preparation for this moment. They parked and both of them got out the car. Science opened the back door and pulled Smack out of the car by his nappy afro. He dragged him across rocks, grass, and sticks to a secluded area in the woods where they dug a hole almost six feet in the ground. Science picked him up and tossed his body inside.

"Come on, yo. Don't do this! I didn't pull the trigger I swear on my kids. Tarik pulled the trigger, all I did was call Gwop and ask for 10 million. The nigga told me he wasn't payin' shit. So Tarik popped him. I promise I thought we was just going to rob him." Smack begged them not to kill him. Mooch stood there with a shovel in hand. He scooped up some dirt and tossed it down on Smack's body with devious grin.

"You bitch ass nigga, who else had something to do with it? Tell us, or I swear on my unborn child, I'll go to ya momma house and blaze that shit until the bricks bleed." Mooch said with a heart full of revenge.

"The nigga Hungry helped us. He was the only other person. The nigga Hungry and Tarik, that's it, I swear." Smack cried out.

"I ain't know you was a hater like that, yo. You helped kill my lil' brother and think I'ma let you live? My mom's cry every fuckin' day because of you. Bitch, you dead. Mooch, go get that shit out the trunk." Science told his brother.

It wasn't long before Mooch came back with two bags in his hands. He looked down at Smack in the hole looking pitiful and confused, but most of all terrified.

"We got somebody to chill with you down there, yo. We don't want you to go alone." Mooch dumped the one bag out and three rattle snakes fell onto the hole with Smack. He screamed as they slithered around his body. He was stuck there on his back, cuffed. His struggling agitated the snakes and one bit his foot and the other followed with a bite to his stomach.

"Ahhhhhh!!" He yelled as the bites felt worse than bullets burning his flesh. Science and Mooch laughed at the top of the hole. "We got some gifts for you, Smack. It's the shit that you risked your life for when you crossed my family." Mooch tossed stacks of money that they discovered at his home down in the hole, too. He also tossed a couple guns, coke, and the keys to his Bentley down there with him.

"Please yo, don't do this, help me." Smack cried out with a swollen eye from the snakebite he took in the face. Science started spraying his body with gasoline. He begged and pleaded but knew they would never let him go for what he did.

Now Smack wished that he had grabbed the .38 he kept under his pillow when he saw the flashes of the light that woke him up. It was no time for wishing so he began to pray as the cold liquid splashed on his face. He closed his eyes when he saw Mooch light a cigarette, take a hard pull and toss it in the air.

Science and Mooch both grabbed a shovel as Smack's body ignited in flames. His screams fell on deaf ears as they began to cover him with dirt. Science did what his mother asked and made him pay worse then Donte. He felt content that Smack was gone forever.

# Chapter 33

Science pulled up in his mom's driveway behind her car. He hopped out with his son by his side and entered the house. The kids were all playing in the living room when Science came through the door. Lil' Cecil joined the fun with his brothers and sisters. Science went to find his mom. He could smell the sweet aroma from the kitchen so he followed his nose.

"Hey mom, what smells so good?" He took a seat at the stool in front of the kitchen counter.

"Just baking some cookies for the kids, that's all," She said.

"I need to talk to you about something." He sounded serious.

"Alright, let me set the timer and we can go out in the den."

Science admired his mom's strength. She had adopted all Damya's kids except Lil' Cecil so they wouldn't get separated by the state. She was a strong independent black woman and he respected her so dearly.

"Go out there and take a seat. I'll bring you something to drink. Let me tell the kids to go play in the backyard." She told him.

Science stepped in the den and took a seat in the wooden chair. Not even five minutes passed and the little army came running past him and out into the backyard. His mom had a small playground built with swings, a sliding board, monkey bars, a sand box, and a seesaw. His mother came out with a tray of milk and cookies.

"Y'all play right, and don't be pushin' them babies around." His mother warned as she took a seat next to Science.

"So what's on your mind, son?" she asked.

"I did like you asked and made them pay, mom. That guy that killed Donte is gone. I found out that some more people were involved." Science could see the tears welling up in her eyes but she sucked it all in.

Her next statement was concise. "Then ain't no need to be wasting time here with me. I'll watch my grandson, you go and get those bastards." Science saw the pain in her face and almost broke down himself, but it was apparent that his mom was serious, and she wanted street justice. When it came to that, Science was one of the best. No more words were shared as he kissed her forehead and left to avenge the death of his brother.

$$$$

Science and Mooch posed as police officers as they woke Hungry and Tarik up. It was 3 a.m. when Science pulled under the Hanover Street Bridge in a black Dodge van. He awaited Mooch's arrival. Science heard the muffled screams behind the duct tape of their mouths. He checked his watch when the lights of an oncoming car were heading in his direction. The car stopped right in front of the van and Mooch stepped out with two green army duffel bags. He was struggling with the heavy bags so Science stepped out to give assistance. They placed the bags down and Science opened the back of the van.

"Hey fellas, I see y'all chillin' real good. Well, this the end of the line for you two bitch ass niggas." Hungry and Tarik both were trying their best to break loose from the duct tape that had their hands and feet bound together. Their pleas of help and forgiveness were unwanted.

"Don't cry now, nigga!" Mooch blurted out and stepped in the back of the van. He had two bottles of honey in his hand. He squirted Tarik first from his face to his feet with the sticky sweet honey.

"You like dat? You sweet ass nigga! Huh? Let me know cause you about to love what we got next for you." Science passed him another two bottles and he did the same to Hungry. Mooch pulled a knife out and looked Tarik straight in the eyes. "You get a say in this part. I'm going to stab you. Now, do you want it in the chest or stomach? Blink once for chest and twice for stomach." Tarik closed his eyes tightly not wanting to cooperate.

"Okay, you did that to yourself!" Mooch hit him once in the chest and once in the stomach with the sharp steel. He asked Hungry the same thing and he blinked once.

"Okay, good, fuck you!" Mooch stabbed him twice in the stomach and backed out the van as they cried out behind the duct tape. Mooch and Science emptied the bags, letting the rats crawl in the back of the van. Hungry and Tarik fought to get away but they wiggled with no avail. Science closed the back of the van as the huge rats went to work on their live prey.

Science and Mooch walked away, leaving the screeching from the rats and muffled screams from the two cowards behind them. They got in the car and Mooch pulled away from the bridge.

"Ayo, you think they gonna be dead before somebody find them?" Science asked.

"Them rats already ate 'em up or they bled to death from the stab wounds. That's a done deal," Mooch said.

Science just laughed and sparked up a Dutch he had rolled already.

"So, what we gonna do about Gwop?" Mooch asked, ready to put a bullet in his head for leaving his brother for dead.

"Let him ball for a lil' bit longer. Then when he least expects it, he'll be taking the same trip Smack did. Chill lil' bro, I got dis. He didn't tell Mooch what else he'd found out about Donte's death. He just wanted to handle it himself. "You surprised me though, Mooch. You a lil' mad man. Where the fuck you come up with the idea of the snakes and rats?"

"The Discovery Channel shows how them mafuckas get down. I just wanted to see if that shit works. That shit was funny as hell with them rats, wasn't it?"

"You crazy, yo." Science and Mooch both burst out in laughter as they hit the interstate.

# CHAPTER 34

Gwop didn't want to wake up, but the banging on his presidential suite door took him from a dream of his being the first billionaire drug dealer. He was just about to cash the check when the loud banging interrupted his dream.

"Mother fuck!"

Gwop climbed out of bed and picked his boxers up off the floor. He looked back at Maliza, Genie and his two escorts that were on a leash and smiled. He had a crazy night of sex and drugs with them. Genie had brought the freak out in Maliza. Ever since he moved Genie in his house with Maliza, the sex had sky rocketed.

The banging took him from his thoughts and he went to see who was waking him up like the police at 8 a.m.

"Who the fuck is it?"

"It's Link." Gwop opened the door and Link put a newspaper in his face.

"I told you to chill, big shot. Ya nut ass made the front cover. Your flashy ass Christmas Party from last night made TV's, magazines and newspapers. I warned you that party would be hot. Now look!" Link said furious. He knew attention meant police and then the Feds, which was something he wanted no parts of.

Gwop held the paper with a picture of him and his two sexy models on the leash stepping out of his Maybach entering his party. The headline read, *Drug Lord Throws Christmas Sex Bash*. Gwop smiled as he let Link in, and closed the door behind him.

Link sat on the couch and kicked his feet up on the glass coffee table. He lit a cigarette and watched Gwop read the paper with a grin of excitement.

"You think that shit funny? You hot and you bringing the heat to the team. The Feds probably already building they case. Wondering who you is and where the money coming from." Link snapped.

"Stop bitchin', yo. I got real estate. I'm covered. I got over 50 properties, so the Feds and whoever else can try me. This drug lord shit is just bogus entertainment. We good."

"Nah, the team ain't having you fuck the paper up. You on a power trip. Fall back for a while. I'll handle the connect and make moves for you until shit blow over."

"What? I said I'm good yo, this—"

"This ain't up for negotiation. It's final, chill until this shit die down. You hot and you can jeopardize a lot of money and people's freedom." Link stated seriously.

"Baby, come back to bed it's cold without you." Genie came in the living room in her birthday suit with her sexy innocent voice.

"Go back to bed, I'll be there in a minute." Gwop saw Link looking Genie up and down licking his lips.

"Somethin' wrong with ya eyes, Link?" Gwop asked.

"Nah Cannon, we good." Link stood up giving Genie one last look over and headed for the door.

"Ayo, Gwop that's an O.G. call from home. Get back to playin' Hugh." Link closed the door and left.

"Bitch, if you hear me talkin', why the fuck you interrupt me? Then you come out naked. Don't get cut when you just made the team. I swear you'll be back to strippin' and callin' ya self Sweet P in a heartbeat if you don't act like you know!"

Gwop walked past her and went to get his cell phone. If Link said it was a O.G. call that only meant the connect must of seen the papers and felt he was out of line. He definitely couldn't mess up a perfect routine. His Arab connect had the kilos of coke and dope coming in by the boatloads. It was nothing for 100 or 200 kilos to come through every five days like clockwork. Gwop stepped out on the balcony to get some fresh air and privacy. He usually didn't call from his main cell phone unless it was a 911 call, but when it came to him playing the backseat, that was an emergency.

"Yo, what's good my friend?"

"I see a lot of flashin' lights around you. A fuckin' high dollar party last night, huh? If you want to be a celebrity then the construction game isn't for you."

"Yeah, that's my fault and I'll take that. Just don't cut me off right now, shit really started poppin'," Gwop said.

"I don't like attention and you bring a lot. I respect you and admire your loyalty but just relax for a minute. Go on vacation and come back refreshed. For now, let your associate do all the construction work." Gwop wanted to argue his point but it wasn't much he could say on the phone and his connect had his mind made up. He would take this one on the chin. He realized he was too flashy and he took responsibility for that.

"Alright, I say a week or two," Gwop stated.

"A few months rather, I'll call you." The line went dead and Gwop let out a sigh.

"Ain't this a bitch!" he said, smashing his phone down on the floor.

# Chapter 35

Almost two months passed with no sign of Gwop. Obviously he understood that the connect would have his balls hanging from a tree if he didn't comply. Genie and Maliza used that time to get to know each other better, enjoying all the material things Gwop's money had provided. Maliza's feelings grew more and more for Genie each day they were together. They shared information about each other, secrets and could talk for hours. Since neither of them had to work anymore, they sexed each other daily and slowly fell in love. Genie was now in love with pussy. She couldn't fight her feelings and she couldn't hide them.

Genie walked in the kitchen still halfway sleep in her black sheer teddy. She opened the refrigerator and searched for some orange juice. She found some Sunny Delight and closed the door.

"Where ya man at, bitch?" The blow to her jaw knocked her straight to the floor and the orange juice went flying in the air. When Genie opened her eyes, the familiar face got closer. Rome's huge frame stood over her body and pressed the cold steel to her face.

"Don't make me repeat myself, shorty." Genie was so terrified that she didn't feel herself pissing on the floor. Her heart raced as the man stood over her with a gun to her face. At that moment she wished she stayed in her little town. She would have never woke up to a gun in her face.

"He's out of the country. I don't know where he at, I swear. I haven't heard from him in almost two months. Please don't kill me." Genie noticed the other man behind Rome with the crazed look. Rome sucked his teeth and put his gun in his waistband.

"You got that, shorty. You don't mind if me and my niggas just wait on this clown, do you?" Rome asked.

"No, do you." Genie stood to her feet feeling the warm liquid between her toes and looked down seeing what she did.

"Don't sweat that, Ma. I seen grown men shit they pants. A gun in ya face will do that. Go clean ya self up and tell that pretty thang upstairs a real Philly nigga tryna holla," Rome said with a grin.

$$$$

Ever since Gwop had fallen off the map, all Science had been doing was thinking. He wished he'd killed him the many times he had the opportunity. Now, no one had seen Gwop or had any inkling about where he has. Science's plan for Gwop had been ruined. He ended up putting his mind on other ventures. Science found a way to show homage to his baby mother and put his money in something positive. He came up with a clothing line and named it Damya Jeans. The jeans would be specifically for women with large butts and wide hips who couldn't find those nice designer jeans to fit snugly.

His mom helped with the designs and he opened up a clothing store in the mall that would market his product. He put his brain to use and realized he loved females, especially big booty females, so why not market to them on an everyday basis?

Science had just finished promoting his jean line and the story behind it on the radio station when he got the call he'd been waiting for. It had been almost two months yet he called out of the blue. Science didn't know how to react. Gwop wanted to meet him under the Hanover Street Bridge. Science contemplated about calling Mooch and taking Gwop on that road trip today, but he decided to just hear him out and do that later on. A few people had tipped him off that the Feds were still watching them.

Science put his business matters aside and headed out. The sun was still fighting with the clouds to come out and bless the sky with its presence. When Science pulled up under the bridge he saw Gwop leaning on a black Benz, smoking like he didn't have a care in the world. Science opened the glove box where his gun sat and put the small .25 in his boot just in case he just wanted to dead Gwop on the spot and move on with his life. He calmly stepped out of the car and strolled over to his long time homie.

"What's good, play boy? You got me out in the sun. What's on ya mind?"

Gwop put his hand out for a shake but Science just gave him the closed fist.

"I really got to talk to you, yo." Gwop inhaled on his Black & Mild and flicked it to the ground.

"Talk," Science barked.

"A nigga took that trip that all blacks need to take, dog. I had to leave town for a couple months. My eyes been opened to a lot of shit though. I now know I was a sheisty cat. I thought I was being real but I let the power of a dollar blind me," Gwop said sincerely.

"What you talkin' bout, yo?" Science asked.

"Africa, yo. I went to Africa and the shit changed my life. All our people out there looking so beautiful without the chains, cars, and big cribs. We got it fucked up and I'm fucked up." Gwop pulled out a .45 from his waistband and instantly Science was pissed he didn't put his gun in a more accessible place.

"I'm sorry, yo. I did get a phone call from some dudes talkin' 'bout they had Donte. They asked for like 10 million, and me being me, I said fuck that shit. I did that, but I'm pretty sure he was already dead. Nonetheless, I was wrong and that shit wasn't thorough," Gwop said.

"So, what now? Why you tellin' me this?" Science felt his fist ball up.

"Because you my nigga and we like brothers!" Gwop shouted, clutching the gun.

"I fucked up and while you was doing ya time, I fucked Damya, yo. I'm sorry, I'm a dirty, grimy dude, yo. I just know seeing those people, our people, made me want to right my wrongs. Here…I told you I'm sorry and I pray you forgive me. If not, let me die by the hand of my brother then by my enemy. I love you, dog and I'm sorry. Blow my shit out right now if you want."

Science extended his hand, and pointed it at Gwop's face. This man fucked his baby momma, probably could've avoided his brother's death and was standing at his mercy. Gwop had stabbed him in the back too many times. Tears came down Gwop's face as he looked Science in the eyes.

"Just do it, I deserve it…."

The sound of the gunshot silenced them both.

Science let off one shot and one shot only, before dropping the gun to the ground and turning to walk away. It was over and he just wanted to live his life and leave the life of mayhem alone. He was tired of an endless lifestyle that only had two endings and bullshit in between. He had out grown the shine and street frame. It was cool at 21 but he was 33 years old with responsibilities. He never thought he would make it past 18 but here he was on a path to guide his son correctly.

"Fuck that shit," He said aloud as he hopped back in his car and pulled away.

# Chapter 36

Genie and Maliza held each other in bed as strangers invaded their home. It had to be at least twenty thugs with enough artillery to take over a small country. The front door opened and Rome was right there to greet whoever it was. He prayed Gwop had slithered back to his home because he was tired of waiting. Rome pointed his gun and smiled.

"What up, Gwop?" Rome said, mushing the gun in his face.

Gwop was taken off guard by Rome's surprise visit. He had just been spared by Science who let off a shot by his head that still had his ears ringing. Now he was in another situation where he didn't know if he would live or die.

"Get dat ass in the living room." Rome pointed his gun in Gwop's back as he slowly led the way to the other room. He dropped to his knees when he felt the butt of Rome's gun hit the back of his head.

"You almost got away with it, fam. Almost. But when ya face came on CNN about a drug Lord in B-More I got curious. I put two and two together and figured you was the cause of my peoples' coming back home in pieces. Then I hear you and the bull runnin' shit." Rome pulled a plastic sandwich bag from his pocket and tossed it in front of Gwop on the floor. Its contents were two round pale brown objects.

"You know what those is?" Rome asked with a smirk.

"I really don't want to know." Gwop said, looking at unknown contents in the bag.

"That's what happens when you disloyal to your family and homies. I live by death before dishonor and any nigga in the game is obligated to live by that too. If not, then it's consequences you deal with. Those Link's balls, he was disloyal to his homie so he was sent home with no nuts in a bag." Rome smacked Gwop with the bag across his face.

"I was just going to put a bullet in your head but that's too easy. I want you to suffer like the country bitch you is. Now open ya fuckin' mouth!" Rome demanded.

"Oh hell no! Nigga, kill me cause I ain't openin' shit!" Gwop said as Rome attempted to stuff Link's testicles in his mouth.

"That's fine, ya aunt and uncle in South Baltimore you moved in that big ass house gonna see bad times. Ya sister and niece in Montgomery county gonna see worse times, oh and moms in rehab gonna see the best time. Now open ya fuckin' mouth!" Rome screamed.

Gwop had no choice. He couldn't let his family be subjected to hurt because of his poor choices. It crushed his pride but he slowly opened his mouth. Rome gripped his face tightly and placed one of Link's testicles on his tongue and closed his mouth shut.

"Chew motherfucker and you better not leave a crumb of nothing." Gwop slowly began to chew letting his teeth sink into the horrible tasting skin. Juices squirted in his mouth as he tore through the skin with his teeth. His stomach flipped and he wanted to throw up as the laughs from Rome and his goons made him want to cry like a baby. He swallowed the remains with a sour look on his face. Rome smiled at him and waved the other testicle in his face.

"Now open up cause you got one more."

Gwop slammed his fist on the carpet and screamed. "Ahhh man, c'mon man, yo chill! Not again, yo. Don't make me do it." Gwop cried out.

Rome gripped his neck up and hit him with two stiff jabs to the nose, drawing blood.

"Wash it down with that!" Gwop opened his trembling mouth. After swallowing the last bits of Link's nuts, Gwop was ready to vomit. He just knew Rome was waiting on that to make him lick it up, so he would save that for later, praying to himself that there would be a later.

"Now since you big money Gwop around this bitch, give me 200 of them birdies and 10 million won't hurt ya pockets. My goons gotta eat, Daddy. Oh yeah, don't shit ya self. I ain't gonna murk ya nut ass. You gonna pay like you weigh, and my nigga, you heavy. Seven days, big guy, seven days have my shit! I'll meet you here at, let's say, noon-ish. After that payment I got a lil' bit more in store for ya ass. But let's leave that a surprise." Rome laughed.

Gwop got to his feet and sat on the couch. A few more big beards came downstairs and Gwop wondered if they hit his safe.

"Ayo, Rome that bitch got some good ass pussy. That shit tight and wet." Laughs echoed throughout the living room as Gwop imagined what these ignorant niggas did to Maliza and Genie.

"Don't trip, Gwop they hit the black bitch. I had ya lil' mixed chick. Make sure she get checked cause she might of got pregnant on you. My jawns swim like crazy. The other bitch though, after all these big dicks, she ain't no good." Gwop clenched his fist wanting to knock that smirk off Rome's face so bad. If he could get him one-on-one he knew he would punish him.

"Let me get the keys to that Lambo, Cannon. I ain't never drive the Gallardo. Me and my niggas out, I know you got shit to do." Rome put out his hand. "And remember, I'll kill ya whole family; momma, sisters, kids, everybody."

Gwop gave up the keys to his ride and watched Rome leave out the door. He knew he meant every threat uttered. He raced upstairs to check on his ladies.

$$$$

When Gwop ran to the bedroom Maliza was in the corner balled up. He ran over to her and she jumped, thinking it was the men that had taken advantage of her and Genie.

"Baby it's me Gwop, you good, yo. I'm here now. I got 'chu and I'm sorry. Baby, I'm sorry. I'ma handle that shit." Gwop cradled her in his arms on the floor whispering in her ear he loved her.

"Nooooo Gwop! That nigga took it, and you told me you would always protect me. Where were you? Every last one of them niggas fucked Genie on our bed! She cried the whole time begging for them to stop. They been here for a while just doing what the fuck they want. Where the fuck was you?" Maliza cried out.

"Where G at?" He asked.

"In the shower." She pushed him off her.

"Chill yo, stay here, I'll be right back." Gwop walked to the bathroom and the water was running.

"Please, just gimme 30 minutes. I can't take it yo, I can't even get wet no more." Genie cried.

"Nah, baby it's me, its Gwop." Genie pulled the shower curtain back and Gwop pulled her naked wet body into his arms. "I'm sorry, G, I should have been here. I'll handle this shit, fuck them niggas, baby."

Genie just embraced him and let the tears flow not wanting to let Gwop go.

# Chapter 37

Gwop hit the streets fast. He had seven days to get this money up, and get the coke. So he hit all the spots over West first to collect what was his. He didn't care if it was the lookout's two hundred dollars, he had to get it. Gwop pulled up to Fairmont and Gilmore that had about five dudes on the corner with white T-shirts on. Gwop rolled down the window.

"You niggas seen Meezy?" Gwop shouted. One of the kids who had some shades on stepped up to the car.

"Oh shit, Gwop! You back in the hood. Niggas thought you went Hollywood, ya boy up the block talking to his shorty." Gwop ignored his comment and rolled up the block spotting Meezy chatting with some hoodrat with a ton of weave.

Gwop double-parked and hopped out with his Gucci duffel bag over his shoulder.

"Meezy, let's go we got business to handle!" Gwop stated in a rush.

"Hold up, Gwop! Let me holla at my b.m. real quick." Meezy, said not paying Gwop any attention.

"Unless you want to holla at Burger King to feed that bitch you better come on." Gwop snapped, not wanting to be fucked with right now. Meezy left his girl and quickly followed behind Gwop. They went into the stash house and Gwop opened the duffel bag.

"Go get every dollar and whatever bricks is left." Gwop demanded.

"For what, Gwop? We just got the re-up, yo." Meezy said, confused.

"I swear to God if you don't hurry up and get my shit. The only thing you gonna re-up on is a bus pass. Get my shit!" Meezy felt disrespected, but didn't want his cash flow to get cut short. His Capo position on the block was too sweet. He was about to jump in the new Benz he stacked for, fuck his pride. He did what he was told and emptied the stash. He filled the bag with five keys of coke and a 100 grand. He made sure he tucked a brick for himself and a few dollars just in case Gwop was on some bullshit.

"That's everything, Gwop. You good?" Meezy asked.

"Yeah, but you ain't. You fired, get the fuck off my block!" Gwop said. He zipped up the bag and left.

Gwop made stops at McHenry and Gilmore, Monroe and Fayette, and Vine Street to pick up more money and drugs. The stash houses on Saratoga and Penrose Street held the majority of the money from the drug trade of his Westside blocks. Gwop quickly shot over East with his truck filled with enough coke to get him 1000 years in prison. He went to every corner he owned and every stash spot. He had a quota to meet and his family's lives were at stake.

When Gwop got back home he emptied everything in his garage. He had 50 kilos and almost 5 million off the streets. He still had a long way to go, but for one day that wasn't bad. He knew he had a few million in his stash but it wasn't ten, and needed 150 more bricks. The clock was ticking. The next shipment would be coming in a few days so he was good on the drugs. He had to get that money so he made a call that could be either detrimental or a lifesaver.

"We need to meet like yesterday," Gwop said.

"I see. Tomorrow, you know the place. Oh and Gwop, I'm tired of the drama! Noon!" Gwop hung up feeling exhausted and mentally drained. It never was like this before when he was a block boy. At that moment he wished he could turn back time.

Noon came too fast and Gwop didn't get a wink of sleep. He laid in the middle of Genie and Maliza with their heads on his chest. He just thought about life, family, Science, his trip to Africa and his future. He took his Benz to a quiet little Chinese restaurant downtown. He walked in and his connect was in the back with two of his bodyguards close by. Gwop always smiled when he saw Hakeem because he resembled Bin Laden so much, but it was nothing to smile about today.

"I heard about Link's death. Did you take care of his family?" Hakeem asked.

"Not yet, I got shit I got to do to save my own family." Gwop took a seat beside him.

"What are you talking about?" Hakeem said.

"Look yo, the people who got at Link are at me now. They think I had somethin' to do with Sheek gettin' popped. These cats want 200 bricks and 20 mill or my family is dead. I got a nice part of the cash but need ten. I need you bad, yo. I can't let my fam die 'cause of me." Gwop looked into Hakeem's eyes for support.

"Looks like you have a lot of trouble on your hands. Let me ask you this and it will determine the outcome. Did you have anything to do with Sheek's death?" Gwop took a deep breath and looked Hakeem in the eyes.

"Yes, Sheek was out of line and crossed me and Link. He violated and had to be taken care of. That's the truth." Gwop stated boldly.

"Good, 'cause if you would have lied I would have not helped you with shit. And that red dot on your forehead would have been messy. I know everything and I knew Sheek was doing his people wrong but it just wasn't my place. When do you need the money?" Gwop was still in shock about the red dot on his forehead but shook it off.

"Before Sunday." He blurted out.

"At the next drop off I'll have my people give you that. The shipment will be three times as much as you usually get. Take what you need and the rest you'll be getting rid of for me. You owe me double what I'm giving you in cash. The next five shipments you work for me. Don't worry about paying the money back for a while. Just do what you do best…sell drugs. Now leave me."

Gwop smiled and his plan was coming together smoothly. He could pay the Philly crew off and still be sitting on millions to escape to Africa with his ladies. He was about to burn the connect; but it was either burn him or let his family suffer.

# Chapter 38

The boat came in at 2 a.m. and Gwop and his top dogs were at the docks to receive the product and cash. Gwop and his goons pulled up in three black vans to separate the merchandise. Gwop stepped toward the docks to meet the Arabs. It was about five of them with very serious looks on their faces.

"500 kilos of cocoa and 50 of the heroin. The money you asked for is in stacks of 100 thousands. I'm sure Hakeem told you of the consequences if you fuck this up." The man stated with a heavy accent, but Gwop understood every word.

"No problem, yo." All of Gwop's people began to unload the drugs off the boat. The van Gwop came in held 150 kilos and the money. The rest of the work was divided between the other two vehicles.

*I swear if I didn't love my family, I'd be going to war. I mean, Philly vs. Baltimore until the last city standing. These bitch ass niggas ain't built like that for real. Yeah they got this for now.* Gwop thought, as his soldiers finished unloading. He turned to the Arab that was giving all the orders.

"Tell Hakeem I said good lookin!" Gwop said.

"Make sure you take care of business." He told Gwop and then spoke in his native tongue and all his people got ready to ship out.

"That's what I do, yo. I got dis." Gwop stated, halfway believing himself, hopping in the van.

Gwop parked the van in his garage and loaded the other bricks and money with the rest. In two days Rome and his goons would be back to pick it up. Then they would be out of his life until he found a way to get revenge. First, he had to get his family out of the city. He was dead tired when he got upstairs but two lovely ladies were wide-awake. He stepped in his bedroom and Maliza and Genie were in black stilettos showing off their birthday suits.

"Hey baby," they both said in unison like they were the double mint twins. With all the problems going on sex never crossed his mind. But seeing his special ladies looking so good had his dick extra hard. They swarmed him and ripped away at his clothes until he was in his socks. Maliza fell to her knees and took his erect penis in her mouth slowly. Genie opened her hand and showed him a few pills. She popped one and slid one in Maliza from behind. Then she stuffed two in Gwop's mouth.

"We need you to last until lunch time. I can't have that big dick getting soft tonight, Daddy." Genie said, pushing the pills in his mouth. Gwop had taken X before and swallowed them with ease. Genie dropped to her knees to assist Maliza. Genie attacked his balls, while the slurps Maliza was giving his dick made him yell her name. Genie crawled to the bed poking her ass in the air. Gwop pulled Maliza to her feet to take the freak fest to the bed. Gwop slowly felt the effect of the pill as he lay on his back and Maliza hopped on his manhood. She gyrated, holding her breasts as she purred for him to nut in her.

"I love you, Gwop. This is ya pussy, baby. Nut in me papi, please cum inside me." Maliza screamed as she bounced up and down on his thick stick. Genie began to kiss him and as their tongues twisted Genie passed him two more pills from her mouth.

"You rollin' yet daddy?" Genie asked, and before he could respond, her nipple was in his mouth. As he attacked her nipples with force she took them away and sat on his face. She grinded on his tongue as her juices flowed down his cheeks.

"Lick dat pussy, Daddy! Eat it, nigga!" She screamed.

Genie sat on his face and Gwop did the best he could at the full course meal of coochie. "Cum for mommy, Gwop. Cum for me!" Maliza said as she turned around on his dick not letting it slide out. With her back towards him she went to work. Gwop felt his heart beat get fast and thought he was about cum. Then it sped up even more and he pushed Genie off his face onto the floor. He grabbed his chest and Maliza came to an abrupt stop. She turned around with a devious grin on her face.

"Something wrong, Daddy?" She smiled.

Gwop held his chest even tighter as his eyes began to water. "Call nine….one…one." Maliza blew him a kiss that he never would of thought was the kiss of death. Gwop felt the unbearable chest pains and the sweat beads fall from his forehead. Genie stood up and sat by him in the bed.

"You a lil' too young to be takin' all them Viagra pills, baby. That and X don't mix good. Just enjoy the feeling and accept it. At least you got fucked real good before you went out. You had two bad bitches before you died. But them two bad bitches…is who got ya dumb ass." Genie spit in his face.

With one hand gripping his chest he couldn't believe what was happening. With all his might he gave Genie a backhand from hell. She fell back to the floor and he felt the pain taking over. At that very moment his heart exploded in his chest and it was over. Maliza looked into his lifeless eyes and said a silent prayer for her longtime lover.

"That bitch ass nigga! I hate you!" Genie yelled holding her face.

"G…look his dick still hard." Maliza pointed and grabbed it. It was still fully erect. She kissed the head of it and felt sorry for him just for a second.

"Whatever, just call the ambulance! Let's get this shit over with. Make sure you give them some good tears. Remember, Gwop was ya boo," Genie told her confidently.

By the time the paramedics arrived, Maliza was in tears. They both gave the police and paramedics the run down on what transpired. Maliza could have won an Oscar the way she performed for the police. Hour after hour, Genie told the cops about the drugs Gwop had given them to take, and how he wanted to last all night. Some additional detectives eventually arrived who searched the house with dogs, and at least ten different agents. They all came up empty handed. Everything was going according to the plan. The girls had convinced Gwop to lock up all the money in the secret safe before their sex session began.

Strangely, when the paramedics covered Gwop up with the white sheet and put him on the stretcher he was still rock hard. When Maliza closed the door behind the last detective who was asking a thousand questions she breathed a sigh of relief.

She turned to Genie and screamed, “We did it, girl! We did it!”

“Now call Science! Let’s go get our cash and get outta here,” Genie said, ready to get their cut of the cash.

It took about an hour before Science arrived. He had Mooch watching Rome and his boys at their hotel, making sure they weren’t headed back to Gwop’s yet. Rome would be in for a big shock when he got back and realized Gwop was dead, and Genie and Maliza were gone.

Science and Genie had concocted the perfect plan. With the feds on their asses, Science didn’t want to worry about ever going back to jail again. He couldn’t bear to leave Lil’ Cecil and Candy. But Gwop had to pay for all he’d done. Science found out that he was behind Donte’s death. He found out his involvement with sending the Mexicans after him and Candy, and killing Damya. He had done too much for Science to allow him to live.

When Science entered Gwop’s house from the back, Genie and Maliza both were at the door to greet him with a kiss.

“Look, here’s the proof,” Genie said, shoving her camera phone in his face. It was a picture she’d taken of Gwop right before the paramedics arrived.

“Damn, my nigga!” Science blurted out and remembered his last words to him. *I rather die by the hands of my brother than the hands of my enemy*. He said a silent prayer for Gwop and talked about how they would split Gwop’s money.

By the time it was all said and done, Science left with 2.7 million dollars in cash, two hundred and fifty grand was in one safe, and the rest was in a safe that only Maliza knew about. Gwop had obviously been stacking for years and only trusted Maliza with the combination. Genie and Maliza ended up with 1.4 million as they piled into Genie’s pink Bentley and rode out, glad that they’d partnered with Science.

“Damn, life is good,” Genie stated with a smile. “Pussy and money.”

# CHAPTER 39

Science stopped at the oncoming red light and a car came to an abrupt stop in front of him at the intersection. Another van pulled up beside him. His heart skipped a beat as he saw men in black ski masks hop out with heavy machinery and began to blast away at his truck. He ducked down to avoid the wave of bullets that made Swiss cheese of his vehicle. When he heard the clips fall to the ground he opened the door and ran as fast as he could.

He was hit in the shoulder as he turned the corner and the chase begun. He reached for his gun but there was nothing there.

"Shit!"

He could hear the footsteps behind him as he ran in zigzags to avoid another bullet.

"Fuck!" He was hit again in his calf and fell to the ground. He quickly rolled under a parked car to hide but heard a bystander say, "He under the green car."

Here it was two o'clock in the afternoon, and instead of ducking a stray bullet, this asshole wants to be a snitch. Before he could even think of crawling to another car, he was pulled from his hiding spot.

He saw the eyes of the person who held his life in his hands and wanted to beg. He had kids, a wifey, and family that loved him. He thought it over and wasn't going out like that. He did his dirt and God was just paying him back. He had to pay his dues. The four masked men stood over him with their guns drawn. He thought of many events in his life and knew it was over.

"Do what 'chu gonna do, yo. My name still gonna ring bells when I'm gone. Pull it! Pull the trigger! I seen everything but God anyway you bitch ass—" His words were cut short as the bullets entered his chest and blood covered his shirt. His eyes rolled in the back of his head and it was over. One of his killers looked around at the people peeking behind cars and looking out of their windows.

"Ain't nobody see shit!" A black van pulled up and the men were gone as fast as they came. They left Science in a pool of his own blood.

"Cut! That was perfect! That's how you do it. Everybody did good, it's a wrap for today. We finish early tomorrow morning." Mooch yelled from his director chair as he walked over to Science who was getting up off of the concrete. They hugged and received applause from everyone around, including Science's mother, and Lil' Cecil.

"You did great, yo. I almost cried when the bullets hit you," Mooch said.

"Word? You think I'm the next Denzel?" Science asked.

"Let's not get carried away, yo. I told you I'd do it. I'm about to take this independent shit over. First this movie *Trigger Happy* then I'll hit em with part two. Walter Brothers Films baby, we in there." They hugged again when Candy came over wobbling with her huge 8-month-old belly.

Mooch finally put his money to good use and his dreams were coming true. He was permanently out of the game and into the movie industry. *Trigger Happy* was going to be the best gangster flick since *Belly*. He was focused and ready to make moves.

Science had so many business deals on the table that life seemed promising for him too. Everything seemed to be perfect until his phone rang from a 215 area code.

"Yo," he answered smugly.

"I told you what would happen if I found out you were involved in any of that shit, right?"

"Huh?" Science pulled the phone away from his face and looked at the number again. He figured someone was fucking with him.

"When your little man gets snatched this time, you won't get him back. Hope ya enjoyed ya legit life while it lasted, time to strap up, nigga."

"Yo, who the fuck is this?" Sadly, Science knew the voice. The caller was out for revenge.

"Prepare to lose everyone you love, nigga."

The line went dead with Science shaking his head. Everyone he loved was now in danger.

# Author's Note

I want to thank you personally as a reader for supporting my work.

Please do not put me in a box as just a street author. This is one of many of my books. I love to write and create stories that people can relate to as well as keep people entertained.

Keep following me and my movement. I promise to give you nothing but quality work. The black James Patterson in the making!

I love y'all. I write!

## For More Book Titles Please Visit

www.lifechangingbooks.net

facebook.com/lifechangingbooks
Twitter: @lcbooks
Instagram:@lcbbooks

Dirty Divorce pt 1
Dirty Divorce pt 2
Dirty Divorce pt 3
Dirty Divorce pt 4
Welfare Grind
Still Grindin'
Welfare Grind pt 3
Game Over
Married to a Balla
Life After a Balla
Gangsta Bitch
Love Heist
Paparazzi
V.I.P
Left For Dead
Good Girl Gone Bad
Woman Scorned
Next Door Nympho
Chedda Boyz
Bruised
Bruised pt 2
One Night Stand
Another One Night Stand
Wealthy and Wicked
Cashin' Out
Bedroom Gangsta
Daddy's House
Expensive Taste
Millionaire Mistress pt 1
Still a Mistress
Millionaire Mistress pt 3
Naughty Lil Angel
Mistress Loose
Charm City
Tricked

Winter Ramos, one of the new faces of VH1's hit reality television show, Love and Hip Hop New York Season 3 delivers a brazen and unabashed memoir of her life in the world of hip hop. In Game Over, Winter puts all of her emotions on the page leaving no experience, emotional abuse, or former lover uncovered. From her days as assistant to rapper, Fabolous and friend to Jada Kiss, to appearing on Love and Hip Hop and being Creative Costume Designer for Flavor unit Films, Winter delivers a tell-all book on her famous ex-lovers and experiences in the music industry. As the chick that was always in the mix and cool with everyone, Winter was privy to the cray beyond the videos, private flights, and limos that the cameras caught for us. Her reality and theirs was no game. Game Over is Winter's cautionary tale for the next generation of young women who believe that the fabulous lives of celebrities unveiled in blogs and on reality television shows are all FIRE! Stay tuned, because this GAME is about to get real.

In Stores Now!!!

# LCB BOOK TITLES

**See More Titles At**
**www.lifechangingbooks.net**

# CHECK OUT THESE LCB SEQUELS

Life Changing Books
LCB
Wealthy
&
WICKED
A Novel By
CHRIS RENEE

# ORDER FORM

**MAIL TO:**
PO Box 423
Brandywine, MD 20613
301-362-6508

| Date: | Phone: |
|---|---|
| Email: | |

| Ship to: | |
|---|---|
| Address: | |
| | |
| City & State: | Zip: |

*Make all money orders and cashiers checks payable to:* **Life Changing Books**

| Qty. | ISBN | Title | Release Date | Price |
|---|---|---|---|---|
| | 0-9741394-2-4 | Bruised by Azarel | Jul-05 | $ 15.00 |
| | 0-9741394-7-5 | Bruised 2: The Ultimate Revenge by Azarel | Oct-06 | $ 15.00 |
| | 0-9741394-3-2 | Secrets of a Housewife by J. Tremble | Feb-06 | $ 15.00 |
| | 0-9741394-6-7 | The Millionaire Mistress by Tiphani | Nov-06 | $ 15.00 |
| | 1-934230-99-5 | More Secrets More Lies by J. Tremble | Feb-07 | $ 15.00 |
| | 1-934230-95-2 | A Private Affair by Mike Warren | May-07 | $ 15.00 |
| | 1-934230-96-0 | Flexin & Sexin Volume 1 | Jun-07 | $ 15.00 |
| | 1-934230-89-8 | Still a Mistress by Tiphani | Nov-07 | $ 15.00 |
| | 1-934230-91-X | Daddy's House by Azarel | Nov-07 | $ 15.00 |
| | 1-934230-88-X | Naughty Little Angel by J. Tremble | Feb-08 | $ 15.00 |
| | 1-934230820 | Rich Girls by Kendall Banks | Oct-08 | $ 15.00 |
| | 1-934230839 | Expensive Taste by Tiphani | Nov-08 | $ 15.00 |
| | 1-934230782 | Brooklyn Brothel by C. Stecko | Jan-09 | $ 15.00 |
| | 1-934230669 | Good Girl Gone bad by Danette Majette | Mar-09 | $ 15.00 |
| | 1-934230804 | From Hood to Hollywood by Sasha Raye | Mar-09 | $ 15.00 |
| | 1-934230707 | Sweet Swagger by Mike Warren | Jun-09 | $ 15.00 |
| | 1-934230677 | Carbon Copy by Azarel | Jul-09 | $ 15.00 |
| | 1-934230723 | Millionaire Mistress 3 by Tiphani | Nov-09 | $ 15.00 |
| | 1-934230715 | A Woman Scorned by Ericka Williams | Nov-09 | $ 15.00 |
| | 1-934230685 | My Man Her Son by J. Tremble | Feb-10 | $ 15.00 |
| | 1-924230731 | Love Heist by Jackie D. | Mar-10 | $ 15.00 |
| | 1-934230812 | Flexin & Sexin Volume 2 | Apr-10 | $ 15.00 |
| | 1-934230748 | The Dirty Divorce by Miss KP | May-10 | $ 15.00 |
| | 1-934230758 | Chedda Boyz by CJ Hudson | Jul-10 | $ 15.00 |
| | 1-934230766 | Snitch by VegasClarke | Oct-10 | $ 15.00 |
| | 1-934230693 | Money Maker by Tonya Ridley | Oct-10 | $ 15.00 |
| | 1-934230774 | The Dirty Divorce Part 2 by Miss KP | Nov-10 | $ 15.00 |
| | 1-934230170 | The Available Wife by Carla Pennington | Jan-11 | $ 15.00 |
| | 1-934230774 | One Night Stand by Kendall Banks | Feb-11 | $ 15.00 |
| | 1-934230278 | Bitter by Danette Majette | Feb-11 | $ 15.00 |
| | 1-934230299 | Married to a Balla by Jackie D. | May-11 | $ 15.00 |
| | 1-934230308 | The Dirty Divorce Part 3 by Miss KP | Jun-11 | $ 15.00 |
| | 1-934230316 | Next Door Nympho By CJ Hudson | Jun-11 | $ 15.00 |
| | 1-934230286 | Bedroom Gangsta by J. Tremble | Sep-11 | $ 15.00 |
| | 1-934230340 | Another One Night Stand by Kendall Banks | Oct-11 | $ 15.00 |
| | 1-934230359 | The Available Wife Part 2 by Carla Pennington | Nov-11 | $ 15.00 |
| | 1-934230332 | Wealthy & Wicked by Chris Renee | Jan-12 | $ 15.00 |
| | 1-934230375 | Life After a Balla by Jackie D. | Mar-12 | $ 15.00 |
| | 1-934230251 | V.I.P. by Azarel | Apr-12 | $ 15.00 |
| | 1-934230383 | Welfare Grind by Kendall Banks | May-12 | $ 15.00 |
| | 1-934230413 | Still Grindin' by Kendall Banks | Sep-12 | $ 15.00 |
| | 1-934230391 | Paparazzi by Miss KP | Oct-13 | $ 15.00 |
| | 1-93423043X | Cashin' Out by Jai Nicole | Nov-12 | $ 15.00 |
| | 1-934230634 | Welfare Grind Part 3 by Kendall Banks | Mar-13 | $15.00 |
| | 1-934230642 | Game Over by Winter Ramos | Apr-13 | $15.99 |
| | | | **Total for Books** | $ |
| | | | **Shipping Charges (add $4.95 for 1-4 books*)** | $ |
| | | | **Total Enclosed (add lines)** | $ |

*** Prison Orders- Please allow up to three (3) weeks for delivery.**

**Please Note: We are not held responsible for returned prison orders. Make sure the facility will receive books before ordering.**

***Shipping and Handling of 5-10 books is $6.95, please contact us if your order is more than 10 books. (301)362-6508**